Lessons From Ducks

By Tammy Robinson

Copyright © 2015 by Tammy Robinson

All rights reserved. No part of this publication may be reproduced, distributed, or transmitted in any form or by any means, including photocopying, recording, or other electronic or mechanical methods, without the prior written permission of the publisher, except in the case of brief quotations embodied in critical reviews and certain other noncommercial uses permitted by copyright law.

This book is set in New Zealand and as such all spelling is in New Zealand English.

Acknowledgments

My thanks to Kerrie Ryan and Lorraine Tipene for their fabulous editing skills and support. Any mistakes are their fault entirely (jokes). No seriously, you guys are wonderful and I couldn't have gotten through the last couple of years and stayed as sane as I have (hey it could be worse) without you. I love you both.

Thanks also to Kate Cooper for her sharp eye in fine tuning the manuscript.

And lastly, thanks to my husband Karl, for coming home from a full day at work and taking on parenting duties so I could sit and write for an hour. This would never have seen the light of day otherwise. I know I kept saying, "I've almost finished!" for the last year, but this time it's true. *It is finished.*

Enjoy.

This book is dedicated to my darling little family - my wonderful husband Karl and my beautiful girls, Holly and Willow.

You guys are my everything

And to my dad, for telling me I could do anything and believing it.

Chapter one

The girl didn't start crying until she saw the blood. Small at first, a scarlet pinprick against the stark white knee of her tights, it spread rapidly, expanding in a circle until it was the size of a two dollar coin. *Then* she started to cry. Her face scrunched up till her eyes were mere slits and her small shoulders heaved like ocean waves.

"Mum-my, MUM-*MY*."

Anna's womb tightened upon hearing the word called in such a manner. She tensed, her body ready to spring into action. But it wasn't her that the girl was calling. It was some other mummy. Anna knew exactly which one; the one with the horrible greasy hair. The one who went tap tap tap at her phone with one talon like fingernail, the end painted incongruous colours that changed from week to week, instead of watching as her child swung on the swing or climbed the ropes. She was a single mother Anna had decided. Young, unemployed, possibly not even sure who the father of her child was, although she could probably narrow it down to a couple of possibilities.

The sort of mother who didn't deserve the title.

"MUMMY!" the girl sobbed, clutching her knee to her chest, staring in horror at the blood.

That was it. Anna could not just sit there any longer. She hurried to the little girl, knelt beside her. The girl eyed her anxiously; this woman was not her mother.

"There, there sweetheart," Anna soothed her gently. "Did you hurt your knee? Would you like me to give you a cuddle to make it all better?"

The girl frowned, her tears temporarily forgotten. This seemed to fall into the kind of situation her grandmother always warned her about. Don't talk to strangers, her grandmother said. Don't take sweets off them and definitely don't get in a car with them.

This lady had a kind face though. A nice smile.

Anna picked her up and when the little arms went around her neck she thought she might faint from the pleasure.

"Give her to me."

The girl turned in her arms and strained towards her mother. Anna reluctantly passed her over.

"She fell and hurt her knee. It started bleeding. She called for you but you didn't come."

"I didn't hear her, but I'm here now."

"She needed comforting."

"Yeah, and like I said, I'm here now."

The mother looked like she wanted to say more but something held her back, and Anna knew what. In her experience there were two kinds of people. Ones who recognised her, who remembered her face from the news, and ones who didn't. This lady clearly did. There was sympathy woven in with the anger in her eyes.

Anna knew she should shut up and walk away but she had never been good at doing what she should do.

"You shouldn't spend so much time on your phone. You *should* be watching your daughter play. You could even get up and play with her, or is that too hard?"

"How dare you –"

"You don't deserve her. You don't deserve to be her mother if you can't be bothered paying any attention to her."

"Look lady," the mother snarled. "I'm going to let that go just this once, because I know what you've been through. But if you ever, and I mean *ever,* come near me or my daughter again I'll deal to you, you got that you nut job?"

"Charming. What a wonderful role model for your daughter you are."

The mother turned briskly and walked away, the little girl blinking owlishly at Anna over her shoulder. Anna waved at her and the girl poked her tongue out in reply. Anna sighed. What hope did the girl have with a mother like that?

She walked slowly back to the seat she had been occupying when the girl fell. It was the same seat she sat at every afternoon on her way home from work. The playground was a little out of her way, adding an extra ten or so minutes onto her journey but that didn't bother her. It wasn't like she had anyone to rush home to.

Picking up her bag she gave one last lingering look around the playground. The young mother had joined the other playground mothers at the far end by the swings and they were huddled together like a first fifteen rugby scrum. No doubt she was recounting her encounter with Anna with a degree of relish. Sure enough, faces popped up to look her way. Feeling cheeky, Anna waved. The faces quickly turned away.

She'd opened her big mouth and blown it. She sighed. What was done was done, no regrets. The mother had needed to hear it. Perhaps, Anna thought, it would be best if she avoided the playground for a few weeks, let the dust settle.

Chapter two

The rest of the walk home passed uneventfully, although she fretted over the playground encounter. She knew there was no sense to be had in beating herself up with unanswerable questions, such as why that woman was a mother. But it was hard not to.

She focused instead on her feet, taking one step at a time in front of her. The pavement was cracked and chipped and occasionally even missing large slabs of concrete, forcing her to find alternate routes along the grassy verge or even in the gutter. Someone should really complain to the council about the state of the path, she thought. But it wouldn't be her. She thought the same thing every day on her way home but had yet to pick up a phone or compose an email.

At the gate to her house she paused before lifting the latch. The sight of the small gate that led through the archway always gave her a thrill and she ran a hand lovingly along its curved top, the wood cool beneath her touch. A fleck of paint came away under her hand, flicking off into the hedge that grew to the side of the gate and she frowned, she would need to give it a new coat of paint this weekend before the cruel heat of summer cracked the rest of the paint. She might see if she could find the colour chart inside and choose a new shade, she thought. The duck egg blue it had worn the last two summers was faded and no longer suited the surrounding gardens, not since she'd uprooted the tired agapanthus and replaced them with roses. Perhaps she'd go for a dusky pink this time, or an antique pale green. The latch, she was satisfied to note, opened seamlessly and she lifted and dropped it a few times just to make sure. Last week it had developed an annoying squeak, but some oil spray and a rub with an old cloth had taken care of it.

Up the path Anna went, placing her feet down as softly as she could, but the crushed shell path that she'd wanted as soon as she'd seen it in a magazine wasn't made for stealth, and the crunch of broken shells under her heels betrayed her presence. From around the corner of her home they came quacking furiously, waddling as fast as their stubby legs and webbed feet would allow them, jostling to be the first to attract her attention.

'QUACK'

"There you are," she tutted at them affectionately. "Sleeping on the job were you? I almost made it to the front door today. Call yourself guard ducks, honestly."

'QUACK QUACK QUACK'

"Hold your horses. I haven't even got the key in the lock yet. Give me five minutes and I'll be back with dinner, ok?"

'QUACK'

"Yes I know I say five when I usually mean ten. Ok give me ten minutes, can you last ten minutes?"

'QUACK QUACK'

"Ten minutes I promise." Then she realised something wasn't quite right. She counted them.

Five. Someone was missing.

"Where's Dudley?"

'QUACK'

She shrugged her bag off her shoulder and put it on the ground beside the front door. Then she kicked her shoes off and peeled down her knee high stockings, leaving them all beside her bag.

"Dudley?" she called, walking barefoot on the lawn, the grass pleasantly cold and soft on the soles of her feet. She wiggled them down deep into the grass, wiping the day and the heat and the sweat off as she walked. The ducks waddled after her, determined to keep her in sight until dinner was forthcoming.

"Dudley?"

'QUACK'

"Dudley," she said with relief as she spied him sitting beneath long ribbons of flax leaves, "there you are you silly duck. I was worried about you. Come here boy."

But Dudley remained underneath his flax, only his beak and long neck moving as he flicked his head anxiously from side to side.

"What is it?"

'QUACK'

She knelt down in front of the flax, trying to get a good look without scaring him away.

'QUACK'

What she could see looked ok, but it was impossible to see all of him clearly.

"Come here Dudley," she coaxed.

'QUACK'

There was nothing else for it; she would have to gently pull him out so she could examine him closer. As tame as her ducks were, in that they would gather at her feet and accept bread from her fingertips, they did not like to be petted or held. She had learnt this lesson the hard way, one nip from a beak pinching the skin on the back of her hand so tight it had stayed bruised for over two weeks. As much as she had no desire to repeat that incident, she could see no other option. He must be hurt, otherwise why hadn't he come to greet her with the others? She knelt down so she was at his eye level.

"Ok Dudley. I'm going to touch you now, if that's alright with you, and I promise I mean you no harm whatsoever. I'm doing this out of complete concern for your wellbeing. You got that?"

'QUACK'

"Was that a yes, I've got that, or a warning to back off?"

'QUACK QUACK'

"Right. Ok. Here goes."

Keeping a wary eye on his beak she edged towards the flax.

'HISS'

"There's no call for that, I'm trying to help you."

'HISSSSSSSSS'

And just as her fingertips were making contact with his feathers he lunged at her, his beak narrowly missing her hand. She quickly withdrew."

"Well will you look at that," she said.

For as Dudley had moved to attack she had noticed something she had not been prepared for.

Eggs.

Dudley was sitting on eggs. She frowned. Were ducks like penguins? Did the male of the species nurse the eggs until they hatched? Or was Mr Dudley in fact a Mrs Dudley? She would have to Google the answer. In the meantime she went back to where she had dropped her things and picked them up, the other ducks quacking furiously at her feet. The promised ten minutes had already morphed into twenty. This was not on.

"I'm sorry," she told them placatingly before she closed the front door on their indignant faces. "But there was a very good reason. I'd do the same for any one of you. Now go shoo and meet me by the back door in ten."

'QUACK'

"Ok, five."

Inside the house she sighed. The place was untidy, with toys and clothes strewn over the floor and furniture.

"Honestly," she said to herself, "you'd think I was the only one who could pick up after themselves."

Although she would rather pour herself a glass (large) of wine, cut off a wedge of that nice blue cheese she bought on the weekend and consume the two in front of 'Who wants to be a Millionaire', she had obligations. After all, she told herself, a mother's work is never done.

So she opened the pantry and took out a loaf of bread which she threw onto the lawn from the back door. Mrs Dudley did not get off her nest to join the others. Anna walked as close as she dared without risking another attack and threw a couple of slices near the mother duck.

"Eat," Anna told her, "you'll need your strength once they arrive."

Then she tipped out the murky brown water from the large stainless steel bowl – "I do wish you lot wouldn't swim in your drinking water," she scolded the others, "there's a perfectly good trough in the round garden and you know it. Stop being so lazy" – and refilled it with fresh clean water from the hose.

Then she bade them goodnight and set about tidying the house. Clothes went into the hamper in the tiny laundry off the kitchen, toys went into the giant wooden toy box in the corner of the lounge. When she was satisfied the house passed muster again she went upstairs and changed out of her work clothes into a pair of black tights and a long blue tunic top. As she changed she mused on what she might cook for dinner. Her husband's favourite was lasagne, but she had no tinned sauces in the cupboard and she couldn't be bothered going to the effort of making one from scratch. His second favourite, very close behind, was meatloaf. But she wasn't in the mood for meatloaf.

In the end she threw some lettuce, carrot, beetroot and cucumber in a bowl and mixed it, then she grated some of the blue cheese over the top and ate salad for her dinner, with a buttered slice of crusty bread and a large glass of merlot.

She turned the television on and flicked through the channels, bemoaning the lack of entertaining programmes. These days it was all reality shows; people stuck on islands trying to outsmart each other, or in houses trying to make out with each other. People dancing, cooking, racing around the world. Where were the classic shows like in the old days? The sitcoms that made her laugh? Friends, Mad about you, Seinfeld; these were the shows she missed. Disappointed, she turned the television back off.

Then she stood in front of the bookshelf for a good twenty minutes, waiting for a title to jump out at her. She'd read them all before but these were her favourites, the ones she kept when the others got donated to op shops or given to friends with the instruction to pass on after completion. These ones were well loved, with fingered covers and ever so slightly folded page tips. Was she in the mood for a travel memoir? Romance? A thick book dripping with literary fiction and poetic prose that would require all her mental attention? No. None appealed.

So she cleaned out the pantry. Checking expiry dates and discarding anything that had passed or was close. There weren't too many; only a box of crackers (unopened) and a jar of fish sauce she'd forgotten all about buying when she went through her Asian cooking phase. Both went into the rubbish bin. The rest she lined up on the bench while she wiped the shelves down with spray and wipe cleaner, lemon scented. Everything then went back in, neatly sectioned into areas, dry goods, bottles, canned foods, miscellaneous odds and sods. Tallest at the back and shortest at the front.

Finally, when the clock over the mantel chimed eleven, she knew she could put it off no longer. But she didn't need to.

She had survived another evening. The rubber gloves went back under the sink, the spray cleaner beside it. She closed the doors on her shiny, ordered pantry and she flicked the light switches off, after first making sure the chain was on the back door and the deadbolt across.

Up the stairs she went, down to the end of the hallway where her tall cast iron bed awaited her. She showered using a shower cap to keep her hair dry, and selected her pink pyjamas from the drawer, the ones with the black cats that Tom's mother had given her one Christmas and which Tom had never really liked as he felt they were more suited to a twelve year old. She pulled back the covers on her side of the bed and slid in, pulling them right up to her chin. It was something she'd done since she was a child and her cousin ghoulishly warned her that if she left her neck exposed at night a vampire would bite it.

Sleep did come, as it always did, at first. A few hours passed uneventfully before she woke sometime after two, heart racing, panicked, craning to hear if it was a noise in the house that had woken her but knowing it was the noises and the pictures in her head instead that had done it.

After that, sleep would remain elusive. She might start to doze but always she jerked to full conscious again, with that horrible start you get when it feels like you have fallen off a kerb. Around three, as she always did, she gave up; sliding out of the covers, pulling them up tidily and straightening the pillows, before making her way quietly down the hallway to the blue door on the room next to hers. Hand on the knob she took a deep breath, as she always did, before she opened it and that familiar smell assailed her. It was weakening, with time, but it still lingered. She didn't look in the cot, just crossed to the lazy boy in the corner, the one that she used for breastfeeding and rocking while singing soft nursery rhymes, and sank down into its familiar curves.

Here Anna slept fitfully, as she always did, for short periods. Until the cracks around the curtains started to lighten and she was able to make out the black blobs that were animal stickers on the wall, and as the room lightened, their faces. That's when she knew it was time to get up. When she could legitimately once again join the world of the awake. She got up slowly from the chair that wasn't designed as a bed, her back making the sort of crunching sound that, really, a human body shouldn't be making.

"Sorry," she apologised to it, stretching into an arch to try and ease some of the tightness out.

Then she gingerly made her way to the window and taking a deep breath, she opened the curtains to watch the sunrise.

It was the eleven hundredth and forty first sunrise she had watched in a row. She knew exactly which number because her life was separated into days before, and the days since. Into days filled with shades of love and laughter and chaos and occasionally anger and impatience, and days which stretched endlessly and quietly and blended into one and which sometimes went by without her hearing a single other living voice or seeing another face.

This sunrise was up there amongst the more beautiful; vivid and orange, peeping cautiously over the rooftops before exploding violently across the sky like someone had fired a paint ball gun. When it had finished, when the colours had settled and merged and the world started to come alive, Anna crossed to the tall dresser, again ignoring the cot, and opened the drawers, selecting a few T-shirts and a pair of navy shorts and red and white striped socks.

She showered, this time without the shower cap so she could wash her hair. She pretended for a moment to stand and consider her outfit options in front of the wardrobe, before resignedly pulling a grey and green shirt and skirt from a hanger. They were identical to the ones she had worn yesterday and to the ones she would wear tomorrow.

She straightened up the bed covers a little more, and then from the wardrobe on the other side of the bed she took down a folded T-shirt from the shelf and slid a pair of jeans off a hanger.

Downstairs, Anna opened curtains to let in the new day. As she made her way around the open plan dining/kitchen/lounge she casually, as if unaware, let items of clothing fall to the floor. The small T-shirts here, the jeans there, the tiny shorts over there.

Breakfast consisted of muesli, eaten from a chipped red and white striped bowl. Coffee was consumed, two cups, one right after the other. For background noise she pushed the button on the small transistor radio that sat on the windowsill, moving the aerial to the right slightly until most of the fuzziness went away. During the night, she learned, a suicide bomber had killed thirty nine people in a Middle Eastern country, and another well known celebrity cook had admitted to partaking in drugs and an extra marital affair. This didn't come as a total surprise to Anna. He'd always seemed to have more energy and enthusiasm than she considered healthy.

As she ate she wandered over to the toy box with her bowl in hand, lifting the lid with a big toe and pushing it back against the wall. Colourful plastic faces greeted her.

"Morning," she said.

Placing her bowl precariously on the small wooden table with the stained glass lamp she selected a few of the toys – different ones than yesterday, she liked to change it up – and scattered them willy nilly around the lounge, as if discarded by small hands.

It was only as she was getting ready to leave, switching the radio off, washing her bowl, spoon and mug and leaving them to air dry on the wooden dish rack, that she remembered the soon to be additions to her household.

The last thing she always did on her way out the door for work was feed the ducks. This morning they brushed around her ankles, tripping her lightly as she threw out their breakfast.

"Anyone would think you hadn't been fed for a week," she said, "but we both know it was only last night. If someone from animal control ever comes knocking I hope you won't pull this starving nonsense on them."

Mrs Dudley remained underneath her flax bush, eyeing Anna wearily.

"Rough night for you too huh?" Anna commiserated, "Just wait, it gets worse."

The bread she had left for Mrs Dudley was gone, no way of knowing whether she had consumed it or the others had. She placed a few pieces even closer than the night before, as close as she dared.

'HISSSSSS'

"Oh give me a break, I'm trying to help you, you daft bird."

Mrs Dudley frowned and then clambered awkwardly to her feet, off the eggs and towards the bread, keeping a wary eye on Anna, who backed away. She could count eight eggs, and for the first time she considered the occupants.

"How lovely it will be," she pondered, "to have some fluffy little babies around the place." Then a thought occurred to her and she looked around anxiously. The garden, normally an innocuous and peaceful oasis of calm, suddenly seemed menacingly evil and littered with death traps. "I'll have to do some baby proofing," she fretted.

Finishing the bread, Mrs Dudley waddled over to the water bowl.

Anna watched her take her time filling her beak with water then throwing her head up and jerking her neck to shake the water down. She knew she was dangerously at risk of being late to work, but she couldn't leave without making sure Mrs Dudley got back onto her eggs.

"Shoo," she said after a few minutes, walking behind Mrs Dudley and waving her back towards her nest. "Get back on your babies you naughty mother."

'QUACK'

"Yes I know you must first look after your own needs in order to be the best mother you can be, but you don't need to be so slow about it."

'QUACK QUACK QUACK QUACK'

"That language is *very* unbecoming of a mother."

'QUACK'

"Honestly Mrs Dudley, I can't stay here all day and argue the odds with you. I have to go to work in order to earn money to buy *you* more bread. *Especially* given your recent behaviour and the resulting fact that our numbers are soon to increase," she added pointedly.

'QUACK'

But with that last defiant quack and a glare, Mrs Dudley settled back down on to her eggs. Anna sighed in relief. She knew she wouldn't have been able to concentrate all day if she'd been worried about the eggs. Then she heard from somewhere over the fence...

'WOOF WOOF'

...and fresh worry sprang anew.

"Damn," she swore. She'd forgotten dogs occasionally roamed loose around the neighbourhood. Indeed, hundreds of them, if Mrs Gilbert - pale cream house at the end of the cul de sac, blue shutters – was to be believed. She told of a cat being mauled to death last summer right in the middle of the street; in the bright light of the middle of the day even, by a pack of vicious marauding dogs. Although she could recite the incident blow by blow with macabre glee and describe how the fur went flying into the tops of trees and the blood ran deep and fast in the gutters, she was a little sketchy on the finer details, such as whose cat it had been (none were reported as missing) and what had happened to the evidence (said mentioned fur, blood or even the forlorn remains of the corpse). Unfortunately, or rather fortunately in this case, no one else bore witness to the supposed Massacre on Oak Street, as Mrs Gilbert had christened the event, so it was left to the residents to decide amongst themselves whether to believe her or not. There was a rumour that Mrs Gilbert was somewhat fond of a midday sherry, although Anna held no truck with rumours.

Still, evidence or no evidence, Anna did not want to risk the same fate happening to the eggs, so she dragged the fireguard from the house, a cane table from the deck and the long bench seat from the other end of the garden and she set up a kind of barricade around a bemused Mrs Dudley.

"Don't help or anything," Anna huffed, dragging the heavy wooden seat into position.

'QUACK'

Satisfied that, although the furniture was hardly Fort Knox it should at the very least act as a deterrent, she quickly washed her hands under the hose and set off to work, flustered and slightly sweaty, and by now very late indeed.

Chapter three

Her supervisor, Judy, glanced at her watch and gave an imperceptible shake of the head as Anna hurried through the front doors of the bank and made her way to her desk. She was fifteen minutes late and normally this should worry her, but it didn't. She had stopped caring about some things in life a few years ago, and her place of employment was one of them.

She didn't need the money anymore, not really. Once upon a time she had enjoyed her job, but a few months back the bank had been taken over by a much larger one, and along with the renovations that saw the old furniture go by way of the back door, customer service and morals and values had gone with it. Now everything was about selling and making money. Fee hikes, staff cuts; none of these made for a particularly happy work environment. Still, Anna stayed because it was somewhere to go each day.

From time to time she made noises about looking for something new to do, finding her career 'passion' in life, but she never did. She wasn't sure whether to put it down to laziness or comfortable familiarity.

"You need something to put a rocket up your ass," her grandfather eloquently told her every Christmas.

"Sorry," Anna mouthed to Judy on her way past, but she was careful to make sure she didn't look sorry at all.

Judy scowled. She was new to this branch and had come along as part of the recent acquisition. She would have loved to fire Anna. She even dreamt about it at least once a week, but the branch manager, Mr Hedley, was a soft soul who treasured all his employees, Anna in particular, so termination wasn't an option. Not yet, anyway. So she hulked down at her desk and bid her time. Eventually the old bastard would have to retire; he could barely see four feet in front of himself as it was. Then she would be in control and a few people were in line to feel her wrath, Anna included.

Judy had a chip on her shoulder a foot wide and four inches deep. It sat there, fat and ugly and radiating unjustness. It must have been a fair weight, Anna considered, because it threw Judy's shoulders out of alignment and caused the left one to droop slightly lower than the right, like the hunchback in that animated kids movie. To compensate, she jutted her right hip out when she walked and the whole effect was rather comical and reminded Anna of an awkward rotund puppet.

The chip was also multilayered; each layer testament to an event in Judy's life when she had felt hard done by. Like the time her sister received the beautiful blond doll for Christmas that she had been coveting through a shop window for months, and she received its rather plain, brunette friend instead. The one with only a book for an accessory. Then there was a layer for not being asked to her high school ball, another for getting passed over three times for promotion in favour of *men*, and a particularly thick layer was courtesy of her fiancé dumping her three weeks before the wedding in favour of the lady hired to do the flowers.

Anna sat at her desk and reached underneath to push the button that powered up her computer. As it whirred slowly to life she noticed Judy still scowling at her, so she grinned and gave her the thumbs up. Judy frowned at her as if Anna were a lunatic and looked down at her desk.

Triumphant with the small victory Anna straightened the gold name plate at the front of her desk – Anna Jenkins, Personal Banker – and squirted some water into the small potted fern beside it from the water bottle she kept in her bottom drawer for just that purpose. The login screen had appeared so she entered her password – *judyhasalargebottom* – and recorded the day's answering machine message onto her phone. They were all issued with official bank passwords that technically they were not supposed to change, but she and the other personal bankers had all changed them anyway. They were all aimed at having a dig at Judy (*judysmellslikevodka* or, Anna's personal favourite and the one she wished she'd thought of, *judylookslikejonbonjovi*).

Blessed with a squat frame and a pug nose, Judy's blonde hair was her pride and joy and she wore it like a mane around her head. Sprayed to within an inch of its life it stood high and proud, and Anna had to resist the urge to pat it every time she walked by. She often spent whole meetings transfixed by it, wondering how it was possible Judy still had hair on her head when it was been subjected to so much bleach, perm solution and fervent teasing with a comb over the years. She looked like an 80's rock bands lead singer, a male one. All she needed was a pair of spray on leggings and a ripped singlet and she'd be a dead ringer, although the mental picture this conjured set Anna shuddering.

"Late again were we?" Judy's obvious question snapped her out of her reverie. She had paused on her way past Anna's desk and was clearly spoiling for a fight.

"We? You were late as well?" Anna gave her a conspiratorial wink.

Caught on the off, Judy's mouth opened and shut as she tried to think of a retort.

"No *I* wasn't late," she finally managed to say. "Unlike *you* I happen to take my job seriously, not flit in and out whenever it takes my fancy."

"Good to know."

"I suppose you have an excellent excuse for being late. What was it this time? Let me guess, you were almost out the door when you suddenly remembered your plants would die unless you watered them right then? Oh no hang on, wait, I know," she smirked and held up a hand, "you saw a squashed cat on the side of the road and you just couldn't leave it there, so you held an impromptu roadside funeral for it. You and your bleeding heart."

"I don't know why you bother to ask when you clearly won't believe me anyway."

"Try me. Go on, nothing surprises me anymore when it comes to you."

"Fine. I was late because I had to build a temporary protective shelter in the back garden."

"To protect what?"

"Not what, *whom*. Mrs Dudley. She is with child."

"And who is Mrs Dudley when she's at home?"

Anna pretended to look confused. "She's only ever Mrs Dudley at home."

Judy slapped her thigh comically. "HaHa. Not. I should have guessed it would be your stupid ducks again. How many times have they made you late now? Five? Six?"

"You'll have to tell me. I'm not the one keeping count."

Judy leant in closer, her pug nose flaring so that Anna could see a fine black hair waving erect out of her left nostril. "You think you're untouchable don't you," she hissed. "You and your smart ass friends thinking you can do whatever you want around here. Well I've got news for you. Whisper is that Hedley's going to announce his retirement very soon. Then your ass is mine."

"My ass is…? Oh! Oh dear, how can I put this. I'm flattered Judy, truly I am, but I'm just not that way inclined. Sorry." She shrugged her shoulders.

"What?" It took a moment for Judy to catch up and when she did she turned a bright shade of puce. "That's not what I meant and you know it!"

"Don't worry. I won't report you for sexual harassment, although should you continue to make advances then I may have to rethink that decision. It's not nice to be made to feel uncomfortable in ones workplace after all."

"I didn't…I wasn't…that's disgusting!"

"There there, Judy. You should know by now that I don't judge people based on their personal preferences. You need not fear prejudice from me."

"I am *not* a bloody dyke!"

Anna crinkled up her nose. "Are we even allowed to say that word these days? I get confused with what's pc and what's not."

"I don't care what you call it, I have sex with men, you idiot, as in someone with a bloody penis!"

Unfortunately as she got more and more heated her voice rose and just as she made that last declaration a hush fell over the bank. Everyone turned to stare at Judy, including Mr Hedley and Mr Ferguson, - the nationwide manager who was visiting for the day - and who both paused on their way up the stairs upon hearing the commotion below.

Any hopes Judy have held that Hedley's decrepit hearing might have spared her were dashed when he spoke in clipped tones. "Ms Pettigrew," he said formally. "Do join me in my office will you."

"Sir I'm sorry, I didn't....*she* started it." She jabbed a stubby finger at Anna.

"*My office,* Ms Pettigrew."

She sagged. "Yes sir." When he continued on up the stairs she rounded on Anna furiously. "You did that on purpose. Just you wait, your turn will come."

"I'm positively shaking in my shoes, Ms Pettigrew."

With one last snarl Judy turned as speedily as someone with her girth could and stomped off up the stairs. As soon as she was out of sight the other personal bankers applauded.

Anna stood up and took a bow. "Why thank you," she said. "I'll be here all season."

Peace restored, she sat back at her desk and opened up the personal bankers shared outlook calendar, where she deleted a couple of Judy's appointments and moved others to different times. It was something they often did to make Judy look unprofessional in front of her clients. Normally it was the sort of the thing Anna wouldn't dream of doing, as she was a peaceful, non confrontational sort of person, but for Judy she made an exception.

That done, she scrolled across and checked her own calendar. Her first appointment - a couple wanting advice on superannuation investments - were due in ten minutes, enough time to check her personal emails first.

A few spam emails trying to sell her Viagra and other such drugs, she moved these to the junk folder. Some more legitimate spam emails from legitimate companies such as Farmers and The Warehouse. It was her own fault; she couldn't resist entering in-store competitions when they were offered, and a side effect of this was that she found herself subscribed to their advertising emails. There was always an innocuous little box somewhere on the form that said 'tick here to receive promotional offers and other exciting news!', and she feared that if she didn't 'tick here' they might throw her form away and she'd not be eligible for the competition. She knew there must be a way she could unsubscribe, especially when months had passed and she clearly hadn't won whatever the prize was that had been on offer (did anyone ever?) but she was yet to figure out how. With a click of her mouse she deleted them. Easy enough.

Then she saw a name in her inbox that made her heart quicken.

From: Frank and Barbara Jenkins

Subject: when are you coming to visit?

She squeezed her eyes shut. How long had it been since she'd fobbed them off last time? Easter? Anniversary Weekend? She couldn't remember. Whenever it had been she'd bought herself months only. They were persistent; her in-laws. Once they had an idea in their heads it would take nothing short of an all out nuclear war to stop them in their tracks.

She couldn't deal with it just then, she couldn't. Not at work and not with clients due in shortly. She needed to be able to smile professionally and act as if she had not a care in the world. Opening that email would be inviting a trip down memory lane and she wasn't prepared to do that to herself. Not today. She quickly closed the internet window and opened up the banks system instead. But still, the email niggled in the back of her mind all day. As she dealt with clients, while she sat through a training session, (how to slash appointment times and *still* double the banks commission!), and even while she ate her sandwiches outside on a patch of grass underneath some bushy green trees. It was like someone had inserted a worm into her ear and it was wriggling its merry way around her brain.

If she tried to think about anything else it wouldn't be long before - *wiggle wiggle squirm* - here it came, back into sight, puffing from the effort and waving its little body furiously at her as if to say, "Here I am! Don't forget about me!"

"Like I could," she muttered, attracting an odd look from a businessman enjoying his own sandwiches nearby. She gave him a friendly, its-quite-alright-I'm-not-insane smile and he smiled nervously back then pretended to study his shoelaces. She sighed. Damn email.

The rest of the day passed much the same. Judy emerged downstairs after roughly half an hour and stomped past Anna loudly. Anna pretended to hold onto her desk, stapler and sticky tape holder as if the ground were shaking.

"Grow up," Judy hissed. Then she went and sat at her desk and stewed angrily for the rest of the day. Anna could feel the hate aimed at the back of her head. It made her ears itchy. Home time arrived and she shut down her computer, swapped her tidy black small heels for sneakers and bid the others, excepting Judy of course, good night.

Remembering the 'incident' the night before she regretfully decided yes, it would be best if she avoided the playground for a time. She stopped at the supermarket, where she eyed the large shiny trolleys, lined up neatly and primed for use. Once they were her weapon of choice, but now she dejectedly picked a small green plastic basket instead. Up and down the aisles she went, admiring the many brands and flavours.

"We really are spoilt for choice these days, aren't we?" she smiled conspiratorially at a frazzled woman pushing a heavily laden trolley. The woman jerked her mouth up briefly in what Anna supposed was some sort of reply, then pushed on by.

"Have a wonderful evening," Anna called after her. The woman grunted.

At the checkout Anna tried again to initiate conversation, this time with the elderly cashier whose gnarled and arthritic hands suggested she was in this job out of necessity, not choice.

"Busy tonight isn't it?" Anna smiled.

"Normal."

"Sorry?"

The cashier sighed. "It's normal for this time of night. Everyone grabbing something for dinner on the way home."

"Oh right."

Anna continued smiling as the cashier, whose name tag introduced her as Betty, scanned her items.

"Bugger. Did they tell you how much this was?" Betty asked, holding up a plastic container of beetroot salad that Anna had decided to treat herself with from the deli.

"No I'm sorry, they didn't. Didn't they put a sticker on it?" She craned her neck, trying to see the bottom. "Normally they put a sticker on it."

"If there was a sticker on it I wouldn't need to ask you how much it was, would I."

"No. I suppose not."

"Wait here," Betty frowned at Anna, as if she considered her a flight risk the minute her back was turned.

"Ok." Anna humoured her.

Betty pushed a button and the number above her head lit up. While she waited for the supervisor to hustle her way over she looked at the people queuing behind Anna.

"Sorry folks," she said, "but this lady bought up a salad without a sticker so we'll need to wait for a price check."

Anna heard dramatic sighs and cursed mutterings over her shoulder.

"It's hardly my fault," she protested to Betty.

"I never said it was."

The supervisor – Irene, according to her own badge - arrived and listened as Betty explained the problem. She looked at Anna, eyes narrowed.

"They didn't put a sticker on it?" she asked, her tone suggesting her belief that Anna had removed the sticker herself.

"I guess not."

She sucked in her breath sharply. "That's not like them." She shook her head as if she couldn't believe what was happening. "They always put the stickers on, don't they Betty."

"They sure do."

"Well, clearly not *always*," Anna pointed out.

They both looked at her as if she had insulted the entire workforce of the supermarket. "Look, maybe it came unstuck and ended up on something else." Anna suggested, turning over a few of her other items patiently waiting their turn on the conveyor belt. "Look, here it is," she held up a can of baked beans triumphantly, the offending sticker stuck to the side of it. The cashier and the supervisor exchanged knowing looks, as if to say, 'see, this crazy lady planned it all along for attention'.

"I didn't move it," Anna said, hand over heart.

"Mmm."

The supervisor hustled off. The cashier continued scanning.

"No really, I didn't."

"That will be thirty four dollars and seventy six cents."

Anna swiped her card through the eftpos machine, entered her account and pin number and tried to protest her innocence one final time. "Honestly, it must have come loose in the basket. I'm sure it happens all the time."

"Here is your receipt, have yourself a nice evening."

Betty the cashier passed over her bag of groceries and in a clear sign of dismissal turned to the next customer. "Sorry about the delay," she apologised to him, a man in his forties buying a box of beer and a packet of sanitary pads.

"That's quite alright. I know it wasn't your fault," he replied.

"It wasn't my fault either," Anna clutched her bag to her chest, reluctant to leave until her innocence was proven.

"Had a good day then?" Betty chirped to the man. Her personality had seemed to undergo a transplant in the last two minutes and Anna struggled to reconcile her with the grumpy old goat who had served her.

"Not bad, can't complain thanks. Of course it's getting better now I'm on my way home," he gestured towards the box of beer, "hahaha."

"Haha," Betty agreed.

Anna wondered if a black hole had opened up and swallowed her where she stood. She leant forward and waved a hand experimentally in Betty's line of vision. Betty frowned in annoyance but otherwise didn't acknowledge her.

Anna gave up.

As she walked the rest of the way home, her purchases heavy and the plastic straps of the bag cutting red welts into her arms so she had to stop every few minutes to readjust, she pondered just what it was about her that had set Betty off on the wrong foot. She'd been nice, hadn't she? She'd tried to make pleasant small talk, as she always felt compelled to do with people in the customer service industry. Anna had always been slightly baffled by the sort of person who could order a coffee, try on shoes or purchase a new car without barely a cursory word spoken. Over the years she'd lined up in queues and watched, a little appalled, as the person ahead of her demanded their double trim lightly whipped full cream macchiato, or something along those lines, without any eye contact or simple pleasantries exchanged whatsoever.

Anna was not one of those people. She had been raised to always look the waitress/salesperson/cashier straight in the eye, smile broadly, and enquire as to their health/day/life or comment on either their delightful name/choice of outfit. It was just in her nature. Somewhere along the way though the shoe had skipped over to the other foot and now it was perfectly acceptable behaviour for the waitress/salesperson/cashier to ignore the customer or serve them with exaggerated indifference, as if they were doing *you* the favour by bothering to assist you. Still, Anna persisted with her niceties.

At the gate she noticed with alarm that yet more paint chips came away under her hand, and she made a mental note to check the brand of paint left in the tin in the shed and avoid it when making her next selection.

Halfway up the garden path they heard her, and with a chorus of QUACK QUACK QUACK QUACK'S they rounded the corner, skidding to a halt at her feet, the two in the rear connecting beak to feathered tail with the leaders after their fruitless efforts to stop on time.

'QUACK' they said crossly, shaking the heads and attempting to restore dignity.

"At least someone is happy to see me," Anna smiled gratefully.

'QUACK'

"Oh I just had a run in with a lady at the supermarket. It has left me a little depressed, if I'm honest."

'QUACK QUACK'

"Yes, I'm aware of the time."

'QUACK'

"Yes I'm sure you *are* hungry, but can I just have a moment to pretend that it's me you're delighted to see and not the bag of food in my arms?"

'QUACK'

"Thank you."

She watched them fondly for a minute before the quacking become quite indignant, and with a sigh she told them – "Meet you round back" – and let herself into the front door. She was filled with an immediate sense of belonging the second she stepped over her threshold.

Home.

Closing the world outside behind her she stepped over a stray t-shirt ("oh", she sighed, "I guess I'll pick that up shall I?") and made her way to the kitchen where she unpacked her purchases. She fed the ducks and checked on Mrs Dudley, who, upon seeing Anna, lumbered to her feet with the duck equivalent of a groan and waddled out through a gap in the barricade to dine with the others.

"I'll just babysit these guys for you shall I?" Anna called after her.

She tried to lift a few flax leaves to check on the eggs and confirm her earlier count but a warning quack saw her drop them again hurriedly. Once Mrs Dudley was sated and comfortable back on the nest Anna headed back into the house. On her way upstairs to change she picked up the clothing dotted around the floor and placed them in the laundry hamper.

"I must do some washing soon," she noted, as the hamper was over three quarters full.

Back downstairs, now in comfortable tights and a long green tunic top, she smiled to herself as she collected toys from various positions and put them back into the toy box. Then she made herself a cup of tea and sat at the kitchen island to drink it. A fly landed near her hand and she watched it; its delicate wings threaded through with what looked like black veins, and its mirrored eyes giving her the uncomfortable feeling that it was observing her magnified times ten. She coughed and it flew away, close enough to her ear that she could hear the buzzing noise it made. Was the noise from its mouth or its wings?

A lawnmower whirred somewhere in the neighbourhood, occasionally spluttering as something temporarily clogged up the petrol pipe. A muffled thud indicated that a kick was all that was required to clear it.

From time to time she heard a quack from one of the ducks as they fought over the most popular sleeping spots in the garden.

She could hear cars in the distance, and someone whistling for their dog on the reserve that backed onto the cul de sac.

In Anna's house, the silence didn't just echo; it bounced off rafters, slid down windowpanes, rolled off benches and skidded across the floor.

Chapter four

Her resolve lasted almost two weeks but on the Thursday at the end of the second week she decided enough time had passed for any furore to have quietened down. After work she stopped by a cafe and ordered a large creamy caramel hot chocolate as a treat – managing to ignore the tempting brownies that beckoned to her from within the cabinet - and carrying the takeaway Styrofoam cup she took the road that led to the playground.

It was one of those late summer afternoons that reminded Anna of her childhood. A hazy sky, streaked with faint pastel pinks that signalled a glorious sunset would at some point be forthcoming. Warm sun beamed down on her head. Unseen birds twittered in trees, a gentle breeze fanned the flowers that lined the road, causing their delicious scents to waft up and treat her with their sweetness. She stopped in front of a particularly pretty rose, a deep gorgeous purple bloom with an abundance of petals curved around each other. She closed her eyes – after making sure there were no bees on the flower first – and inhaled deeply.

"Ohhhh," she sighed, "that is simply divine."

A man walked past at that moment with a black and white dog tugging at its lead, his mouth open as he panted, sharp white teeth smiling as a long pink tongue lolled out the side. The dog stopped at her feet and smiled up at her excitedly, tail wagging.

"Sorry," the man said, "he's a friendly wee chap."

"No need for apologies," Anna smiled, patting the dog on the head and admiring his long silky ears. "He's lovely."

"He is," the man smiled back at her gratefully. Not all who he met on his daily walks were as appreciative of the dog's attentions. "I tell you," he laughed, "It takes me a fair while to just get around the block some days, what with all the people he wants to stop and greet."

"What's his name?"

"Sully."

Anna started to say that it was an unusual name for a dog but then she thought how some people might find the name Mrs Dudley odd for a duck so she stopped. The man read her expression.

"My kids named him, after some monster in a cartoon movie I believe."

"Oh you have children? Why aren't they walking Scully?"

If the man was perturbed by her personal question he didn't show it.

"Oh you know," he said, "usual story. Couple of Christmases ago they were all, 'Please dad, please can we have a dog! We promise to feed him and clean up after him and walk him every day! Pleeeease!'" he laughed. "So I bought this fella," he paused to fondly touch the dogs head. Then he shrugged ruefully. "Of course the novelty for the children wore off after a few months when he destroyed toys and soiled their cricket patch."

He saw Anna frown.

"Don't get me wrong," he added hurriedly, "they adore him, and they'll throw a ball in the backyard for a while if I nag hard enough. But it's me who feeds him, who picks up his messes and who walks him. I don't mind though," he patted his stomach and winked conspiratorially; "I need the exercise."

"Hardly," Anna said, because it seemed to be expected from her.

The dog, satisfied that he had found another fan in Anna and spotting children ahead - more potential fans - tugged at the leash, anxious to be off.

"Woah," the man laughed, "you have a good day miss," he said to Anna, and then he was gone.

"You too," she called after him. She watched as Scully pulled him off up the road towards where the children were playing, his tail wagging energetically. She'd considered getting herself a dog once, some time ago when the loneliness and the sound of her own breathing had become almost unbearable. She'd imagined their life together; one sided conversations – at least there would be someone to listen - and cosy cuddles by the fire in Winter, the dog with his head on her lap or feet while she read. At her desk she daydreamed of walks after work around the neighbourhood. She would take the dog to the river for swims and to fetch sticks and dig holes and do whatever else it was that dogs liked to do. She'd even spent time in the pet store one Saturday morning planning the bed she would buy it – a stylish black and white number – and bowl – green, with black bones around the rim. The collar had taken more deliberation. She ruled out the awful ones with studs – they looked sadistic – but was torn between the lovely leather ones with the white stitching, or the more practical heavy duty canvas ones, guaranteed, according to the label, to stand up to any amount of activity your dog could throw at it.

      The decision was unnecessary in the end. She spent an hour, crouched on the floor, gazing into the cage where the puppies were housed - a litter of black and chocolate Labradors - watching as they chased tails and nibbled enthusiastically on ears and noses and clambered over the top of each other, tumbling to the ground head over bum before shaking it off and repeating. They were absolutely adorable, no question. A soft, wet inquisitive nose left a smear of something wet on the back of her hand through the bars and she thought her heart would melt into a puddle right there in her chest.

"Precious little things aren't they," a voice had said indulgently over her right shoulder.

Anna stood up, too quickly as it were, the blood rushing into her head with a deafening and dizzying roar. She'd wobbled on her feet.

"Whoa," the female owner of the voice, who also happened to own the pet shop, reached out a hand to steady her. "Are you ok? Do you need some water?"

"No I'm fine, thank you," Anna had smiled, embarrassed. "I just forgot how long I'd been crouching down."

"Are you sure? I can have my husband fetch a chair -?"

"No really, I'm feeling much better already," and she'd let go of the shelf she had grasped a minute earlier, stood as straight as her spine would go and smiled broadly to prove her point.

"Ok then," the woman had smiled back at her. Her badge introduced her as Pam, Owner/Operator, and there was a cartoon picture of a dog's paw print in the top right hand corner. "I can understand why you lost track of time though," Pam continued, turning to face the puppies. "These guys have been proving very popular since they turned up a few days ago."

'They're all from the same litter?"

"Oh yes. There were originally eight of them but three have already found homes."

Anna turned back to the puppies again. For the first time she read the words on the sign tacked to the front of the cage. The price – eighty dollars a puppy – seemed reasonably cheap, at least according to the furtive research she'd done on the computer at work. "Are they purebred Labradors?" she'd asked.

"No, not at that price I'm afraid" Pam had shaken her head. "The mother is a champion purebred chocolate breeding dog who has produced some very fine litters. But she got a little, shall we say *frisky*, and made out with a dog of indiscriminate breed from the farm next door. Her owner was not impressed, let me tell you."

"Oh dear, no I bet he wasn't."

"It's not the first time he's caught them together apparently, but it's the first litter they've produced. Says he's tried all sorts to keep them apart, from barbed wire fences – bit over the top, if you ask me – to keeping her on a permanent chain. Somehow they keep getting to each other."

"Sounds as if they have a romantic relationship," Anna mused.

"That's what I said to him, a modern day Romeo and Juliet, albeit canine. Star crossed lovers. He didn't find it as amusing as I did," Pam chuckled.

"Well they're very cute regardless of their parentage. I'm sure you won't have much trouble finding homes for the rest."

"Are you interested in adopting one?"

"I was," Anna had admitted. "But now I'm wondering if it would really be fair."

"Fair?"

"I work," Anna elaborated, "full time, five days a week. I do have a nice yard but it's not big by any means. These little guys look like they need a bit of exercise." They both observed the puppies wrestling energetically.

Pam nodded. "They sure do, otherwise they'll start getting up to mischief. A walk every night should see them right – if you can manage that?"

Anna thought about it. Summer wouldn't be too much of a problem, with its lengthy daylight hours, but in winter she tended to hibernate once home from work. It became dark by quarter past five and she didn't fancy venturing out in that. Not on her own. Then there were the ducks to consider as well, of course. She didn't know enough about dogs and ducks as species to know whether they could cohabitate her backyard in harmony. In fact, once she thought about it, didn't Labradors retrieve ducks for hunters? Reluctantly, she'd decided not to rush the decision and commit herself, not when she couldn't be sure of meeting all of the puppies needs. More time was needed for the decision, to think on it. In the end she never went back to get herself a puppy. The timing was never right. But the desire was still with her. One day, she often told herself.

Now, watching Scully drag the man off down the road she felt more confident than ever that she'd made the right decision.

Sighing, she turned back and continued her walk home via the playground. As she neared she felt her shoulders tighten and her breathing quicken. Would that horrible poor-excuse-for-a-mother be there? Would she have started some sort of trouble with the other mothers regarding Anna's presence? But no, she was relieved to see as she scanned the heads present that the woman was not amongst them. The tension left her shoulders and she took her usual place on the bench seat furthest from where the mother's congregated.

She'd done well nursing her drink all the way here and from the weight she estimated it was still approximately half full, perhaps a touch over. She would take her time and enjoy it while she also enjoyed the sound and sight of the children. Their sweet melodic laughter was already working miracles on that spot inside of her that withered and blackened when she went too long on her own and without pleasures like this. The smile that creased her cheeks was not the smile she wore at work; the one that lied to customers and told them how delighted she was to meet and help them. It was her genuine smile; the one only seen in rare glimpses over recent years.

The warmth of the sky warmed her soul. Reflections of pale lemon yellow and amber from the slowly sinking sun coloured the clouds. Leaves rustled. Flowers bloomed. Songbirds sang. Nature had primped herself up in her finest and was now ready for admiration. Anna duly obliged.

She took a sip of her drink and enjoyed the warm chocolaty taste.

The chains on the swings nearby creaked in protest as they were swung back and forth to eager cries of 'higher!'

The seesaw thudded to the ground as one child, obviously much heavier than the one perched on the other end, lifted his feet up. The smaller boy - the one left in the air - tried jiggling up and down, legs dangling, in an effort to budge his smirking friend off the ground, but to no avail.

"Aw it's not fair Duncan," the smaller boy pouted. "You fat bastard."

Anna choked on her drink and a small amount was sucked up into her nose instead of swallowed down her throat. She started spluttering and coughing, her eyes watering as she fought to take a clear breath, fumbling in her pocket for the clean tissue she always kept there in case for emergencies.

She didn't see the boys on the seesaw stop arguing and eye her with interest, a new subject of mirth.

"Haha she's choking, silly cow," fat Duncan said.

"Yeah looks pretty bad, maybe she'll die right here in front of us," the other boy added hopefully.

Anna didn't hear them. Neither did she hear the child who had approached from her left, cautiously and unseen, when he asked, "Are you ok Miss?"

It was only as he was repeating his question for the third time, right after she had finished noisily blowing her nose into the tissue to expel all last traces of the errant hot chocolate, that she noticed him.

And then for the second time in five minutes Anna found she had lost the ability to breathe.

She was frozen in place, mouth open slightly, eyes wide and staring at the child standing in front of her. All colour drained from her skin till she was left milky white, like freshly fallen snow. The boy had never seen snow, but he did have a grandmother who had gotten very sick and died once. Before she died she went the same colour as the woman before him now was. He frowned nervously.

"Dad?" he called over his shoulder.

Anna started to shake. "No," she mouthed softly, reaching out a hand towards the boy, who was starting to regret his decision to approach her.

The boy took a step away from Anna. "Dad!" he called again, louder this time, and with a fearful tone. It worked and a man appeared seemingly from nowhere to scoop the boy up into his arms.

"What's up?" the man asked the boy. The boy squirmed until his father put him back down – he was too old to be picked up in public - and pointed at Anna.

"I think there's something wrong with her," he whispered loudly to his father. "She looks like nanny did before she became a star in the sky."

The man appraised Anna, her arm still outstretched - although it had drooped somewhat – her mouth still formed in the shape of the letter O.

"She does a bit, doesn't she," he remarked. He took a step closer to Anna and tilted his head to one side like a budgie.

"Hello there," he said jovially, "please excuse my son's intrusion, he was raised by wolves."

When this failed to evoke the expected chuckle, or even a smile, he tried the direct approach.

"Excuse me, but are you feeling ok? You look awful."

Anna couldn't look at him, gave no sign she had even heard him. She was transfixed on the boy, her eyes tracing the contours of his face, the way his cheek curved down towards the small dimple in his chin. The way his lashes curled up so when he blinked he had the look of a baby deer.

"Ben?" she finally said, gently like a breeze through wispy curtains, the word dissipated in seconds.

The man looked behind him in case someone else had approached, but there was just his son. He narrowed his eyes, concerned, and stepped to the right so his body became a shield between them. She seemed harmless, delicate even, but you never could tell these days. You heard stories. His ex-wife was full of them, scanning the news sites on the internet all day and warning him about all the bad things that could happen every time he collected Oscar. *'Don't let him out of your sight even for a second!' she'd warn him.*

"I'm sorry," the man said, "but I'm afraid you've mistaken my son for someone else. Are you sure you're ok? Is there someone I can call?"

For the first time the woman looked at him, and when she did he felt himself fall briefly, like he'd tripped on a crack, and he became woozy on his feet. It was her eyes. They were like whirlpools sucking him in.

"Dad?" Oscar said, breaking the spell.

He blinked. "Yes?"

Anna gave a little sob and the sound was the saddest thing he could ever remember hearing. Her eyes were sorrowful now, but nothing more than that. All the emotion he'd seen, in its most pure and rawest form, was now gone.

"Lady I don't know who you are but you're really starting to freak me out. Are you sick? Has something happened?"

Anna shook her head wordlessly.

"Well something's wrong, that much is obvious. How about you just stay sitting right here and I'll call an ambulance, or the police." Perhaps they could get to the bottom of the mystery the man thought, reaching into his pocket for his cellphone.

"No!" The volume of her voice startled him and he dropped his phone. The corner of it hit the concrete first and the back separated from the front, the battery landing somewhere between the two.

"Dammit," the man swore.

"That's the fourth phone you've broken this year dad," the boy said behind him.

"Yes, smarty pants, I'm aware of that. We don't know it's broken yet though, might still work." He stooped down to collect up the pieces, the woman momentarily forgotten. Slotting the battery back into its place, he pushed the two sides of the phone back together and held his breath as he pushed down the button to power it up again. It made a few half-hearted beeps and the screen lit up.

"Aha!" he grinned triumphantly, turning to wave the phone in his son's face, "see, still works."

"For now," his son shrugged. "Won't be long before you drop it down the toilet like the last one, or leave it on the roof of your car and drive off, like the one before that."

"Those were all innocent mistakes," the man protested, "could happen to anyone."

The boy looked sceptical. His father remembered the woman then and turned back to her, but the seat was empty. He hadn't heard her leave.

"Hey, where did she go?" he muttered, scanning the playground.

"She left while you were trying to fix your phone —"

"— I *did* fix it —"

"Whatever. She's over there." The boy pointed towards a path that led from the playground across a small playing field — where children played soccer and cricket in summer and rugby in winter — and back to the main road. The woman could be seen weaving her way up the path at a pace the purpose of which the man assumed was to put as much space between herself and them as quickly as possible.

Well, he wasn't having any of that.

"Quick come on," he gestured to his son, "let's catch her up."

"Why?"

"To make sure she's ok of course. You saw her; she might need some help getting home."

They both observed the figure rapidly disappearing in the distance.

"Looks like she's doing ok to me," the boy commented.

"Yeah, well who's to say she won't collapse into a heap around the next corner and lay there all night, helpless, just waiting for someone to help her? Could you really live with that on your conscience?"

The boy sighed. His father clearly had a bee in his bonnet and from past experience he knew the only way to remove it was to let his father do whatever it was he wanted to do. "Fine," he said, rolling his eyes.

"I saw that."

"You were supposed to."

"Quick, we'll have to hurry if we want to catch her."

"Even though she obviously doesn't *want* to be caught."

The father chose to ignore this last statement. He couldn't explain to his son why he needed to follow the woman, because he couldn't explain it to himself.

Chapter five

"Keep up," he said over his shoulder when he saw his son's shadow fall away.

"You have longer legs then I do."

The man stopped. "You want me to carry you?"

"No." But the offer had the desired effect of making the boy pick up his pace.

"Sure?"

"Of course I'm sure. I'm eight, dad. Eight year olds don't get carried around by their fathers, it's totally embarrassing."

"Really? Since when?"

"Since forever."

"Guess I missed that memo."

They had rounded the top of the path that disappeared over a small grassy hill and down to the road. The man held his breath, worried that she would be gone but there she was, standing next to the road, her face upturned to the sky, her eyes closed. Was she praying? As they neared her he slowed down a little. He hadn't actually planned what to do if they managed to catch up to her and now that they had, it seemed kind of creepy, following her like this. His son sensed the change in pace and looked up at him questioningly.

"Well?" The boy said loudly. "There she is. Hasn't collapsed or fallen down dead. We've done our duty, *now* can we go back to the playground?"

The woman's eyes flew open. She gave them a look that suggested she thought they were kind of creepy.

"We meet again," the man said with a small wave and a smile.

Without a word she turned on her heel and hurried off down the street, dodging cracks and stepping over loose stones in the pavement like she knew their location expertly.

The man sighed. "Was it something I said?"

"Come on dad," the boy said, "she obviously doesn't want to talk to you. And I'm hungry."

But his father shook his head. "Sorry son, but your stomach's going to have to wait a bit longer. Come on." And he set off determinedly after the woman. Come hell or high water, her rudeness aside, he was going to make sure she made it home safe and sound. Something had upset her in the playground; he'd seen it in her eyes and he'd heard it in her voice. It had tugged at that primal part of him that most men have, that pocket somewhere inside that can't bear to see a woman in distress. Call it chivalry, or gallantry or even just plain old good manners. He was going to set an example for his son, and that was that you never abandoned an upset woman, whether she wanted your assistance or not.

Anna paused at the next street corner and glanced over her shoulder while waiting to cross. She frowned when she saw the man and the boy still following. Crossing, she picked up her pace, but when she came to the next street crossing and saw they were still behind her she stopped and turned to face them, hands on hips and glare firmly attached to face.

"What?" she demanded when they caught up to her. "What do you want? Why are you following me?"

"What makes you think we're following you?" the man retorted.

"Aren't you?"

"Maybe," he shrugged, "maybe not. Maybe we live in this direction too, did you think about that?"

"Well do you?"

"Do I what?"

She gritted her teeth and spoke slowly as if he were an idiot. "Do you live in this direction?"

"Yes," the man said, at the same time as the boy said "no."

"Well? Which is it?"

"No," the man admitted, at the same time as the boy came to his father's defence and said "yes."

"Look, I don't know what you two are playing at, but if you don't stop following me I'm going to call the police."

"Hey," the man took a step backwards, hands held up placatingly. "There's no need for that."

"Dad why does she want to call the police?" the boy was confused. "We were only trying to help."

"I know son, it's ok." The man put an arm across his boy's shoulders and drew him in against his side. He looked at Anna again. "I'm sorry if we scared you, we meant you no harm I promise."

"Then why were you following me?"

"We wanted to make sure you got home ok, that's all. Back in the playground, you seemed so upset over something. You really didn't look well at all." He shrugged his shoulders. "We were worried." He caught his son's expression. "*I* was worried."

Anna's face softened and she even bestowed them with a small smile. 'That's sweet of you,. But there's no need for concern, I'm fine."

The man admired the way her face had altered with the smile, like the world washed clean after a rainstorm, or the way a penny shines bright after a good rub with some baking soda. When her frown lines disappeared so too did the faint impression of anger she'd worn. She seemed to have discarded years off her age with that one single smile. And if he'd thought her pretty before, which he had, she'd become even prettier. Her lips were her best feature, he decided, although it was stiff competition between them and her eyes. Her lips were perfectly proportioned to each other, no thin top lip, like the one his ex-wife sported - which had narrowed even further over the years he'd known her from all the times she'd tightened it into a straight line in anger and bitterness - usually directed at him. No, this lady's lips were full and fleshy and soft, he could see that without even needing a touch for confirmation. They were the colour of just ripened strawberries, but from this distance he couldn't be sure whether it was natural or an enhancement. When she had blessed them with that brief smile they had drawn apart ever so slightly and curved up in the middle like a pretty letter *m,* and on her left cheek a dimple had creased her cheek.

   They were, without a doubt, the most remarkable lips he had ever seen, and he found it hard to take his eyes off them to look back up into her eyes.

   "Are you sure?" he finally answered her, "we don't mind walking the rest of the way with you, do we Oscar?"

   Beside him Oscar sighed. His stomach was actively protesting now and making the kinds of noises that suggested it was about to start eating itself, but he didn't want to be impolite.

   "No," he said, "we don't."

"Oscar? What a charming name. You don't meet many Oscars in this day and age do you," Anna mused. "Named after any Oscar in particular –?

"Yes, but not the one you're thinking of."

"How do you know which one I'm thinking of?"

"Tell me I'm wrong and you're not thinking of Oscar Wilde then."

"I can't," she admitted. "He was the only Oscar that sprung to mind."

The man laughed. "He always is."

"So if not him, then who?"

"I don't want to say."

"Why not?"

"I'm worried you'll judge me."

She was astounded. 'Oh well now you *have* to tell me."

But the man shook his head and clamped his lips shut, "Mm-mm," he mumbled, so Oscar himself spoke up.

"I'll give you a clue; he lives in a rubbish bin." His flat tone suggested he was used to conversations like this.

It took a few seconds for Anna to reconcile this information. "You mean –?"

The man squeezed his eyes shut and nodded warily.

"You named your child after *Oscar the Grouch?*"

The man opened his eyes. "Guilty."

"Oh," Anna didn't quite know what to say about that. Then she rallied, "Well he's always been my favourite character on Sesame Street, anyway."

"Really?" Oscar asked hopefully.

"Really," she confirmed. "Independent, speaks his mind, doesn't hold back – a straight shooter, the best way to be."

The man smiled at her gratefully. "My thoughts exactly. In fact, that's why I chose the name. That and I just loved the way it sounds, *Oscar,* is there any more perfect name?"

"No," Anna agreed quietly, "there's not." But she downcast her eyes as she said it and the man remembered her earlier confusion.

'Ben,' she had called his son at the playground.

There was a story there. And in that moment he became determined to get to the bottom of it.

He held out a hand, "Matthew," he introduced himself, "but everyone calls me Matt."

She placed her cool fingers into his warm ones and felt her blood thaw a degree. "Anna."

Chapter six

"This is me," Anna said, placing her hand on top of her gate, and turning to face Matt and Oscar.

"Wow," Oscar breathed, his eyes wide as he took in the jungle that was her cultivated garden, and the red house in front of him. "You live in a barn?"

"I do," Anna affirmed. His reaction pleased her; it was similar to the one she'd had when the estate agent had first shown her the property.

"That's so cool!"

"Thank you."

"Dad, why don't you live in a barn?"

"According to your mother the inside of my place often *looks* like one."

Anna smiled while Oscar groaned. "No, she says it looks like a pigsty, not a barn."

"My mistake."

Matt couldn't help but notice that Anna kept herself between them and the gate, as if to ward off any possible entry attempts.

"Have you lived here long?" he enquired.

Again a shadow flitted across her face as if a cloud had just blown in front of the sun.

"A few years," she answered.

If he were waiting for any further information none was forthcoming.

"Well," he said finally when it was clear he would need to do the talking, "it looks like an amazing place to live. You do the gardens yourself?"

She nodded.

"That's incredible. Personally I've never been able to keep a pot plant alive longer than a week; I could never create something as amazing as this." He was not quite as bad as that, but he was desperate to keep the conversation going.

Anna turned to admire her own gardens, pretending she was seeing them as Matt and Oscar were, for the very first time. He was right; they *were* incredible, and she felt proud at all that her hard work had achieved. A mass of creepers; roses, wisteria, jasmine and clematis had been teased and nudged gently until they had grown along the fence, over the archway above her gate and along the decking and pillars that made up her front porch. The garden in front of the porch was boxed in by a small hedge – due for a trim soon she noticed – and inside the hedge salmon pink impatiens, crisp white chrysanthemums and a dazzling colourful mix of dahlias jostled for space. Along the inside of the front fence grew sprays of delicate gypsophila and deep golden marigolds. In large terracotta pots framing the front door grew bushy purple petunias plants. The whole effect could have been a horrible confusion of colours, but balanced by the soothing greens and the deep maroon of her house it all came together beautifully.

In the deepening light that was twilight, the whole garden was bathed in an iridescent glimmer that made her feel as if - in this window of time between day and night when children slumbered and lovers stirred - magic was somewhere afoot.

The lawn could do with a mow she realised, although she preferred to keep it longer than some of her neighbours considered fashionable. The pink and white clovers that sprung up overnight when she allowed the grass its freedom attracted bees, and without bees to pollinate her garden it wouldn't be anywhere near as magnificent as it was.

Entranced, she had forgotten the presence of the others until Matt said softly behind her, "it's stunning," and she knew from his tone that he could feel the magic in the air too.

"Right," she spoke briskly and turned back to them, "thank you once again for seeing me safely home. As you can see I'm absolutely fine now so please don't let me hold you up any longer."

"We'll see you to the door," Matt made to step forward but she blocked him.

"There's no need."

He lifted an eyebrow at her as if she was being purposefully difficult but she refused to back down.

"I think I'm capable of making it the last five metres without you," she told him defiantly.

"But –"

A loud noise interrupted them.

"Oscar, was that your stomach?" Anna looked at the boy in astonishment.

He placed his hands over his tummy. "Yes," he assumed a hangdog expression. "I'm starving. I told dad earlier –" he paused to scowl at his father, "but he still made us follow you to make sure you were ok."

"Oh." That rather complicated things for Anna. She couldn't have Oscar's hunger on her conscience. If she sent him away it would haunt her all night. Matt assumed an expression similar to his sons, something akin to what she imagined the phrase 'puppy dog look' referred to. She sighed.

"Fine," she told them begrudgingly. "You can both come in while I fix Oscar something. *For the road,*" she added just to be clear.

Normally Matt didn't make a habit of guilt tripping other people into feeding his child, but he decided tonight he would make an exception.

"Splendid," he beamed, sidestepping Anna neatly, lifting the latch of the gate and striding off up the path. "Come along son," he called over his shoulder. Anna stared after him with an open mouth for a moment then quickly shut the gate and followed them.

"Wait," she called, "watch out for the —" but she didn't get to finish before the ducks rounded the corner, quickly and furiously. If they were at all fazed by the strangers in their garden they didn't show it, tripping each other up as usual around Anna's feet.

'QUACK QUACK QUACK QUACK'

With an apologetic look at Matt and Oscar, Anna turned to soothe the ducks.

"Yes I know it's late and I'm very sorry. It's not my fault though, there were some, er, *unusual circumstances* which were completely beyond my control."

'QUACK QUACK'

"I'd rather not get into it right now. Besides, as you can see we have visitors, and I don't think it's polite to argue in front of them, do you?"

'QUACK'

"Thank you."

She turned back to Matt and Oscar, whose turn it was to stand there open mouthed. Matt recovered first, shaking his head a little and giving her the sort of smile someone might give a person when they weren't sure whether all their marbles were present and accounted for.

"So," he said, drawing out the o slowly, "you keep ducks."

Beside him, Oscar finally managed to shut his mouth. He tugged at his father's jersey.

"*Dad*?" he said.

"Well I wouldn't say I *keep* them," Anna frowned. "That's an odd choice of word."

"Odd?"

"*Dad!*"

"Yes, odd."

"You're saying *keep* is an odd choice of word?"

"In that context, yes."

"Well in that case I apologise. I've never met anyone who owned ducks before. I wasn't aware there was a wrong and right term of reference."

"*Dad, was she –*"

"I mean, you wouldn't say to someone, 'I see you *keep* cats, or a dog,' would you? Seriously, have you ever heard anyone say 'I see you *keep* a parrot'?"

"Well no. Not like *that* -," he admitted.

"*Dad! Was she just talking to the ducks?*"

"Exactly," Anna said, "they're normal pets, just like anything else. A more correct term would have been to point out that I 'have' ducks."

"I'm sorry, but are we really standing here arguing over the unintentional misuse of a word?"

"Like they were people?"

"I just thought I should inform you of the correct term in case you ever meet anyone else who 'has' pet ducks."

"Now see," said Matt, "I've always wondered; should that be 'who', or 'whom'?"

He was mocking her, Anna knew.

"I give up," Oscar muttered. "If no one else thinks it's crazy then who am I to care?" He stooped down to look at the ducks closer. They tilted their heads and studied him back.

Matt and Anna reached an impasse and simply stared at each other, eyes narrowed.

Matt was the one to break it. "You know," he told Anna, "you and Kirsten would get along nicely. She's labouring under the mistaken impression I need to be constantly improved as well."

"Kirsten?"

"The soul sucking black hole that devours the contents of my wallet."

"He means my mother," elaborated Oscar.

" Your mother! Of course you have a mother, why wouldn't you," Anna exclaimed, unsure why she hadn't before now stopped to consider the woman who completed the set-up.

Oscar looked at her like a couple of marbles had just fallen out of one ear. "Doesn't everyone?"

"Yes of course."

"Has anyone ever told you that you're a little bit weird?" Oscar asked her.

"Oscar!" Matt grabbed him by the shoulders and pulled him against him. "Apologise to Anna please."

"No it's quite alright," Anna said. "Children speak without filters, it's refreshing. Right, let's see about getting you some food Oscar, *yes and you*," she added when the ducks puffed up their chests indignantly. "Back door in five. Won't Kirsten be wondering where you are?" she directed this last question to Matt as she turned her key in the door and let them into her home.

"Nope. We're divorced. It's my week with Oscar."

"I'm sorry to hear that."

"Don't be. Its better this way, believe me. She'll be off spending my money on something ridiculously luxurious."

"You sound bitter."

"Not at all, I'm much happier now. This way there's no one trying to improve my speech all the time," and he winked at her as he crossed over the threshold.

"That's not what I was doing," Anna protested after him, but he didn't hear. He was too busy taking in her house. He whistled.

"Oscar, come check this out," he called to where Oscar was still loitering outside with the ducks. Reluctantly Oscar left them to join his father inside.

"Cool," he said, after a few minutes observation. Because, really, when it came down to it, it was just a house and he was an eight year old boy.

"Cool? It's better than cool son."

Oscar tried again. "Great?"

Matt sighed.

"It's a house dad."

"House? Son, it's so much more than that." He opened his arms in a sweeping gesture that encompassed the room. "Look at this place, why, it's a work of art. And you," he whirled swiftly back to Anna who stepped back, startled. "You clever thing you, creating this!"

"I'm afraid I can't take all the credit," Anna told him, puzzled by his passionate reaction.

"Oh," Matt seemed crestfallen, "you bought it like this?"

'Well, not exactly like this. I painted it these colours. And I knocked out a wall there," she pointed, "to make it all one big living area downstairs. But it was built by someone else."

Matt was quiet while he pondered what she'd said. Finally he clapped his hands, "well," he said, "what you've done has enhanced it, for sure. And these colours are perfect. I like how even though it's all one room you've separated each area with a different colour. What was it painted before?"

"Cream."

"Ugh," he shuddered. "Is there any colour less imaginative?"

"Isn't your lounge cream dad?"

"It's ivory, son. That's different. And it's only temporary until I can find the right colour to replace it."

"Are you a designer?" Anna asked.

"Merely a frustrated closet one, I'm afraid."

"Meaning?"

"I graduated as an accountant, worked two months on the job and realised I'd made a horrible mistake and went back to school to study design. Then I met Kirsten, and *life* -" he pointed downwards with his fingers to indicate Oscar silently, "- got in the way and I had to leave to get a job to pay the bills."

"Did you go back to accountancy?"

"Sadly. Stuck with it for years – even though each day a little part inside of me died – but as soon as Kirsten left I quit and now I'm a groundskeeper. It's not glamorous, and the money is absolutely rubbish, but I'm outside each day enjoying the elements." He smiled and Anna could tell he really enjoyed his work.

They heard a scuffling noise coming from the back door off the kitchen.

"I'd better feed the ducks before they mutiny."

"Go right ahead, I'll just look around while we wait, if that's ok?"

Whether it was or not Anna was polite, so she nodded, before hurrying to the kitchen and fetching the ducks bread from the pantry.

"Can I help?" Oscar asked her.

"Sure," Anna smiled at him, "that would be nice." She was struggling to act naturally around him. From the moment she'd set eyes on him in the park her composure had deserted her. Luckily, she had become accustomed to putting on a brave face, something she'd found was expected of her by people who'd stopped inviting her into their homes in case she melted into a basket case in their arms. She found if she maintained a pretence of normality, of 'getting on with things', they found it easier to be around her. It was her that stopped accepting the invitations in the end though. She just found it easier to be in her own company. That way, if she felt like crying uncontrollably for three hours and throwing things at walls, she could. She'd once smashed an entire dinner set – white with blue trim, an engagement present that had sat forgotten in its box under a bed in the spare room - on the cobbled patio out back like she'd seen the Greek's do in movies. She was curious to see if it would make her feel better but it didn't really. All it did was make a big mess that she'd then had to clean up.

Having Oscar in such close proximity was testing every ounce of strength to feign normality though. If she didn't know otherwise she would have sworn, on a bible in any courtroom with hand held over heart, that he was –

Obviously a lot older, but how she imagined Ben would have looked if -

No. She couldn't allow herself to think like that. It was merely that they had a similar hair colour – a sandy pale colour like the fluffy bunny tail plants that grew along the beach – and eyes – such a clear, startling blue, like –

Stop it, she scolded herself.

"Would you like to feed them?" she asked him, holding out the bread. He was standing back, unsure still about this woman who looked at him like she might devour him. However, his dad was nearby and seemed to think she was harmless, and the ducks were about the coolest thing he'd seen in a while, so he accepted the bread and followed her to the back door. Anna had to nudge it open slowly with a foot to stop it from crashing into the ducks who were gathered in an angry mob on the far side.

'QUACK QUACK QUACK QUACK QUACK'

"Now now, calm down. You lot need to remember your ancestors weren't spoon fed like this. Neither are your friends in the park, no, they have to forage for their food. Imagine what they'd think if they saw you carrying on like this just because your dinner's a little late. They'd think you're a bunch of drama queens."

But the ducks weren't listening. They'd spied the bread in Oscars hand and waddled towards him. He backed away. Their beaks looked like they could do some damage.

"It's ok," Anna told him. "They won't bite unless you try and pet them. Throw the bread out over their heads. That's what they're after."

He did as she said and was relieved when the ducks turned and rushed towards the bread. He watched as they gulped it down eagerly, scooping up a bit and shaking their long throats to swallow it down.

"Hungry aren't they?" he said.

"Always," Anna sighed. "I don't know why, it's not like they're running marathons or anything particularly strenuous."

Oscar chuckled at the mental picture this conjured up.

The sound made Anna sag against the doorframe and clutch a hand to her chest.

"Are you ok?" Oscar asked her.

Anna straightened. Now who was being the drama queen? She had to stop scaring the poor boy.

"Yes I'm fine," she said brightly, 'just twisted my ankle a little on the step." She held her left foot off the ground and rolled it in a circle a few times to back up her story. "Seems ok again now though."

"I think dad and I better get going," Oscar said. "Thanks for the offer of food but I'm kind of past the hungry stage now. I'll just grab something at home."

"Nonsense. It's my fault your dad dragged you here so the least I can do is feed you. There's one more duck we have to feed first though. Follow me."

Oscar watched her head off down the garden and swallowed. The night sky had darkened even further and the first stars were making themselves known. He looked nervously over his shoulder to where he could just see his father on the opposite side of the lounge studying book spines on a shelf. Looking back to where Anna was disappearing into the shadows, he tried not to think about garden sheds and shovels. Surely if this woman intended him harm she wouldn't do it with his father nearby? He knew he was being silly. It was his mothers fault for the dangers she was constantly filing his head with. As well as the usual, *don't get into cars with strangers* and *don't accept sweets/gifts from strangers,* she had also warned him:

- *Not to walk down side streets on his way to and from school, stick to main roads only. (More witnesses to any abduction attempts.)*
- *To cross the road if anyone remotely odd looking approached. (This often resulted in a complex zig*

zag journey home – never mind the fact he had to dodge traffic)
- *To always pause before driveways in case a car backed out in a hurry*
- *Never to cross or walk behind parked cars (see above)*
- *Never engage in small talk with ANYONE he didn't know. You never knew who was fresh out of the Looney bin or in need of a visit. (Concealed weapons were dangerous because they were just that; concealed.)*
- *Never go off on his own with anyone not first sanctioned by his mother*

There were other, more odd ones- - *never swim in jeans* for example. It was at times like these he wished his mother would keep her fears to herself. She had made him overly cautious, untrusting. He wanted to be more like his father; open to new people and experiences.

"Coming?"

Something in the timbre of her voice told him he could trust her, so he took a deep breath, and then he took a step forward.

Later that night, in the taxi on the way back to the playground to fetch his father's car, he found it a struggle to keep his eyes open. He fought as long as he could against gravity, kneeling up on the back seat to wave out of the rear window until the car reached the corner. It paused for a second under the yellow streetlight, indicator blinking, before turning. Anna's house and street were swallowed up into inky black darkness.

"Right you," his father said softly, "sit down and buckle yourself in properly."

Oscar did as he was told, snuggling in against his father's comforting side, finally surrendering to it and letting his so heavy eyelids close.

He thought back over the night and how much fun it had turned out to be. He was so glad he'd decided to trust Anna. When he'd followed her down the garden she had introduced him to Mrs Dudley, another duck, and her soon-to-be babies; although he'd had to take her word for that as the eggs were hidden safely underneath Mrs Dudley's plump feathered body. Anna did try to coax her off the eggs to eat some bread but, perhaps due to his presence, she refused to budge.

"We'll just have to leave her be," Anna said eventually, "I'm sure she'll eat something once we're back inside."

Then Anna had whipped up a quick meal of spaghetti bolognaise, but nothing like he'd ever associated with those words before. The one his father sometimes served up was mince in a watery tomato sauce. Served with packet noodles it was ok, but nothing to rave about. His mothers spaghetti bolognaise was even less amazing, due partly to her tendency to buy the cheapest mince available. Once you've seen that stuff raw, all white bits of tubing and weird, unspecified gristly bits, it was hard to enjoy it cooked. His mother didn't use pasta sauce, just a tin of tomatoes and a squirt of tomato ketchup from a bottle. No, his past experiences with the dish had certainly left a lot to be desired.

Anna's though? Wow. Her bolognaise was rich and thick and delicious. She'd diced onion and grated garlic into the oil first which added a flavour burst that surprised him. She served it with crusty bread to mop up the leftover sauce, grated cheese sprinkled over the bowl and a dollop of sour cream on top. The cheese had become gooey and the sour cream melted slightly, and it all blended together to become a creamy and delicious concoction that had made him close his eyes and moan with the pleasure of it. His father had been surprised as Oscar wasn't normally one for getting excited over food.

"That's because you never give me food as yummy as this," Oscar said with his mouth full when his father pointed this out.

"Hey now, that's not true," Matt protested.

"Yes it is."

"You ungrateful sod. How many hours do I slave away to prepare you extremely delicious – also nutritiously designed to meet a growing child's needs, I might add - meals."

"Nutritious? Dad do you even know what a carrot looks like? Or an apple?"

"Oh ha ha. You see the cheek I have to put up with?" he said to Anna, shaking his head in mock upset.

"What would you have been having for tea tonight if you weren't here?" she asked him.

Matt open his mouth then abruptly shut it again. He looked down and mumbled.

"Sorry? Couldn't quite catch that."

Matt sighed, knowing the game was up. "Fish and Chips," he admitted. Then over loud laughter from the other two he defended himself, "but he loves Fish and Chips! And fish is healthy."

"Not when it's under a thick inch of batter it's not."

After they ate, despite Anna's insistence that she needed no help, the three of them washed and dried and put away the dishes, and then Anna served them creamy Hokey Pokey ice cream in little blue bowls and they ate it at the table while they played a round of last card with a deck of cards Anna had pulled from a drawer.

The only weird part of the evening was when he had found the toy box in the lounge, and asked Anna if she had a son too and if so where was he? She had gone a funny colour again then, like earlier in the playground, and she had turned away and pretended she hadn't heard him. He would have repeated himself but a warning look from his father made him close his mouth instead.

Grownups, he had shrugged it off.

The taxi driver was playing some quiet ethnic music, Indian perhaps. It was gentle and soothing like a lullaby.

"Dad?" he murmured, before he let sleep claim him.

"Hmm?"

"Can we get a duck?"

"We'll see," his dad said, which Oscar knew more than likely meant no. Oh well, it had been worth a try. He thought about the ducks, smiled, and drifted off to sleep.

Chapter seven

It was odd. Nothing physical had been altered in her house by Matt and Oscar's visit, but something less tangible, something *atmospheric,* had. She couldn't quite put her finger on it but it was if something had been awakened, a memory perhaps, of echoed conversations and the sound of laughter. These were sounds that, until last night, the house had not heard in some time, but the memory of them was still there, in the dust on the skirting boards and the cobwebs in the corners. Traces remained.

Apart from filling in the hours before bedtime, her previous night's unexpected visitors failed to impact on her life in any other way. She still showered with her shower cap on, slept half the night in one room and dozed fitfully in the other room. She still showered – without the shower cap – and selected an identical grey and green shirt and skirt to the ones she had worn yesterday from the wardrobe.

The moment the taxi had turned the corner and disappeared and her waving hand had dropped back against her side, she had allowed herself a moment to dwell on the events of the evening, before turning and heading back inside the house, banishing them both from her thoughts for good. She could not allow herself to fixate on a stranger's child and any appearance coincidences between him and Ben that made the hairs along the length of her arm stand erect. Too much time had passed and she'd worked too hard at a semblance of closure.

She *did* allow herself a moment to be pleased that she had not forgotten how to entertain guests, something she had once been reasonably renowned for. She still had the gift; she smiled, remembering Oscar's pleasure with the food she had served him.

As Anna ate her breakfast in her bowl over the sink, she couldn't shake the feeling that something was observing her. Not in a sinister way, quite the opposite. The air felt expectant, eager, and desperate to please.

Like a puppy.

She turned and eyed the empty expanse of the room. "Don't go thinking that what happened last night heralds the beginning of dinner parties or BBQ's or anything," she warned it, "because it doesn't. It was a one off. You're stuck with just me for company again; deal with it."

As she got ready to leave she sensed a definite sulk in the air, and when she tried to open the back door she found it was stuck fast. Tugging failed to free it, so she was forced to put her handbag and the bag of bread down in order to brace a knee against the wall and pull with all her strength. This time the door flew open as easily as if it had never been stuck at all, and she fell backwards onto the kitchen tiles, landing heavily on her tailbone.

"Ouch," she said. For a minute all she could do was sit there awkwardly, unable to move or stand up until the pain lessened, and when it did she rolled over onto her hands and knees and pushed herself off the floor. Upright again, she leant against the bench top and rubbed the sore spot.

"You did that on purpose," she scowled. Of course, no one answered. But she *did* sense a slight feeling of chagrin in the air.

"I should think so," she scolded, leaving and slamming the door closed behind her. The moment the door clicked shut behind her was the same moment she realised her bag and keys were still on the other side of it.

She groaned and checked her watch.

Throwing the bread to the ducks and telling them they would just have to suffice with the bowl of dirty water today – "like I've told you a million times, it's for *drinking,* not swimming" – she went around the side of the house where she knew she would be able to climb – awkwardly with a fresh back injury to contend with – up onto the top of the porch and with a little bit of elbow strength, jimmy the bathroom window open. After she'd done that it was simply a case of squeezing in over the windowsill – trying not to land a hand or a foot in the toilet – and voila, she was inside. Out of breath and aching, but inside.

She scurried downstairs and back through the kitchen – pausing only to cast a dark look around the room – and this time, before she slammed the door shut, she made sure that she had everything she needed in hand first.

There was no denying it; she was going to be late again. Judy would have a field day with her excuse – *"wait, you're telling me that your house, got shitty, and locked you out??"*

Oh well. Anna figured she may as well be hung for a sheep as a lamb, so she stopped and closed her eyes and took several deep breaths until she felt her heart return to its normal rhythm, then she opened her eyes and smiled. She was going to enjoy every minute of her walk this morning.

Chapter eight

Anna once owned a car, back when everything was different. Back then she barely walked further than the letterbox at the end of her driveway. But things had changed, and now she found her walks peaceful and therapeutic. She walked everywhere; work, the supermarket, doctors appointments. In fact, it was her doctor who made the suggestion she take up walking.

"Anna," he'd said in his office a couple of years previously, "I'm worried you're not making the right choices when it comes to taking care of yourself. *Obviously* I can understand why," he hurriedly added when he saw her face drop, "but as your doctor it's my duty to try and help you. Are you still taking the medication?"

She nodded.

"And is it helping? With the thoughts, I mean."

She shrugged.

"Well. We can't expect miracles. These things do tend to take time. I know it's a trite thing to say, but time really does heal. I promise."

'How much time exactly are we talking about here?" It was the first time she'd spoken since taking a seat in his office, and her voice was raspy and tortured and the sound of it made him wince. He wished most sincerely that he had an answer for her. But he didn't.

"Look, keep taking the pills. Call the number I gave you if you ever feel, you know, like you can't handle things and need a bit of extra help. Don't be afraid to ask, it's what we're here for. And in the meantime, ditch the car and get out more often into the sunshine and fresh air. Nature really can help with achieving a more serene state of mind." He'd rummaged in a drawer underneath his desk – disorganised, she noticed with indifference. Loose papers, pens, paperclips and, bizarrely, a bright orange golf ball – and pulled a brochure out with a flourish. "Here," he wiped something that looked suspiciously like it had come out of someone's nose – but which she hoped was something less disgusting, like glue - off with his sleeve and passed it over.

"What is it?" she asked. She really didn't have the energy for reading. Or eating, or talking for that matter. But the doctor was only trying to help, and if she didn't attend these scheduled appointments – marked out on the calendar that hung on her pantry door in big black block letters - it was entirely possible someone would call in the men with the white coats. So she went to humour them.

"Read it if you get a minute," he suggested. 'It's a relatively new theory, or movement, I'm not sure exactly what you call it. My wife swears by it though."

Anna looked down at the brochure in her hands.

'Mindfulness', it said in wavy blue letters. 'Experience the conscious life."

It sounded like something that people with more joy in their lives did, she'd thought, but she tucked it into the purse at her feet to keep him happy. She had no intention of reading it, and it sat forgotten amongst the old tissues, coins, loose tampons and other assorted detritus that make up the bottom of a woman's handbag. There it stayed for at least four months, until the next appointment.

That time, a vase of lilies graced the table in the corner of the waiting room and before she sat Anna bent over to smell and admire them. Unfortunately she misjudged the distance and some of the thick orange pollen that coated the stamen brushed off on her nose. Immediately she sneezed, then sneezed again.

Eyes watering, she scanned the room for a tissue but there were none in sight. What kind of doctors' office doesn't have a box of tissues on offer she wondered? She looked questioningly at the receptionist, who ignored her and kept her eyes fixed on the computer screen directly in front. There was no way the girl could have failed to see what happened, the room was barely big enough to swing a cat. Anna sighed and rolled her eyes at the only other inhabitant of the room - a man in his fifties flicking through one of the magazines off the table -

and said in a loud whisper, "I bet she's checking her Facebook page."

His smile floated over her briefly without landing before he returned his attention to his magazine, obviously not wanting to be a part of any anti-establishment conspiracy or ruckus that she might cause.

Anna took a seat and rummaged inside her handbag. She knew there was bound to be a tissue in there somewhere; there always was even if she couldn't remember ever putting one in. It was just one of life's tiny mysteries. Aha! She triumphantly pulled one out and with it came the brochure she had forgotten all about. She had time to kill now, she figured, plus she was slightly worried that the doctor might quiz her on it, so she sat back, figuring she'd scan the pertinent details. That was soon forgotten as she became engrossed in the words on the pages in front of her. They connected. Somehow, they became more than mere words; each one was like a light bulb illuminating her mind. She didn't even realise how excited she was getting or that she was becoming ever more vocal until a particularly loud "Of course!" sprang forth from her lips and the man got up hurriedly on the pretence of switching magazines but after choosing one he moved to a seat further away from her instead of returning to his original one.

"I'm sorry," Anna had smiled apologetically at him, "it's just this article on mindfulness. I'd never heard of it before but it's really very interesting. Have you heard about it?"

The man shook his head. "No."

"Would you like to read it when I'm finished?"

The man looked at the receptionist for assistance but she remained resolutely fixated on her computer screen. "No. But thank you," he finally said, when it was obvious he would have to answer. Then he put his magazine down on his lap and regarded her. "I don't believe in all that mumbo jumbo, hippy nonsense."

Anna's eyebrows shot up. "Nonsense?"

"You know," he waved one hand, clearly on his bandwagon now, "spiritual enlightenment, meditation, aromatherapy, Buddhism – all that guff. You don't want to start dabbling in things such as that." He said it as if she had expressed an interest in learning the dark arts. "No," he shook his head dismissively, "that sort of stuff is for hippies, people that go around not bathing and wearing those god awful baggy trousers without a crotch to speak of." He shuddered. "Not professional people such as ourselves." And he crossed his fat fingers across his generous stomach and gave her a smile that suggested she need not thank him for doing her a favour by pointing out the error of her ways, he was happy to help.

"Hippy stuff?" She leant forward, puzzled. "I did offer you an article to read, didn't I? Not an ecstasy pill or a gram of LSD?"

He frowned. What was she on about? "Yes."

"Oh! Good," Anna sat back and relaxed. "I just wanted to clear that up. Make sure I hadn't inadvertently offered you a fat joint or snort of cocaine."

The man grimaced distastefully at her crass words. Why was speaking to him like this? Hadn't he just pointed out to her that they were of the same ilk? He sniffed derisively; he'd been mistaken, misled by her appearance. She was one of the great unwashed after all. Perhaps not on the outside, but the inside clearly bore the predilection. He sniffed again and lifted his magazine to his nose, indicating the conversation had reached an end as far as he was concerned.

But Anna wasn't finished. "Hippy stuff," she scoffed, "how very small minded of you."

The magazine dropped once more into his lap and the man's fuzzy eyebrows met in the middle, a deep canyon forming above them. "Small minded? Madam, I resent that accusation."

"You can resent it all you like, doesn't make it any less true."

"You don't even know me!"

"No, a fact I'm greatly relieved about."

His mouth gaped open. He was not used to being spoken to like this, especially by a woman. "You are rude and annoying," he said eventually, closing his mouth and giving her his best contemptuous stare, the one he employed in his workplace to great effect.

"And you, sir, are pompous and ignorant. You do know that Buddhism is a religion, don't you?"

"Well I know some people *believe* -"

"One of the top five in the world," she continued as if he hadn't spoken. "In fact, some of the happiest, most non-materialistic and non-judgmental people in the world practise Buddhism. You'd do well to take a leaf out of their book." She eyed his expensive leather shoes and garish gold wristwatch pointedly.

They both jumped as a door opened with a bang. The doctor stood framed in the doorway, the receptionist hovering to his side, her eyes wide with amusement. Obviously she had finally seen fit to fill the doctor in on the drama currently unfolding in his waiting room.

"Mr Thomson," the doctor smiled, "please come this way."

Glowering at Anna, Mr Thomson stood and picked up his briefcase. "Thank god," he growled. "It's about bloody time."

"You do know God is also a religious deity, right?" Anna said brightly. "Only I'd hate for you to take his name in vain in front of the wrong person. You could easily offend someone."

He ignored her and swept past, muttering to the doctor while still within earshot, "That woman is in entirely the wrong place. She needs the services of a mental health professional if you ask me."

Anna sighed as the door swung shut behind them, muffling any reply the doctor may have made.

Perhaps the illustrious Mr Thomson was right, she mused.

She never used to let throwaway comments by random strangers annoy her so much. But then, she never used to say much at all to anyone. It's easier - and usually the more mature path - to let the small things go, she knew. But it was *so* much more fun to say what you really think. She chuckled quietly to herself and to her surprise she heard the receptionist giggle along with her. She smiled at the girl who smiled warmly back.

"You certainly told him off," the girl whispered loudly.

How nice. She had earned the girls respect, Anna realised with a pleasant surprise. And that made it worth it.

Back home later that night, after apologising to the doctor for causing his previous patient to be so irate, she had looked up Mindfulness on the computer. She read up on it for over an hour, including how to put it into practise and some interesting testimonials from people who had.

Over the next few months she'd begun to implement it into her life in small ways. She soon learnt that any form of meditation wasn't for her – her mind refused to empty itself of thought, instead, inexplicably it would fill and become busier – but other things slotted in quite well. Take breathing for example, something she had never really given much thought to before – after all it was something you just *did,* because if you didn't you wouldn't survive. Everyone knew that – but she learnt to slow down her breathing, and to breathe deeply from her belly instead of shallow from her chest. She'd sometimes found that if she closed her eyes and really focused on the next few breaths, both the sound and sensation, she could stop tears from overwhelming her at inopportune times when they threatened to.

She practised using the mindfulness technique in normal everyday activities. Mundane ones like brushing her teeth or washing the dishes. Instead of letting her mind wander as it wanted to do, she reeled it back in and focused instead on what she was doing. She savoured the minty taste of the toothpaste, or the intense lavender of the dishwashing liquid. She marvelled at the satisfying feel of the bristles on her gums or the soft caress of the soap suds against her skin. Of course sometimes these activities were just chores to be got on with, resentful ones at that – the dishwashing, not the tooth brushing – and she rushed through them as quickly as she could.

But where she found mindfulness the most beneficial was when she walked. It became an opportunity to clear her thoughts and have a cry if she needed one. She could use the occasion to pause and admire nature, and of course, as per doctor's orders, to keep her health on track. She paid attention to her surroundings, feeling the breeze on her face and the warmth of the sun on her scalp. She listened to the sounds around her – birds, bees, wind, cars, conversations of people she passed, a plastic bag blowing along in the gutter – and she absorbed the feel of the earth through the soles of her shoes. The soft cushioning feel of the grass and the hard inflexibility that is concrete. The crunch of an autumn leaf underfoot.

Introducing these things into her days helped to ground her. To bring her out of the past and the dark thoughts that inhabited it, and into the present and the things, however small and seemingly insignificant, that could bring her pleasure. No matter how fleeting those pleasurable moments might be. Sometimes a moment's joy, be it from the smell of a flower, a clear blue sky or the smile of a child, could be enough to change the path of her thoughts and hence, the course of her day.

It brought her a sense of peace at a time when her heart and soul had been ripped asunder. It did not heal them, nothing could do that. But it helped to numb the pain.

Chapter nine

The following Wednesday Anna did not go straight home after work, nor did she go via the playground.

It was the twenty first of the month, and on the twenty first she always did the same thing.

First, she walked to the florist on the corner of Churchill and Fenton Streets, where she purchased a bouquet of colourful flowers. It was ready for her when she got there, as it always was on the twenty first. They expected Anna on that day - staying open until she got there even though they normally closed at five - and as always they bowed their heads in sympathy as the transaction was made. The flowers were the only thing that changed, depending on the season. On this twenty first of the month she was happy to see they had taken full advantage of the season's offerings. Colourful orange and pink Gerberas, purple Irises, a smattering of pale sweet peas. Some greenery to set the whole thing off and some closed buds that Anna guessed were a type of lily, although she wasn't sure. But it was the two large sunflowers in the centre that took her breath away, and not just because of their beauty.

"Are you ok Anna?" the owner – Cheryl – asked, concerned. She had been waiting for Anna to enter her four digit pin number into the eftpos machine on the counter, but Anna was frozen to the spot, her attention elsewhere.

Cheryl coughed and flicked a sideways glance at her assistant, Naomi, who shrugged.

"Anna?" Cheryl tried again.

"Yes?" Anna blinked back into the present.

She had been remembering other sunflowers, a bunch of them, in a plastic vase on a shelf. Brightening up the corner of a hospital room, a crib in the corner housing the small and quite unaware recipient.

"Are you ok? You've gone a bit pale."

"Sorry yes, I'm fine. Thank you." Anna entered in her pin number and waited, eyes firmly on the counter while the little machine decided that yes, she had enough money, and promptly spat out a receipt.

Cheryl tore off the little piece of paper and passed it back to Anna with her card. "Same again next month?" she asked, as she did every month.

Anna nodded.

As she did every other twenty first of the month, she headed for the little town cemetery. It was located down a side street, not too far from the bowling greens and the small racecourse whose overgrown grassy tracks saw more mileage from dog walkers than horse hooves. As she passed the greens she could see they had been freshly mown, and the smell of cut grass was heavy in the air. The smell always reminded her of the Saturday mornings of her childhood, when her dad – fuelled by a hearty fry up of bacon, eggs and tomatoes on toast – would kiss his wife on the cheek and disappear out to his shed, from whence the sound of a lawnmower being lovingly coaxed into life would soon emanate. Anna's father treated his tools with respect, and they lasted well beyond their expected years because of this.

On those Saturday mornings Anna would sit on the back door step and watch as her father – wearing his black gumboots and bright red earmuffs - made large circles around the yard, starting at the outside and working his way in until there was just one tiny strip left in the centre to be shorn. That bit he would go over twice, as if reluctant to admit the job was finished. Anna guessed that after a week cooped up inside a windowless office he was glad to be outside, with the sun on his head and the breeze through his hair. Every time he pushed the mower passed where she was sitting he would smile and wave and she would blow him a kiss and he would pretend to dive and catch it, sometimes tripping theatrically over his boots which would cause her to collapse in fits of giggles.

This twenty first day of the month she paused for a minute by the greens to close her eyes and breathe in the fresh scent. The memory this aroused helped soothe the trace of unease left by the incident with the sunflowers. She would try and focus on that happier time in her life, not dwell on the one for which she was here to recognise this day.

Calmed again, she turned down the grass walkway just past the bowling club, between it and the old church. The church was faded white weatherboard, old and peeling in places. Its slate grey tiled roof was badly in need of repairs but its parish numbers were not swollen enough for this to happen. Truth be told, Anna had no idea whether anyone still tended to the church or not, she barely paid it more than a cursory glance. It was just there, a hulking remnant of the past, a stain on the landscape of an era gone by.

She had never been a particularly religious person in her life, although she had never outright claimed herself an atheist either, preferring to stay silent and hedge her bets. Any Jehovah's witnesses who had the misfortune to knock on her door were treated to an earful that sent them scurrying back up the garden path, tails between their legs. Even when they sent in the big gun, the man with the beard who, in his own words, 'thrived on lively religious debate', he left her house meek and at a loss for words. It was hard to look someone in the eye who had lost what she had and find the words to justify it.

So as she always did, she walked past the church as if it were not there. It was the graveyard out the back she was here for. She lifted the latch on the gate and stopped to fill up the bright green watering can that was hanging off the fence by the tap.

The grass had been freshly mown here too, she noticed. The place seemed different, and she frowned as she walked, carrying the watering can in one hand and the flowers in the other, trying to work out why. Nothing was overtly obvious, as far as she could see. The weeping willows – did anyone else ponder the irony, she always wondered? – were in their place along the back of the cemetery, their sweeping long branches fondling the ground at their feet. Many years back, before she'd had cause to start visiting this place; the town council had been dismayed after a week of heavy rains to find that a portion of the cemetery had been devoured by the hungry river that ran alongside it. Several coffins had been swept away with the earth from the banks, and although most were recovered one had never been seen since. For the council there was a bright side; according to records the missing coffin belonged to a man buried some hundred and fifty years previously, and no trace of descendants could be found still living in the area. The council breathed a collective sigh of relief upon this discovery; there would be no request for compensation.

However, there *was* an outcry from relatives of the deceased who *did* still live in the area – the relatives that is, not the deceased - and a town meeting called for action to be taken to ensure no other loved ones received such an undignified uprooting from their resting place. They demanded action be taken to ensure such an event didn't happen again. The council consulted people educated in such matters, and were advised to plant Weeping Willows along the bank, as the beautiful trees were renowned for their ability to grow large and hardy root systems very quickly. Willows, they were told, had a natural born tendency to search out sources of water, so they need not fear soil disruption amongst the graves from the large roots, as some people were concerned about.

The trees were planted one bright Saturday afternoon amongst much fanfare, with a ribbon cutting ceremony attended by the mayor. An article duly appeared in the paper on Monday, the accompanying photo prompting much hilarity when it was noticed the mayor appeared to have sprouted a pair of human fingers from his head, courtesy of a local mischievous teen.

No, Anna decided, the trees were simply their usual beautiful selves, leafy and delicate and like big green umbrellas. But something was different. Something she couldn't pinpoint. The usual crickets were in the trees, unseen but definitely not unheard. Some found the noise annoying but it didn't bother Anna. In the distance she could hear the cars in town, the sound muffled enough so that if you chose you could almost pretend it was the sound of waves breaking on a shore instead.

These things were all normal. Yet the whole place just seemed, fresher, if that was the right word. Brighter, more alive? No, that last one wasn't the right word at all.

She was still musing over it as she walked down the centre path, careful not to step on any graves. The newer graves were at the front and there was a freshly dug plot that hadn't been there last month when she'd visited. Her heart fell as it always did when the graveyard gained a new resident. As much as she would have liked to ignore it, pretend she hadn't seen the dark dirt piled up in a rounded mound, ill concealing the contents underneath, she couldn't. The usual curiosity got the better of her and her feet led her towards it. As she got closer she squeezed her eyes shut and repeated the words, "please be old please be old please be old." Then, like ripping off a bandage she opened one eyelid and quickly scanned the dates on the small white cross temporarily erected to mark the grave.

Charles Herbert Stevenson, 08/03/1943 – 11/01/2014.

Maths had never been Anna's strong suit, which was ironic really considering where she worked, and it took her a moment to do the mental arithmetic.

Seventy one.

The late Charles, god rest his soul, had been seventy one years old at the time of his death.

Anna let out the breath she hadn't been aware she was holding. She quickly crossed herself, unsure if she got the order right – was it head, chest left then right? Or head chest right then left? - but figured the intention was clear enough, then she bowed her head and backed away from the final resting place of Charles Herbert Stevenson.

He'd had a reasonable innings, she mused, as she made her way further down the path. Not as good as some people had, admittedly, but better than some others.

Colourful. That was the word she was looking for, she realised. The place was normally a riot of colours anyway, with all the plastic flowers and spinning flower wheels that adorned a lot of the graves. In fact if you squinted your eyes from the front gate of the cemetery it looked a bit like a child's painting; green with splodges of colour splashed around.

But today it was even more colourful than normal, and as soon as she made that realisation she also realised why. Someone had been adding flowers to the graves. Not the ones with spinning wheels or tinsel and faded Christmas baubles, or the ones with the vases stuffed with plastic flowers. But the other graves, a dozen or so. The ones which, in the whole time Anna had been coming here, had remained unadorned, either because the family had also since passed away or because the deceased had no family to speak of, Anna wasn't sure. But now each of these graves wore a small bouquet of flowers. Not from a florists shop; the sort of wildflowers that grew wild along the train tracks leading out of town. They were in an assortment of jam jars and placed by the headstones.

How odd, thought Anna. I wonder who would do such a lovely gesture.

And then she arrived at her destination and all thoughts of the mystery flowers fell away.

Fourth row from the back, left side, fifth grave in.

As she did every other twenty first day of the month Anna allowed herself a moment to expel a long breath before sinking down to her knees on the grass.

"Hello my darlings," she whispered, even though there was no one around to hear her. She pulled out a few stray pieces of grass by the edge of the concrete that the lawnmower had missed and swept away some dirt thrown up by its blades. Her eyes scanned the headstone anxiously, lest some vandal had inflicted damage since her last visit, but everything was as it should be. The white lettering was fading in places though she noticed, and she made a mental note to bring some paint and a brush with her next time to touch it up.

She set about removing the old flowers, now brown and brittle, from the large crystal vase she kept on the grave. Then she poured a small amount of the water from the watering can into the vase and using her fingers she scrubbed the grime that had accumulated on the bottom before pouring the now murky water out. Not on the grave mind you, but at the end and slightly to the side, where she knew there was nothing below but simple dirt. Then she poured the rest of the fresh water from the can into the vase and set about arranging the new flowers attractively.

The sunflowers made her pause again.

"Do you remember these, Tim?" She spoke slightly louder now, it always took her a while to find her voice here without feeling like she might be disturbing someone.

"Not these ones, obviously, but the ones in the hospital, the day Ben was born. I can't remember who they were from now, but I remember they were beautiful. Do you remember?"

She pushed the sunflowers down amongst the other flowers in the vase and then, satisfied with the result, she placed the vase back up by the headstone. Not in front of it, just to the right where it wouldn't obscure any of the details. Then she scrunched up the coloured paper the flowers had been wrapped in and tucked it in her purse to be taken home with her. Happy that everything was clean and tidy again she sat cross legged in front of the stone, and for a time she spoke nothing, just held her head in her hands as she let her mind roam free amongst its memories.

It was the only place she would let her guard down and truly remember. The only place she allowed herself to think of them so unreservedly; to recall the sight of their smiles and the sound of their voices. The feel of her arms around them, her lips against them, and the smell of their skin as it mingled with hers.

Here, on the twenty first day of each month, she let the tears fall without check and soak into the earth underneath her where they lay. She traced the photos of their faces through blurred eyes and she cried and she swore at the unfairness of it all.

And when there were no more tears left inside, when she was weary to the bone and devoid of all energy, she lay down with her cheek against the cool earth, and she imagined she was lying with them once again.

Chapter ten

Nearly knock off time, Matt noted, switching off the mower slowly and letting it idle down to quietness. He used the back of his hand to wipe the sweat that had accumulated on his hairline before it could run down into his eyes and sighed. He loved working outside, but there were times he missed the air conditioner in his old office. Not the office, nor the people or the job that came with it. Just the air conditioner. Perhaps I should have ripped it off the wall when I left, he thought with a smirk. Would have been a better leaving gift than the potted fern and twenty dollar gift card for Harvey Norman they'd given him. What the hell was he supposed to buy from there for twenty dollars? A door knob? Perhaps a half price reduced WELCOME HOME door mat? The card was still in his wallet somewhere, but now that he thought about it he realised it had probably long expired. Oh well.

"Are we done now dad?"

"Nearly, I've just got to spray those weeds poking through the fence then we can get out of here. Can you hold out for another ten minutes?"

Oscar sighed dramatically. "I don't know. I'm pretty hungry."

Matt laughed. 'You're always hungry! Soon I'm going to need two jobs just to be able to afford to feed you."

"If you learnt how to cook we wouldn't have to spend so much on takeaways."

"You know what happened last time we attempted that."

"We?"

Matt ignored him. "I'm thinking of your safety. You think I like eating takeout all the time? No one warns you how dangerous cooking can be," he said darkly.

"That only happened because you had the tray too high in the oven and the oil splattered on to the elements. It was just smoke."

'It was just bloody scary, is what it was. Smoke alarms going off everywhere, flames licking the ceiling."

"There were no flames."

"But there could have been though, couldn't there? Another few minutes and the whole place would have gone up."

'You're exaggerating."

"I don't exaggerate, not when it comes to your safety."

"Whatever. So what's for dinner tonight?"

"I thought I'd let you choose this time."

"I chose last time. We had Chinese."

"And it was delicious wasn't it? That's why I'm letting you pick again."

The prospect of choosing dinner brightened Oscar up, and he sat back on the grass with his back against the church to give the matter some serious deliberation.

Matt, sensing he'd temporarily placated his son, pushed the lawnmower around the front of the church to where his truck and trailer were parked, and after securing the lawnmower to the trailer with a chain and padlock – you could never be too careful - he got his spraying apparatus out of the back of his truck and shrugged the straps onto his shoulders. It had been a hot day; he was looking forward to knock off and a beer. It was his week on with Oscar and he didn't like to work late on those weeks, but the lawns at the cemetery and bowling greens had experienced rapid growth after a summer rainstorm, and hence needed cutting ahead of his scheduled visit.

The council employed him to maintain their properties around town, such as the cemetery, the greens and, once a month, the racecourse. He also looked after the lawns outside the council building and eight roundabouts dotted throughout town, plus a few other properties as well, and the whole lot kept him busy. It was certainly a change to working in the office, but a good one, and although the pay was about half of what he used to earn, he considered the sacrifice worth it. Besides, his needs were simple. Food in the fridge – and the odd bottle of beer on hot weekends - and making sure Oscar had everything he needed; these were the only things he concerned himself with these days. Now that his wife was no longer in the picture wanting new clothes, a bigger telly, or to renovate the lounge for the third time in twelve months, money wasn't such an issue.

Making his way back around the church and towards the fence that separated it from the bowling green his attention was caught by a figure near the back of the cemetery. The woman – even at this distance the long hair and delicate form were unmistakable - was lying prone on the ground atop one of the graves he had mown only an hour or so before. The sight of someone lying on top of a grave was slightly unnerving, and he turned quickly to check that Oscar was still where he had left him. He was, and when he saw his father look his way he called out something that looked a lot like 'hurry up', but the wind carried it off in the other direction so he couldn't be sure.

He walked over to the fence, head bowed in the pretence of fiddling with the on switch of his spray nozzle, but at the same time he was peeping out under his lashes to watch the person in the distance. Were they ok? Should he maybe go and check on them? He decided he should leave well enough alone, after all people came to cemeteries to grieve, not to be bothered by well-meaning strangers.

He started spraying and promptly forgot about her, busy making sure he got every tendril of Ivy that had worked its way through the cracks in the fence. Left unchecked, he knew it wouldn't be long before the fence was more Ivy than wood, and although that kind of wild, untamed look didn't bother him, it did bother the Reverend who preferred his cemetery remain creeper free. He was half way down the fence when he heard his name called, and straightened up to look back at the church in the direction the voice had come from. Even though the weary sun was sinking lower in the sky it was still bright enough to impair his vision, and he held his hand up to shade his eyes. The Reverend himself had emerged from the back door of the church and was making his way over to him, smiling broadly and nodding as he surveyed Matt's work.

"Matt," he smiled, offering a hand. "I don't know how you do it, but as usual the place is looking marvellous. It always does when you've finished with it."

"Thanks Reverend."

"Please, call me John. Tell me, how do you get the grass so green? I used to pay someone to mow my lawn but my wife bought me a mower last Christmas so I've started doing it myself. I quite enjoy it, very peaceful pastime, but my blasted grass is getting browner and browner. I don't know what I'm doing wrong. Any tips?"

"It could be a variety of things Rev -"

"John."

" - sorry, John. What level have you got your blades on?"

John gave him a blank look. "Level?"

"You know, the lever on the side that makes the blades go up and down. What have you got it set on?"

"There's a lever that makes your blades go up and down?"

"Um, yes. On the side. Near one of the back wheels usually."

John sagged. "Oh. I think I've seen that. Had no idea what it was for so I haven't touched it."

Matt shrugged. "That could be your problem. If the level's too low you might have scalped your grass."

"Oh dear. Sounds painful."

"It'll kill it, that's for sure."

"How can I fix it?"

Matt shrugged. "Depends how far gone it is. Leave it for a few weeks, let it get some rain." He looked up at the clear sky. "Hell, even give it water from the hose if you need to, council restrictions be damned." Then the language he had just spoken caught up to his ears. "Shit, sorry Rev," he apologised, then winced when he realised he'd sworn again. "I didn't mean to say the H word."

John laughed. "It's alright Matt, I've heard worse. Right, I'd better not hold you up anymore. I can see Oscar is waiting. Thanks for the advice, I'll give it a shot."

"No problem."

John started back towards the church but had only gone a metre or two before he stopped suddenly.

"Oh Matt," he turned around, "what level should I set the lever on?"

"Start with six and see how you go, Five at a push, but I wouldn't go any lower than that. As well as scalping it, if you go too low prickles will invade."

"Six it is then. Wonderful. Thank you Matt."

Matt watched John walk back to the church and when he was safely out of earshot he allowed himself a chuckle. 'I guess we're all clueless about something or other,' he mused aloud. He hoisted the spray pack a little higher and readied himself to finish the job. But just as he faced the fence a movement by the church caught his eye. A woman, the same woman who had been lying on the grave, he could see by her clothes. She was nearly out of sight, heading up the path around the church that would lead her back to the road. There was something about her, something familiar, and he frowned as his mind worked to place it.

Anna.

She had her hair tied up today but it was her, he was almost certain.

"Anna!" he called, but the woman kept walking. If anything, she sped up.

"Anna!" he tried again, louder. And this time the wind favoured him and carried his voice right to her and she paused, hovering, just before she was about to disappear from sight around the church. She didn't turn though, not straight away, which made him doubt whether she *had* heard him, or if it had been something else that had caused her to pause.

But then she slowly turned and looked straight at him, only for a second, before whirling and disappearing quickly from his view.

It was her. He was sure. Maybe she hadn't recognised him from this distance? Or maybe she simply wasn't in the mood for talking. He remembered the sadness in her eyes and her voice that day he had met her at the playground, and he thought about the toys at her house and the man's shirt he had noticed on the floor in a corner. There had been no photos, he had checked while she was outside with Oscar. No frames on the walls or dotted around shelves, nothing - apart from the shirt and the toys - to indicate another presence in her life.

He finished the rest of the fence quickly, mulling over the mystery as he worked. Perhaps she was widowed? But then how did that explain the shirt on the floor? She didn't seem an untidy person. It didn't seem likely she would just leave things lying around for any great length of time.

And the toys, did she have a child? Or were they there for the use of visiting nieces and nephews? If that was the case, why did she go all funny when Oscar brought them up?

No, there was definitely more to her story than met the eye. And although his brain was telling him to run and leave well enough alone, he knew it was already too late. He had to find out more about her.

Finishing the spray, he waved and shouted out to Oscar – "one minute," but Oscar had his nose buried in a book he'd checked out from the school library– a book which, as he'd made a point of showing his father, happened to be about ducks - and either didn't hear him or chose not to acknowledge he had. Matt walked to the back of the cemetery, the same area he had mown earlier, and tried to remember exactly where Anna had been. But he couldn't. He wasn't sure which row she'd been in, and he wasn't sure which grave she'd been visiting. He read some of the names on the headstones to see if he could garner any clues, but nothing leapt out at him as obvious. He didn't even know her last name, he realised. In the end he gave up. The shadows from the trees were lengthening and the sky was turning light purple, like a three day old bruise.

He walked back to the church and his son. Anna could keep her secrets to herself a little while longer.

"Come on," he said to Oscar. This place, with the desperate longing and love and grief and sadness that tainted the air so you could actually taste it, left him with a feeling of melancholy that always lingered long after he drove away. It made him want to scoop his son up into his arms and squeeze him as tight as he possibly could and never let go.

"Finally." Oscar got to his feet.

"What did you decide on for dinner?" Matt asked, slinging an arm over his son's shoulders, half expecting him to shrug it off as parental public displays of affection had been outlawed in recent years. But whether he sensed his father's melancholy, or whether their surroundings had got to him as well, Oscar let it hang there, even closing the distance between them slightly, his arm bumping against his father's leg every second step.

"Pizza," he said. "I feel like pizza."

"Now see why I left the choice up to you? I would never have thought of something as delicious as that. Pizza it is."

Chapter eleven

As soon as the first hints of light illuminated the room on Saturday morning Anna was up, drawing back the curtains to admire the dawn just starting to edge out the darkness. She arched her back until it clicked into place, walking barefoot across the soft carpet to the drawers where she selected a green and white striped onesie, one of those all in one baby outfits with the feet attached. She remembered how it used to take a marathon effort to get all four flailing limbs in successfully. Often, she remembered with an ache, she would bend and twist and poke and, red faced from the effort, manage to get one leg in, but before she could make a start on the other, Presto! The first leg would be triumphantly waving somewhere near her left ear, having wiggled its way out again, and her golden haired child would lie there gurgling up at her with great mirth.

She lifted the onesie to her face and inhaled the scent of it. His smell had long gone, despite her best attempts to preserve it, and the cloth smelt slightly musty from being cooped up in a drawer, unworn. The thought of time moving on, a million dawns and dusks and births and deaths and changing of seasons, while these clothes stayed at a standstill, broke her heart, and her throat heaved up a sodden gulp.

"No," she shook her head, swallowing it back down. "I can't do this. I can't think like that." She left the room without a backward glance, pulling the door closed behind her. Those thoughts would lead her back into a dark place where she'd dwelled too long already; where madness was but one heartbeat away and thoughts of leaping off bridges came as often as breaths.

She showered, not bothering to blow-dry her hair, merely sweeping it up messily into a loose ponytail and securing it with a frayed elastic band. At her wardrobe she took great delight in thumbing her nose up at the horrible green and grey skirts and shirts, and pushing them to the side she selected a plain red t-shirt and a pair of white shorts. There were on the shorter side than what she deemed publicly acceptable, as she wasn't terribly confident when it came to showing off so much of her legs – spidery veins from her pregnancy still marked her skin in places like roads on a city map – but she would be in the garden, she figured, and no one would see.

Downstairs the radio informed her – while she waited for the kettle to boil - that overnight another famous cricketer had been charged with match fixing and a rare baby panda had been born in a Chinese zoo. It had been christened Tai Shan, a name Anna thought had a pretty ring to it.

She stood in front of the kitchen window drinking her coffee and watching as the day spread itself out, streaks of vivid yellow, pink and orange staining the horizon. The dawn chorus was already out in force, and she turned the radio off and pushed open the window so she could admire their song while she washed her cup and bowl and set them on the big wide bench to air dry.

Things never took as long when there was just the one of you, she reflected. She remembered a time when she had bemoaned the unwelcome sight of a mess in her kitchen; a pile of dishes, food smeared across the bench and unidentified stains on the floorboards.

If only she'd known then how much she would one day long for that sight.

If she *had* known, she would have shrugged off the dishes, left them to be done 'later.' She would have sat at the bench and joined in the laughter as her husband attempted to feed their son and the mess itself was created.

But of course she didn't know. No one had the ability to know what was coming. That was the whole pointless point. The knowledge that the world can be turned upside down in a moment was what kept her from sleeping, or subscribing to a magazine, or biting her tongue in waiting rooms instead of telling a man what an idiot he is. It kept her from becoming a fully functional paid up member of society again, not that this bothered her because it didn't, not in the slightest. For Anna, life had become about getting through each day. She refused to plan any further ahead than that. Yes, she had made the decision not to wallow in the past anymore for fear of where that might lead her, but she was determined not to allow optimism to worm its way in either.

She existed.

It would have to be enough.

Dishes done, clothes and toys scattered, she opened the back door and was greeted by a loud chorus of QUACKS.

"Morning," she said cheerfully. "Sleep well I trust?"

'QUACK QUACK QUACK QUACK QUACK QUACK'

"Now now," she shushed them as she tipped the murky water from the bowl – accompanied of course by deep sigh and a pointed look at the unrepentant culprits – "we've discussed this before. Yes, I'm sure you would be more comfortable inside the house, but no, that's not going to happen. Can you imagine what the neighbours would think?"

'QUACK'

"Well you might not care, but I know they're just waiting for me to become the odd lady who wears cardigans and keeps forty cats. I've seen the way their curtains twitch when I arrive home each night." She fetched a load of bread from inside the house and started to throw it on the lawn for them.

'QUACK'

"Oh," she stopped, hand still in bag, "you're absolutely right. I just said 'keep' cats, didn't I?"

'QUACK'

"How odd. The conversation from the other day must be still on my mind."

'QUACK QUACK QUACK'

"Keep your feathers on." She finished throwing more bread to them. "You know, you lot really need to work on your gratitude. I feel as if this relationship is very one sided."

But the ducks had stopped listening and were busy devouring their food.

"Right, ok then." She wandered across the lawn to where Mrs Dudley was, dragging the heavy lawn chair out a tad to squeeze through.

"Good morning, mother to be," she said.

'QUACK'

'How are the babies today?"

'QUACK QUACK'

"Good. I keep meaning to tell you that you're doing a splendid job. I know it's not easy, giving up your lifestyle and um, career I suppose, to raise a family. I know there are sacrifices to be made, but it'll be worth it in the end, I promise."

'QUACK'

"You wait, the first time you lay eyes upon their fluffy little faces you'll forget any –,"

Here Anna stopped and sat back on her heels. Did ducks feel pain when laying eggs? She had no idea. She leant forward again.

"– well you'll forgive them anything."

'QUACK QUACK QUACK'

"Yes of course, sorry." Anna reached into the bag for the last few slices she'd reserved for Mrs Dudley and threw them just out of reach. Mrs Dudley looked at her enquiringly.

"Yes I'll watch them, you enjoy your breakfast. But don't take all day, I have things I want to do."

Mrs Dudley clambered stiffly up onto her webbed feet and headed gratefully for the bread. Anna sat back on the cool damp grass and watched fondly as she ate and joined the other ducks for a drink and a morning dip in the water bowl.

"Oh come on, seriously guys? I just changed that water. And right in front of me too," she tutted.

Closing her eyes she enjoyed the stillness of the morning, while most of the world around her was still slumbering. She'd never been a morning person in the past. In fact, up until a few years ago she'd never even seen a sunrise, none that she could recall with any great clarity anyway. These days she found it the most beautiful part of the day, especially on days like this when she felt as if she were the only person awake in the world to enjoy the peace. She stretched her arms up to the heavens and took in a deep breath, before expelling it slowly, letting her arms settle back down against her sides.

"Oi knob, walk on your own side of the path."

"Shut up dick. I'll walk where I wanna walk."

Anna sighed. Living next to a big empty section that was a popular shortcut to town had its drawbacks.

"Don't call me dick, you dick."

"But you are a dick, so what else am I gonna call you eh?"

There was an 'Ooof' sound as one of the boys pushed the other, and then the voices dwindled off into the distance, the word 'dick' still occasionally travelling back to her on the breeze.

Mrs Dudley returned and assumed the position with a weary look at a sympathetic Anna. "Sorry. If I could sit on them for a day to give you a break, I would I promise," Anna told her, before heading for the garden shed. Her quick step and ramrod straight posture echoed the determination she felt, after all, she had been looking forward to this day all week and she was not going to waste a minute of it. A to do list had been drawn up in chalk on the blackboard that hung in a corner of the kitchen and she had no intention of calling it a day until each and every item had been crossed off.

She started by trimming the box hedges out front, which took her the best part of an hour and a half. Lopping off the last stray branch, she straightened and noticed that the sky was now bright blue but covered by a fine layer of cloud, as if someone had draped a sheer piece of chiffon over it.

By the time Anna finished mowing the lawns it was lunchtime, and the fine layer of cloud was long gone; burnt off by the heat of the sun. Grateful for the coolness of her kitchen, Anna made herself a sandwich – ham, lettuce, tomato and cheese with a small dollop of mayonnaise – and drank down two large glasses of water thirstily. She swapped the T-shirt for a tank top and rubbed a generous amount of SPF 50 sunscreen into all exposed areas of skin. The pale and insipid look might not be terribly fashionable, but she preferred it to melanoma.

Back outside she was a little dismayed to feel that the sun had cranked the dial up even further. She liked summer, but she wasn't a fan of looking and feeling a bit like a boiled crab.

Earlier in the week she'd visited the paint shop on a lunch break and, after careful deliberation, had chosen a shade called Oyster shell. It was a soft blue/grey that she felt would enhance the beauty of the gardens surrounding it. Using a screwdriver to prise the lid off the tin, Ana dipped her paint brush in and started on the gate arch.

It wasn't long before she could feel sweat trickling down between her shoulder blades. When it reached the top of her shorts it paused momentarily as if unsure, before continuing on its journey south, causing her to squirm uncomfortably as it ventured its way into places she really would rather it didn't. A quick check over her right shoulder to make sure Mrs Gilbert wasn't out in her front yard – coast was clear – before she adjusted her shorts and pushed against the material to stop the sweat in its tracks.

"Ahem. Do excuse us," said a voice behind her left shoulder.

She jumped, yanking her hand away from her bottom area, and turned in the direction the voice had come from.

"Didn't your mother ever teach you it's rude to sneak up on people?" she asked crossly, embarrassed at being caught in such an undignified situation.

"If she did I obviously forgot," he grinned unapologetically. He crouched down and with his hands on Oscars shoulders turned the boy to face him. He eyed him seriously.

"Learn from this, Oscar," he said. "Make plenty of noise when approaching a woman, *especially* on a public street in broad daylight. They startle easily, like deer. Sing a song or bang a drum or something."

Anna frowned. He was making fun, but she could hardly call him what she felt like calling him, not in front of his son. "What are you doing here?" she asked.

Matt stood up and rolled his eyes. "I've had this annoying little voice in my head all day, nagging at me to come here."

"You've been hearing a voice?"

"He means me." Oscar said.

"Oh." Anna wasn't sure what to think about that. While the knowledge that Oscar had asked his father to visit her gave her a pleasant feeling of warmth in her chest, she also felt that lines were being crossed somewhere.

"Don't feel too flattered," Matt added, sensing her thoughts. "It's not you he wants to see."

"I'm sorry?"

"Show her your book," Matt nudged Oscar, who held out a large book he'd been hugging to his chest. 'New Zealand Ducks', the cover read, accompanied by a large photo of a few ducks beside a lake.

The penny dropped. "You're here to see the ducks?"

"If it's ok with you," Matt held up a hand questioningly. "I can see you're busy but we won't stay long and we'll keep out of your way. He just wants to sit and watch them awhile, don't you Oscar?"

"Yes please," Oscar agreed.

She studied his hopeful little face. How could she possibly say no?

"You'd be doing me a huge favour" Matt persisted, "he hasn't shut up about them all week and it's driving me a little mental, to be honest. We brought our own snacks this time," Matt threw in his final sales pitch. He held up a small blue backpack. "Like I said, you won't even notice we're here."

"Snacks?" she echoed doubtfully. It sounded to her like they were in for the long haul.

Matt shrugged. "What can I say? He gets hungry often."

"We brought some bread for the ducks too," Oscar added eagerly.

Anna caved. "Go on then," she said, opening the gate carefully by touching a section she was yet to do. "Watch out for the wet paint."

"Nice colour," Matt commented as he passed through. "Not very exciting, but nice."

"Not exciting? You would rather I paint it bright orange or something equally as show stopping?"

"Orange? Hell no, I'm not completely tasteless. But a cheerful turquoise, now *that* would have given your neighbours something to look at."

"And complain about, probably."

"It's that kind of neighbourhood is it? Where everybody knows everyone's business?"

Anna shrugged. "My neighbours could be considered by some to be nosy, yes. But in my experience, people only discover your secrets if you're unguarded enough to let them."

"Is that a warning?"

"Of course not. Merely an observation."

Bored with the conversation taking place above his head, Oscar piped up. "Can I go see the ducks now? Please?"

"Of course," Anna said. She hadn't realised he was still there. "They're around the back somewhere, sleeping off breakfast in the garden. Feel free to observe the main flock, but please stay away from Mrs Dudley and her eggs. I would prefer she remain undisturbed."

"Ok."

"What do you say?" Matt prompted Oscar.

"Thanks," Oscar said over his shoulder as he was already half way up the garden path.

"You're welcome," she called after him.

Chapter twelve

"Aren't you going to go with him?" Anna asked, when it became clear that Matt intended on hanging around the front with her.

"Nah he's ok. Ducks aren't really my thing, to be honest."

"Oh." She cursed inwardly. Despite his assurances that they wouldn't be in the way, she was already annoyed by his presence. "As much as I'd love to stand around and chat," she lied, "I have things to do." She picked up her paintbrush and without thinking grabbed at the gate to pull it towards her, forgetting she'd already painted that section.

"Damn," she cringed when she realised her hand was coated in paint. She hoped he hadn't noticed but luck wasn't on her side.

"Nothing a little turpentine won't get off," he said, and she heard the teasing in his voice.

Ignoring him, she dunked the brush in the paint, sweeping it against the wood, covering her tidy, neat strokes from earlier with messy, uneven ones. When it had been silent for two minutes she turned her head to one side to check. He was gone. She let her shoulders relax, rolling them backwards a couple of times but the tension refused to be dispelled. She was annoyed. The equilibrium of her day had been destroyed by their visit. Before, she could enjoy the silence and the sun on her skin. She was surrounded by lush nature that had flourished by her doing, and the feeling of peace this brought her was immeasurable. Days like this were for Anna like being plugged into an electrical socket to be recharged. The physical activity eased her body, and the calm of her surroundings soothed her soul.

She closed her eyes and inhaled deeply.

"I will not let it ruin my day," she whispered to herself softly.

"So, how's your week been? How about that weather eh? Phew, hot or what."

Her eyes flew open. He was making himself comfortable on the front porch steps, leaning back, a hand shading his eyes against the sun. He grinned up at her.

"What are you doing?" she asked.

He looked around puzzled, then back at her. "Is that a trick question?"

"Where is Oscar? Why aren't you with him?"

Matt pointed to the side of the house. "I left him around there, safely camped out in your garden with the ducks."

He could see by her expression that this answer had failed to appease her.

"Don't worry, he won't damage anything. I gave him strict instructions not to touch."

She shook her head. "I'm not worried about that. What are *you* doing?"

"What do you mean, what am I doing? I'm sitting here making small talk with you."

"Yes, I can see that, but why?"

He looked genuinely baffled. "Why not?"

She sighed. He was being deliberately dense. She would have to spell it out. "You promised you wouldn't disturb me."

"Did I?"

"Yes. You said, and I quote, 'you won't even notice we're here'."

"Huh. That doesn't sound like something I'd say."

But she could tell from his tone and the way his eyes were crinkled around the edges like screwed up paper that he was playing with her again.

"Well you *did* say it. And now you're just sitting there, right where I can see you. It's distracting."

"Sorry," he said, looking anything but. He made no move to go, if anything he made himself more comfortable on the step. He opened the blue backpack and after rooting around inside pulled out a banana, which he proceeded to peel and take a large bite from. He noticed her still watching him. "Oh I'm sorry," he said, "would you like one? We brought plenty."

"No. Thank you. I've just eaten lunch."

"Ok, well let me know if you change your mind. There's plenty to go around." He took another bite and looked at the gardens around him. "These really are spectacular gardens," he said. "Did you plant them all yourself?"

Anna sighed and turned back to her painting. He was not taking the hint. Perhaps if she refused to participate in the conversation more than necessary he might lose interest.

"Yes."

"No help from a landscaper?"

"No."

"A gardener?"

"No, just me."

"Did your husband help?"

She gave him a fed up look. "Which part of 'just me' do you not understand?"

"Sorry, just making conversation."

"I don't *want* to make conversation. I want to get on with painting my fence."

"Well don't let me stop you. Just pretend I'm not here." He took another large bite to finish off the banana and folded up the peel, looking around for some place to dump it. She watched. He saw her watching and smiled guiltily. "I'll just take this with me, shall I?" he said and started to put it back into the backpack.

She took a deep breath, counted to five then expelled it. This man required levels of patience she no longer had. "Pass it here." She held out her hand.

He gave it to her and she pulled it apart, tucking the pieces into the soil underneath a nearby hydrangea.

"Now why didn't I think of that?" he said.

"I have no idea. We do all have differing levels of intelligence though."

He had just taken a mouthful of water from a bottle and spluttered at her words, spitting the water out like a fountain. A few droplets landed on her feet and she looked down at them distastefully.

"You're insulting my intelligence now?" he managed to cough out.

She frowned. "No, you asked a question and I offered an answer."

"By insulting my intelligence!"

"That wasn't my intention, but if you choose to take it that way I can't stop you."

He put his head to one side and observed her sardonically. "You," he said, "are what my grandmother would have referred to as 'an odd duck'."

"Oh I see. This is payback is it? You believe I insulted you – when I was merely pointing out a fact – and so you resort to childish name calling. Not a very mature response is it, but perhaps I shouldn't expect any better."

Her remark made his eyes flare and he got to his feet swiftly, striding up the garden path to stand in front of her. It was the closest anyone had stood to Anna in a very long time, and immediately she felt her body tense and little pinpricks of skin pop up, as if someone had just tickled her with a hundred feathers. She held her breath.

"Now that's not fair," he said, quietly but sternly. "You're judging me based on what? Casual conversation and your mistaken belief that I was stalking you when in fact I was only showing concern?"

Anna's ears were listening but her eyes, deprived of another person in such close proximity for some time now, had a curious life of their own, and while he talked they were busy examining the colour of his skin up close – rich like polished rimu wood – and the little trees of stubble that were sprouting from his chin – some grey dotted in amongst the black, she was surprised to see. She tried to think of a word to describe the colour of his eyes but the closest she could come up was a kind of sea green, like the colour of smooth glass washed up on the beach. He had a small scar that extended from the edge of his left eyebrow and ran across his temple before disappearing into his hairline. She wondered briefly at its cause before remembering that actually he was of no interest to her, and took a step backwards. Even so, it was a minute before the scent of him – he smelt of nature and soap, the plain white one you could pick up at any supermarket for fifty cents apiece – left her nostrils.

He was still talking.

" – and I don't know why or when exactly you formed this opinion of me, and I have no idea why it bugs me as much as it does - because it *really* does – or why I feel the urge to correct you, but if you could see the way *you* yourself come across to people you've just met I'm guessing you wouldn't be so quick to judge."

"Really."

"Yes, *really*."

"How do I come across?"

"You sure you want to know? I wouldn't want to offend you."

"I wouldn't ask if I didn't."

"Alright then. Uptight. You come across as a bit uptight."

She defined the word in her head and concluded that he was probably right. "I can accept that."

"And rude."

"Rude? I am not rude."

"You can be, and I haven't finished. You also come across as arrogant."

She opened her mouth to protest. No one had ever accused her of being arrogant before, and she resented the application of the title now. "I am not arrogant."

"What would you call it then? Correcting someone you've just met on their speech when the word they've used is actually perfectly acceptable by most people's standards? See, I checked around and no one else thinks there's anything wrong with the term, 'keeping' ducks."

"What would I call it? I'd call it, 'teaching'. Doing you a favour. And the reason your friends don't see anything wrong with it is probably because you all speak the same language."

"Of course we do. And that language is English."

"You can call it what you like. As I told you then when this conversation originally took place, I meant no offence. I apologise if it came across that way."

"Apology accepted."

"Oh how very gracious of you."

"I'm a gracious kind of guy. It's one of my many wonderful traits."

"Really."

"Yes, really."

"Anyway what are you, an elephant?"

He was confused by the sudden turn the conversation had taken. "Elephant?"

"Yes, holding a grudge about something so silly. It's very tiresome."

He laughed, all traces of his earlier anger gone. He held up his hands in a conciliatory gesture. "No grudge, and I promise that's the last time I mention it."

"Good. I hope so."

He held out his right hand, "Deal?"

She gave the question serious consideration before reaching out her own hand and sliding it inside his. "Deal."

"As long as you promise you'll give me another chance to show you what a lovely guy I really am," he said, not letting go of her hand. He wondered if she were feeling popping tingles up her arm too, like the small ones you get when you place your tongue on the end of a battery to check if it has any life left.

"Says who?"

"Ask anyone around town, they'll all tell you the same thing. Matt Pritchard is a stand up bloke, honest as the day is long, loyal as a Labrador. The ladies might add that he's not bad to look at either," he winked at her.

"And modest, don't forget modest."

"Yes he's very modest."

Anna enjoyed the way his smile made her feel for a moment, warmed through to the creamy marrow inside her bones. Her body had been subjected to a long and particularly cold and brutal internal winter. It was testament to her very character that she had survived. But now, with his full wattage smile, she felt the first icicles start to melt – *drip, drip* – and the snow begin to thaw and recede, revealing pockets of new green growth. Hopeful and optimistic, blinking under the bright glare of the sun.

Oh no, she thought. *No this won't do at all.*

"Shouldn't you check on Oscar?" she asked, but managed to make it sound more of an order than a question. She turned back to the gate, almost kicking the paint tin over in her haste.

Matt watched her shut down from him. He knew it wasn't because she was suddenly desperate to continue with her painting. He had seen the joy in her eyes, the unreserved moment of pleasure she had allowed herself to feel, even if it *was* only for a moment. Now that he knew he could elicit that kind of response from her, that she wasn't always gruff and curt and all rough edges, he wanted so badly to do it again.

"I guess, although I did tell him to scream out if he ran into any trouble." Matt wandered off around the side of the house but came back almost immediately, a wide smile on his face. He indicated with a finger for her to follow him.

"What is it? I'm trying to paint a gate here."

"That can wait. You have to see this."

Sighing heavily, she put the brush down with the wet end on the upturned paint lid and followed him.

"Hardly notice we're here, you said –" she muttered and got a fright when Matt turned suddenly causing her to bump against him. He held a finger up to his lips. "Shut up and look," he whispered, pointing towards her large back garden, where raspberries grew wild amongst white roses, Daphne bushes, lavender plants and some self seeded cherry tomatoes. She peered in the direction his finger was pointing, at first seeing only the lush green of her garden. Then her eyes adjusted and she saw Oscar, sitting beside a large ornamental rock beneath a climbing rose. He hadn't notice them approach, and she soon saw why. His attention was utterly focused on the ducks sitting all around him. To her astonishment, she realised one was even in his lap, and she took a step forward because she figured he must have captured the duck against its will. Why else would it be sitting on his lap? Then she saw his hands. One was cupped against the ducks breast gently and the other was making soft gentle strokes down its back. If Ducks could purr she imagined that duck would be doing so.

"Huh," she said, forgetting to whisper in her astonishment. Oscar looked up and several of the ducks clambered to their feet, startled.

'QUACK QUACK'

"Shush, it's ok, it's alright," Oscar soothed them and they settled down again, casting reproachful looks at Anna.

Matt waved a greeting and then led a dazed Anna back to the front of the house.

"But, but how -?" she stammered.

"I take it from your expression that they don't do that for you."

She shook her head, outraged. "No, they certainly don't do that for me, the ungrateful little –" but she didn't finish the sentence, not being able to think of a word suitable to say in front of him. "They've never let me so much as touch a feather," she said instead. "I feed them and care for them and what do I get for it? A few pecks on the hand if I get too close, that's what."

"You shouldn't take it personally," Matt pacified her. "The kid has read every book in his school library on the subject of ducks, plus burned through my month's data plan on the internet in one week. Maybe he picked up a special duck whispering trick you don't know about."

"Maybe," but she didn't sound convinced.

"You're not really upset are you?"

"No, not really. It's nice that he's made a connection with them. Do I wish it was me instead? I'd be lying if I said no. But it's just one of those things, no point dwelling on it. Right," she bent down and picked up her brush, "back to the work I guess."

"Let me help."

"No thank you."

"Please, it's the least I can do for gate crashing your Saturday."

"I guess when you put it that way. Here," she handed him the brush she'd been using. "I'll get another one."

He looked at where she'd already almost finished the arch and had just the front section of the gate left to do.

"Where do you want me?"

"I beg your pardon?"

He smirked, aware of how it had sounded and how, he could tell from the pinpricks of colour on her cheeks, she had heard it. "To paint. Where do you want me to paint?"

"Oh right." She pointed. "There. The whole front of the fence needs doing."

He frowned. "I can't paint that."

"Why not?"

He looked at her as if the answer was blindingly obvious. "Because you can't even see half the fence, that's why."

"You're exaggerating."

"I am not." He walked to the fence and kicked at some stray Ivy that was creeping along the bottom. Then he pointed wordlessly to where long grass poked up and out through the cracks between the boards and lastly he used his arms to sweepingly indicate the delicate baby pink rose that had settled heavily along the top of the fence, draping herself majestically, her flowers perfectly formed and begging to be admired.

"It's not covering half the fence," she said when he had finished making his point, "maybe a third."

He sighed heavily. "I am not going to argue details with you. My point is that I can't very well paint the fence properly with all this lot hanging all over it, can I."

"I didn't ask you paint it properly."

"I may regret asking this, but explain."

She walked over to join him, muttering, "This would have gone much quicker if I'd just done it myself."

"I heard that."

At the fence she gave him a look she usually reserved for her most difficult customers and then using both arms she gently lifted up a section of the rose. "There, see."

He crouched down to see what she was showing him and when he did he whistled. "Ok now I've seen it all."

She dropped the rose and brushed her hands against her shorts. "Questions?"

"Yes. Have you always been this lazy?"

"I'm not lazy."

"What would you call it? He lifted the rose again. Underneath where it normally draped, the fence was old and a faded ivory colour. You could see where Anna had painted *around* the rose, each coat covering less area as the rose had grown bigger, leaving a concentric rainbow of Anna's previous fence colour choices.

"I call it practical. Why paint an area that no one can see?"

"Because that's just what you do."

"Why?"

He struggled to come up with an answer that would beat her child's logic. "Because you just do, he feebly came up with.

"A compelling argument, but let's just agree to disagree. You paint your own fence whichever way you choose, and I'll paint mine the way I like it painted, ok?"

"But...it looks *weird*."

"Only if you lift the rose up, otherwise you can't even tell. You never noticed did you?"

"No," he admitted.

"There you go then. Now if you don't mind, I would like to finish this job today. You can either help or leave me to it. Which will it be?"

"I'll help."

"Fine." She turned her back on him and walked out to the back shed to fetch a clean paintbrush. When she was around the side of the house she laughed quietly. The expression on his face had really been quite comical. She knew it was the cheats' way to paint the fence but she was loathe to cut back the beautiful rose, so painting around it seemed the kindest thing to do. She checked quietly on Oscar on her way back – still happily ensconced in the garden with the adoring ducks – and popped inside briefly to gulp down a glass of cool water. Then she did something that took her completely by surprise. On her way back out she caught sight of her reflection in the old round mirror that hung by an assortment of coats and to her great surprise, she paused. Her startled expression in the mirror confirmed the uncharacteristic manner of this action. After all, she passed this mirror several times a day and never stopped to even glance at it. In fact, she'd almost forgotten it was even there. But today, for some reason, she stopped. Today she took a moment to study her image reflectively, and it was just a moment because when she realised what she was doing she flushed, cross with herself.

Matt wasn't sure what he'd done to earn the particularly irritated glare that was cast his way when Anna rejoined him back out front, but he wasn't about to ask either. He kept his mouth shut and his brush strokes even.

Chapter thirteen

With the two of them painting the job was finished in another hour. They stepped back off the kerb to admire their handiwork.

"Phew," said Anna, wiping the sweat off her brow, "it's hot."

"That has got to be the understatement of the year," Matt croaked beside her, "I need water."

Anna observed his damp hairline and rosy skin. "I'm sorry. I probably should have offered you some before now."

"A more considerate boss would have."

"I'm not your – oh. I see, you're joking."

He grinned at her.

"I should leave you to suffer," she said primly. "But for the sake of your son I won't. Follow me."

She led him carefully through the gate,

"Don't touch the paint"

"Of course I won't touch the paint!"

Around the house to where the hose and tap were neatly coiled.

"There you go," she said.

"You're kidding."

"What?"

He shook his head, amused. "Nothing, this will do fine." He uncoiled a couple of metres of hose and turned the tap on, waiting for the first rush of water warmed by the sun to make its way through the pipe. She had turned her back on him, craning to catch sight of Oscar, and he silently whipped his shirt off over his head, thrilled by the feel of the slight breeze against his hot skin. The water started to run cold and he tipped down his head and held the water above it, gasping when it hit his skin.

"Oh god that's good," he groaned, letting the water soak though his hair and run down his back and chest. When he was satisfied with the relief that brought him he held the hose in front of him and gulped thirstily from it, not stopping until his thirst was temporarily satiated.

He flicked his hair out of his eyes and shook like a sheepdog, enjoying the sensation of being half naked in the sunshine. Often, during his hours of work, he found himself hot and sticky and bothered by the physical exertion and it was all he could do not to stop himself stripping off like this and doing the same thing with his water bottle. Only the fact that his places of work were generally public, and that he was employed to tend grass not put on a show, stopped him. Today was the culmination of many a hot days fantasy.

"You want a turn?" he asked Anna, who was still facing away from him. She looked over her shoulder and opened her mouth to answer but then she noticed his half naked state of undress. "Oh!" She turned quickly away and sucked in her breath sharply. She started to turn back towards him but stopped, completely at a loss for where she should look.

"What do you think you're doing?" she asked him.

"What does it look like I'm doing? I'm cooling off after a hard day's work. I should have thought that was pretty obvious."

"Oh please. You worked for an hour, that's it. And what if one of the neighbours sees you?"

"So I'm not wearing a shirt, it's hardly a big deal."

"It *is* around these parts," she said. "Mrs Foster at number 5 would have a heart attack if she saw you like that."

"Thanks for the compliment."

"I wasn't complimenting you."

He shrugged. "I choose to take it that way."

"Put your shirt back on," she ordered him, her back still turned on him and her eyes nervously scanning the six foot fence line in case someone should be spying.

"Why does it bother you so much?"

"It doesn't bother me," she lied. "It's others I'm worried about. What will Oscar think?"

"He'll think his dad got hot painting a fence and hosed himself off to cool down, which is, incidentally, what happened."

Anna knew her reaction was over the top, but she couldn't help it. It had been years since she'd been so close to a half naked man and it was making her nervous. Still, nervous or not, she couldn't help but notice that working outside was clearly good for him. It was certainly good for muscle definition. She had to fight the urge to sneak another furtive glance.

"That looks like fun," Oscar had approached them unseen.

Matt squirted the water at him playfully and laughed when he squealed.

"Had enough of the ducks yet?" Matt asked.

"I could never have enough of them. They're so cool and so, so soft, aren't they," he directed this last remark to Anna.

"I'll have to take your word for it."

Matt smiled at the bliss radiating from his son's face. "I think you've found your calling in life. A duck specialist, if there is such a thing."

"There is, it's called an ornithologist. They don't just deal with ducks though, they study all birds," Anna informed them.

"An orni… what now?"

"Ornithologist."

"You made that up."

"I did not."

'I know, I'm teasing."

"You have an odd sense of humour."

"Yes, but odd-weird? Or odd-hilarious." Matt winked knowingly.

"That doesn't make any sense. Odd is not a definition of hilarious."

"Here we go again," Matt rolled his eyes at Oscar. "Another language lesson."

"Well if you choose to butcher the English language as you do then you should expect people to correct you."

"Yet somehow I've managed to get through life ok until now."

"Dad," interrupted Oscar.

"What?"

"Did we bring a drink?"

"We did," his dad answered sheepishly, "but I kind of left the bottle in the sun and now the water is boiling."

"It's hot but it's not technically boil –"

"For the love of god, *it's a figure of speech Anna*."

"Oh," she sighed. He really was a difficult one to understand. "Follow me Oscar, I'll get you something to drink."

"How come he's allowed inside and I get the stinky old hose?" Matt called after them.

"Don't be silly. He's a child. Of course I'm not going to make him drink from the hose."

She disappeared into the house with Oscar trailing along behind her.

"I'm not being silly, *you* are," Matt mumbled childishly as he coiled the hose back up neatly onto its holder. He found them in the kitchen, Oscar sitting at the bench on a tall stool, legs dangling, a tall glass of something clear with bubbles fizzing away in front of him.

Matt peered at the glass. "He even gets ice cubes?"

"For goodness sakes, here," Anna handed him his own glass, "now stop complaining."

"Deal," he accepted the glass happily.

She arched her eyebrows at him expectantly.

"What? Oh right, thanks."

"You're welcome."

The three of them sat around the bench, enjoying their drinks and the cool shade protection offered by the house.

"I think this might be one of the hottest days we've had this summer," Matt broke the companionable silence.

"It's certainly up there, for sure," Anna agreed.

"And you picked today to paint your fence. Now who's the clever one."

"Excuse me, but if you hadn't come along when you did and interrupted me I'd have been finished hours ago."

"You can never admit when you're wrong can you?"

Oscar sensed his father and Anna were gearing up for another disagreement. For two people who barely knew each other they sure argued a lot. Most of it went over his head, and he wasn't entirely convinced they were really upset with each other, but it brought back echoes of the final years of his parents' marriage. They'd done their best not to let it affect him but he wasn't stupid. He heard them once they thought he was asleep in bed, the raised voices reverberating through the thin walls. He'd hated it, which is why he was relieved when they called it a day. This way, he got to enjoy both of them and they got to enjoy him and no one had to listen to his dad tell his mother to stop buying so many unnecessary tea towels and cushions just because 'they're on sale," or his mother growl his father daily for leaving his underwear on the bathroom floor.

This was different arguing though, between his father and Anna. For one, his father still had a smile on his face, which was reassuring. But still, he worried that his father might annoy Anna so much that she'd ban him from coming to see the ducks. He needed a distraction and looking out the window at the heat haze that hovered above the ground he thought of just the thing. He tugged at his father's sleeve to get his attention. "Can we go for a swim at the pools dad?"

Matt checked his watch. "It's a nice idea but the pools close in about an hour. It'd be a waste of money. By the time we got there we'd only get five or ten minutes to swim."

"Oh," Oscars face fell.

Seeing the sad expression on his face made something shuffle inside Anna's chest.

She surprised herself by saying, "I know a place we can go."

"Yeah? Where? Is it nearby?" Matt got up and took his glass to the sink, turning on the tap to rinse it. He was still shirtless and Anna took the opportunity to examine him while his back was turned. She'd seen bodies like his of course, although not in person. Not on anyone she knew, anyway. Obviously at beaches and other places where a lack of attire was more acceptable she'd seen other muscular men, but always from afar and never so close she could reach out and poke one.

Tim had been more of an 'indoors' specimen. His general genetic make-up and desk job accounted for that, although he did like to ride his mountain bike on weekends and once a year at Christmas played a game of rugby with extended family and friends. His skin also never tanned, merely turned pink with the first summers sun then peeled to reveal an even whiter shade than he'd started with.

Matt's upper body was as brown as her wooden floors, although without the scratches and scuff marks. He had a small smattering of freckles on his upper shoulders, but for the most part his skin was blemish free.

Anna didn't realise she had forgotten that he'd asked her a question until he finished rinsing his glass and turned, catching her studious look upon his body. He smiled knowingly which made her cross because she knew he was making the wrong assumptions. Just because she found herself slightly intrigued by his physical presence *did not* mean she found the man himself intriguing.

"So where is this place?" Matt prodded her.

She was glad he hadn't made any snide comments about her staring because if he had she might just have ordered him to leave, and that wouldn't have been very fair on Oscar.

She got up and rinsed her own glass. "It's not far. Let me just change into my swimsuit and grab some towels. You'll have to swim in your shorts I'm afraid," Anna told Oscar, "I don't have anything here that would fit you."

Oscar shrugged. "My shorts are fine."

"Don't worry about us," Matt told her, "we can swim in our underwear if need be." He was wearing a pair of knee length denim shorts that were entirely unsuitable for swimming.

The thought of Matt in his underwear made Anna drop the glass she'd been drying with a clatter. Luckily it was made of sturdy stuff and bounced rather than shattered, rolling and coming to a stop against the bench cupboards.

"Whoops," she said.

"You ok?"

"Perfectly fine. I'll be back in a moment."

Upstairs Anna fetched a one piece swimsuit from the back of a drawer – navy blue with white spots, very flattering – and grabbed three towels from the linen cupboard. On her way out the bedroom door she stopped, and without giving the action too much thought she opened Tim's drawers and pulled out a pair of faded baby blue swimming shorts, a modest knee length. She knew if she stopped to think about it too hard she might change her mind.

Making her way downstairs again she felt odd. Like a sore tooth, she isolated the feeling and prodded it. It *was* a nice feeling, she decided, an air of an excited expectation, an anticipatory buzz like when you wake up on Christmas morning and remember what day it is. It felt pleasant to be doing something spontaneous.

For some time now she had operated on a basis of routine, each day mapped out and thoroughly planned in advance. Occasionally things had tried to throw her days off course, like tiny fissures working their way in silently. Impromptu drinks after work, BBQ invitations; all politely but emphatically declined. There was comfort in familiarity, solace in solitude. Today she would make an exception.

Downstairs the guys were waiting for her outside the back door.

"Here," she threw the shorts to Matt. "You can borrow these."

He caught them and she saw his curious expression. She tensed herself for the inevitable question.

"Are you afraid I'll scare people away in my underwear?" he joked instead, and she relaxed.

"I'm afraid you'll get arrested for public indecency."

"You think I'm indecent? I rather like the sound of that, like I'm some wicked, dastardly pirate." He pretended to stab at Oscar with an imaginary sword. "Argh me matey!"

"You know what I meant."

"Yes but it's more fun to imagine it my way."

Anna made a humming noise and locked the back door, conscious of Matt's eyes on the back of her neck.

"This way," she said, leading them towards a gate nestled in amongst the giant back hedge. It was a rickety old thing that gave the appearance of having been bunged together from driftwood and bits of old wire. It also looked like it might fall apart if you were to apply too much pressure to it. Anna opened it confidently and left it ajar for Matt and Oscar to follow her through.

"I didn't realise there were empty fields behind you," Matt said. "No neighbours throwing noisy parties until all hours, or using the pathetic square patch of grass you call a front lawn as their dog's personal toilet."

"I have neighbours."

"Yes, but you're not surrounded on all sides though. You have what, eight? Nine? Other houses down a little cul de sac? But nothing behind you. Just look at this," he spread his arms wide, "It must be so peaceful."

After the divorce he had moved 'temporarily' into a one bedroom flat in town. It was conjoined to four other flats at ground level, with another five on top. The inner walls were cold white brick that were about as useful at keeping warmth in as they were at keeping noise out. He kept meaning to find somewhere a bit more suitable to have Oscar stay – he was fairly sure the guy in number eight was dealing drugs and the woman in number four entertained too many men to just be considered, 'popular' – and had even visited a few open homes, but nothing had grabbed his attention yet. Now, seeing where Anna lived, he realised why he'd been holding back. He didn't want to find just any old place, he wanted somewhere like this. His own piece of paradise.

They traipsed through the long grass in the field, knee high and crackly from the sun, along a narrow path that was slightly overgrown, as if no feet had travelled this way recently. Although they barely walked a few hundred metres it may as well have been a mile for the difference it made. The sound of a working town completely dropped away. Even though Anna lived on its outskirts there was still a distant hum in the air, of traffic, sirens and people going about their day to day lives. Like a hive of bees, there was a low cloud of noise that hung over any populated area, a sign of life happening.

Now though, all Matt could hear was his own footfall, and that of his son behind him and Anna ahead. He could hear the rustle as she pushed through the dry grass, and the sweet sound of birdsong, unseen in distant trees. He let the peace soak into him, felt his body relax with every step. As they walked he became aware of something else, the gentle babbling noise water makes as it travels over stones and along river beds. He tried to orientate his mind on a virtual map. Let's see, Anna's house was here, his mind pointed, so we must be heading towards – yes, he could see it now, the blue line running alongside the town, overlapping at one point as it made its way under a bridge on main street to travel past the cemetery, then bend in a semi circle and travel back out via a bridge on Old Mill Road by the school.

"We're heading to the river?" he asked.

"No," Anna stopped short in front of him, "we're already here."

He came up beside her and took a moment to absorb his surroundings. The river was around fifteen metres across, and although Matt could see the sandy bottom for a few metres out from the bank, after that it darkened into a dark green then almost black colour, indicating it dipped quite deeply in the middle. Bushy trees lined the far bank. Upstream the river stretched away off into the distance and about a hundred metres downstream the river turned a corner to the left and disappeared.

"This place is amazing," he said, dropping the towel he'd been holding into the long grass and stretching his arms above his head. "I bet you come here every day in summer."

Anna turned away from him so he couldn't see her face, kicking off her sandals and lining them up neatly on an old log. "Once upon a time I did," she replied in a flat tone, "but I haven't been in awhile." She pulled the elastic from her hair and put it on her left sandal, and placed her folded towel beside them.

He shook his head. "What a waste. If I lived here I would swim every day."

"The novelty wears off eventually."

"I doubt it." He looked around. "Where am I supposed to change into these?" He held up Tim's shorts and grinned at her wickedly. "Or shall I just change right here?"

Anna knew he was trying to get a reaction so she shrugged casually and said "wherever you like, it doesn't bother me." She didn't expect him to call her bluff and drop his shorts right in front of her and she thanked heaven for small mercies in that he was wearing underwear, even though they were a pale blue colour and snug, leaving little to the imagination.

"Oh!" she dropped her face into her hands. "What are you doing?"

"What does it look like? I'm changing. You said it didn't bother you if I did it right here so I am."

"I didn't mean it though."

"Then you shouldn't have said it. You can look now, I'm decent again."

Anna waited another minute to be sure, before risking a peek between her fingers. He was standing there in Tim's shorts, laughing at her.

She dropped her hands and scowled at him. "You're a scoundrel."

"It's not my fault you react the way you do."

"Dad?" Oscar had trailed behind them slightly on the walk, stopping to pick up sticks and whack the tops of grassy stalks off with them, typical boy behaviour. But now he had caught up and was standing at his father's elbow with a nervous expression on his face.

"What's up?" Matt asked him, still chuckling to himself as he recalled the horrified look that Anna wore when he'd dropped his shorts in front of her.

"I think I forgot to close the gate behind me."

"That's ok, we'll get it on the way back." Matt's attention was on Anna as she lifted her t-shirt over her head, folding it and placing it on her towel. She then lingered a moment, dipping her toes gently into the water, before quickly unzipping her shorts and wiggling them down over her hips. With a flourish she kicked them off and, unlike with her previous belongings, dumped them unceremoniously on the log before making her way down the bank. With a splash she dove in headfirst, causing ripples to fan out in large circles. He waited with bated breath for her to pop her head up again, a good four or five metres from the bank.

"Don't you know you're supposed to test the depth before you dive?" he growled at her. "You could have hurt yourself."

She shook the water from her face and hair and started making long languid strokes in front of her, enjoying the shock of the water against her heated skin and the embrace of the current. "Not likely," she answered him, "I've swum here a hundred times remember. I know exactly how deep the water is."

He knew he was overreacting but he couldn't help himself, he'd felt real fear when she'd disappeared beneath the surface. "Maybe, but as you said yourself you haven't been here in some time, it could have changed. That's the nature of rivers."

"Well I'm fine, so you can stop with the lecture." She flipped over onto her back and drifted further out into the water.

"Dad?"

"What?"

"I'm worried."

Oscars tone finally broke through Matt's distraction and he dropped to a crouch in front of his son. "What is it? What's wrong?" He could see Oscar's bottom lip starting to wobble, a sure sign tears weren't far away.

"I didn't mean to leave it open," he said, "but I did and now Anna will never let us come back again." The last word was high pitched and as he flung himself into his father's arms with a sob.

"Hey now, it's ok," Matt soothed him, stroking the back of his head. "It's just a gate, there's no need to get upset. Anna won't be mad at you."

Oscar drew back and wiped his nose noisily on his sleeve. "But look."

Matt followed the direction of his wobbling finger. "Ah," he said. "I see. Anna?"

"Yes?"

"We may have a situation."

"What sort of situation? Are you two going to get in or not? This water feels amazing."

"Yes, we will. But first I think we need to tell you something."

"That sounds rather ominous."

'QUACK QUACK QUACK QUACK'

Waddling furiously as if their lives depended on it the ducks bustled past Matt and Oscar and made a beeline for the water's edge, jumping fearlessly and landing almost on top of each other with splashes.

"Oh!" Anna spluttered as they splashed her while joining her in the water. "Where did you lot come from?"

"I'm really sorry Anna, I forgot to close the gate," Oscar kept his eyes on the ground. "They must have followed us."

Hearing his voice and realising how upset he was, Anna waded through the water to the bank. "Oscar it's ok, don't worry about it. This isn't the first time they've followed me here."

"It's not?"

"No," she said. "It's not. The first time they did it I got such a fright, like you just did. But they were fine. They swim and then they go home when they're ready."

"You're not angry?"

"Do I look angry?"

He studied her face. She looked the opposite of angry.

"Now get in here and have a swim, before it gets too dark," she told him, splashing water up the bank to wet both his and his father's feet.

"Last one in does dishes for a week!" Matt hollered, dive bombing off the bank despite his earlier misgivings. When he surfaced, laughing and shaking off water like a long haired dog, Anna gave him a pointed look.

"What?" he said innocently, "I jumped in the same place you did."

"Hypocrite."

The three of them enjoyed a leisurely swim, forgetting all sense of real time. Anna floated on her back and enjoyed the weightless sensation of the water. She knew why she had stopped coming here, of course. The memories had been too painful. It was a shame because it was a pleasure she had once thoroughly enjoyed, but there had been days it was all she could do just to get out of her bed in the morning, and some days she'd failed even at that. There had been no time, nor energy, for pleasurable pursuits. She'd neither wanted nor expected to feel pleasure ever again.

Life marches unwaveringly on though, and when she didn't kill herself in the first year afterwards, her family and friends gave a sigh of relief and held a dinner party, of all things, where they silently congratulated themselves on 'seeing her through the darkest patch.' Unaware that the whole time Anna sat on the couch, numb, nursing a drink that she feared drinking lest she be unable to stop herself from drinking the whole bottle, cursing her cowardice and her inability to do what needed to be done to end the pain.

She was not over it now and she knew she never would be, but she was through it enough to be grateful that she hadn't given in to those early desperate thoughts. She wondered what other simple pleasures she had denied herself, but that hurt to think about so she decided to just enjoy the wonder of the moment instead.

Matt also floated on his back and enjoyed the tranquillity, but it wasn't long before he became bored with that and started to investigate his surroundings. He poked with sticks in the bushes to see if he could rustle up some eels, much to Anna's dismay. To his disgust - and her relief - there were none to be found. Then he and Oscar started collecting large stones the size of two fists from the riverbed and built a small dam on a part of the river where the water was only ankle deep. When they'd finished, only succeeding in rerouting the water thirty centimetres from its previous path, they pumped hands in congratulations of a job well done and patted each other on the back, as proud of their efforts as if they'd just built the Panama canal.

The ducks swam around them in lazy circles, protesting if Anna or Matt got too close, but perfectly content to let Oscar swim in their midst.

They stayed in the water until the sky was smudged yellow and gold, the horizon a blur of orange as the last of the sun's rays relinquished their hold on the sky above.

"Time to get out I think," Anna finally said reluctantly, holding up a hand and studying the wrinkled effect the water had wrought on her fingertips.

"Do we have to?" Oscar protested.

"I guess so," Matt sighed, not ready to leave, but knowing that as the parent it was up to him to lead by example.

"But it's not even dark yet."

Matt pulled himself up the bank and picked up his towel, dabbing at his face and chest. "It will be in about twenty minutes though. And unless you feel like finding your way back by yourself in the dark, I suggest you do as you're told."

He was joking but it worked, and Oscar reluctantly got out of the water. "Can we come back next weekend?" he begged his father.

Matt glanced over at Anna, who was also out of the water and towelling herself down, her earlier body inhibitions washed away by the water. She was half turned away from him, silhouetted against the sun. He already knew she had a lithe figure, but now he could see that she bordered on almost too slim, her ribs pushing against her swimsuit as she reached up to rub the towel over her hair. When she lifted her arms her breasts rose up too, their perky tips standing to attention against the coolness of the breeze against her wet swimsuit, and he found he couldn't take his eyes off them.

He'd never wanted anyone more in his life than he wanted her in that moment. The feeling came from nowhere, the intensity of it stealing the breath from his lungs. In that moment he needed to touch her, to taste her, to feel her skin against his own. He wanted to tear the swimsuit from her body, fall to the grass with her and feel her legs around his waist while he made her moan his name into the sky.

If Oscar hadn't flicked him with his towel just then, reminding him of his presence, he might have reached out for her. It took a moment for his head to clear and for his eyes to focus on his son.

"You ok dad?"

"What?"

"You look funny."

Anna finished wrapping her towel around her waist and turned to see what Oscar meant, and in doing so she just caught the tail end of longing before it fled from Matt's eyes. Not before it had burnt her with its force though.

No one had ever looked at her like that. She thought men only looked at women like that in the movies, or those Mills and Boons books her nana used to devour. She straightened up and bit her bottom lip without even realising she was doing so, and busied herself checking the log to make sure she wasn't leaving anything behind. When she risked a glance at Matt again the look was gone, replaced with his normal jovial one.

"What about the ducks?" Oscar asked, oblivious to the atmosphere.

"They'll follow us, you'll see," Anna said briskly, and she headed back along the way they had come. The shadows cast by the night swallowed her quickly, until they could only tell her passage by the sound of disturbed grass.

Chapter fourteen

"Penny for your thoughts? Of course, I'd expect you to bank it safely away for a rainy day haha," Mr Hedley chuckled, pleased with his own wit.

Anna smiled. He would have to twist her thumbnails out with a corkscrew to get her to tell him what had been on her mind; specifically, the 'look' Matt had given her last weekend. Annoyingly, it was pretty much all she'd thought about in the minutes and hours and days since, despite varying attempts to distract herself.

"Morning Sir. I was just mentally making sure I've got everything ready for my next client," she lied. "She wants to open her own business and needs a start up loan."

"What sort of business?"

"Bookshop."

"Oh dear, a risky venture in these hard economic times. Food, on the other hand; people will always buy food. Has she thought about opening a cafe instead?"

"I'm not sure."

"Perhaps you should mention it."

"I'll do that Sir."

"Good. Good." Mr Hedley's eyes momentarily glazed over. "Oh I miss those days," he said wistfully. "The thrill of being the one to change someone's life. Literally holding their dreams in your hands. There's nothing like it is there?"

"No," Anna agreed. "It's the reason I walk through the door every single day." This was also a lie, but a harmless one.

His face turned serious. "When you have a minute pop up to my office will you, I need to have a quick word."

Anna's heart quickened. Was this the day when he saw through her faked enthusiasm for the job and let her go? Despite her declarations that she couldn't care less if she had her job or not, she'd never been fired from anything in her life, and would be mortified if it were to happen now at her age.

"I have a few minutes now, if that suits?"

Might as well rip the band aid off quickly.

"Your client?"

She consulted the clock on her computer. "Not due for another fifteen minutes."

"Excellent. Come along then. No time like the present."

She could feel her heart beating a little faster than normal as she followed him up the stairs. Keeping her gaze fixed firmly on the scuffed heels of his shoes she imagined this was akin to being summoned to the principal's office, something else she'd never suffered the indignity of. It occurred to Anna that she'd led a pretty sheltered life, in terms of rebelliousness. Never parked anywhere she shouldn't, littered, or shoplifted even so much as a pack of gum, despite her high school friends pocketing lipsticks and mascaras willy nilly as if it were the easiest thing on earth to do. Upon reflection, as Mr Hedley led her to his office and held the door open for her, she wished she had lived a little, kicked up her heels, let her hair down. Clichés like that. Then she remembered she was merely being summoned to her bosses' office, not the hangman's noose.

"Come in Anna," he said, closing the door behind her and taking his seat behind his giant wooden desk.

Anna sat in one of the two green chairs on offer, dithering for a second over which one to choose – the one closest to the door in case she needed to run? – and settled for the one closest to the window for the view.

"How are you Anna?"

She gave him a bright smile. "Fine thanks Mr Hedley, just fine."

His face clouded over. 'It was a terrible thing, what happened to you. Still breaks my heart when I think about it."

Anna clasped her hands in her lap and studied them.

"I know I've told you this before," he continued, "but I do really admire the way you coped with everything. Not everyone has your strength, Anna."

"Thank you." She didn't want to hear this. If he only knew how fresh the pain could feel some days, as if it had been only yesterday. She didn't believe him either. If he knew how many nights she had sat on the floor in the dark, clutching an empty bottle - having consumed enough alcohol to fell a normal, healthy medium sized man - and fantasised about the various ways in which she could end it all, he wouldn't think her strong. To her eternal regret, she lacked the courage and conviction to see them through.

He watched her eyes squeeze shut and realised he had inadvertently set her mind on a path into the past. He set about bringing it back. "Right," he coughed loudly, "that's not what I brought you up here to discuss. Anna I'm sure you've heard the rumours already, the ones concerning my retirement."

Anna made a vague noise that could be construed as agreement.

"Sadly, they're all true. It's my time, I'm afraid. It's probably been due awhile, truth be told." He swivelled in his chair to survey the view out his window. From up here you could see all the way down Main Street, right from one end to the other. Anna followed his gaze as he watched people scurrying about their business on the street below. He sighed.

"I just wasn't ready to give it all up." A memory assailed him and he looked at her questioningly. "I lost a friend recently, John Cunningham, you know him?"

Anna shook her head. Should she?

"No, I don't suppose you would." He looked back out the window. "Forty five years that man dedicated to his business. One of the hardest workers I've ever had the pleasure to meet. Dropped dead last week on the golf course from a heart attack, just two weeks shy of retirement." He shook his head sorrowfully. "Poor guy didn't even get to finish his game, only had one hole left to go. He was winning; at least he went out knowing that I suppose. It's one thing to be grateful for."

Anna nodded, not sure if it would have been of any consolation to the deceased.

"Funeral was yesterday. The family are devastated, understandably. It's the wife I feel sorry for. She's stood by him for all these years, running the household and raising the children. She's been waiting for him to retire so they could finally get around to doing things together. Holidays all booked, cruises and safaris and the like. She'll be lucky to get her deposits back now."

Anna murmured sympathetically. She was starting to wonder how much longer this story was going to go on for, and its relevance to her.

"Life isn't always fair, Anna." Then he remembered who he was talking to and flushed. "But you of all people know that."

That was enough. She didn't need him to keep reminding her of what she had lost; she had an empty house and a permanent ache in her heart to do that. She tapped her watch pointedly. "Sir, was there something you wanted to discuss? Only I have a client due in, remember?"

"Yes, of course. I mustn't keep customers waiting." He straightened up at his desk, instantly looking less frail old man and more dignified businessman again. "Right, so as I was saying, the time to move on to the next chapter in my life is here. Obviously we need an efficient branch manager to take my place, -"

Anna's heart quickened. Was he about to tell her she had the job?

" – and after much deliberation the decision has been made to award the position to Judy."

He smiled at her, waiting for her reaction.

Anna relaxed again, relieved. It was a position she held no desire for.

"I am aware she's not the most, *popular*, person, but that's part of the reason why it was decided she might be better suited up here and off the shop floor. Although please keep that little bit of information just between us." He winked at her, his co-conspirator.

"Of course." Fat chance.

He leaned forward and spoke quietly. "Also between us, I put your name forward for the job, but it was felt by others that Judy has more experience over a broader range of areas."

"Thank you anyway sir. I appreciate the thought." And she did. Although she held no desire for the position it was nice to know he thought she was capable. It was just unfortunate that Judy had been the one chosen. Anna had a hunch things were about to become insufferable.

"I'd appreciate it if you keep it to yourself until it's announced officially at the next staff meeting. I just wanted to let *you* know personally beforehand, as I know you and Judy don't always see eye to eye. You will try to get on with her though Anna, will you? I know you have your differences but the others look up to you. If they see you making an effort to get to know Judy better they might make an effort also."

This was putting things rather mildly. The differences between her and Judy were as obvious as the difference between a spade and a chair.

"Forget any past slights," he continued, "let's have a fresh start, a clean slate. I have every faith this bank will go on from strength to strength under her leadership."

His optimism was misplaced, thought Anna. It was more likely to self combust with Judy at the helm. Not for the first time, she was in awe of the poor lack of judgment shown by management.

"I appreciate the heads up sir. For the record, I think the wrong choice has been made. Louise would have been a much better choice for the job, but only time will tell."

Louise - forty something, kind face, pleasant natured and friend to all – was the one they'd all been hoping would get the promotion. She would be devastated by the announcement and Anna wondered if she should risk giving her a heads up. It was the nice thing to do and she knew if the shoe were on the other foot she would want someone to warn her. She would have a quiet word in her ear later, she decided.

Mr Hedley had the look of a man tempted to agree, but forty years of managerial diplomacy got the better of him. He stood up slowly, his bones taking their time to process the instructions from his brain so it looked for a moment as if he might fall, but at the last second the message got through and he rallied, straightening up intact.

Anna felt a small flooding of fondness towards him. As an employer he'd been more than a little understanding; after all, to put it mildly, there had been times when she'd been a rubbish employee. Days when she'd not bothered coming in to work, without even a phone call to let them know not to expect her. She had simply not shown up. Other days when she'd left suddenly without a word to anyone. Overwhelmed by too many people and too much noise she'd just picked up her handbag from under the desk and walked out.

Her unreliability had driven Judy wild. But not Mr Hedley. He'd had no words, but he'd smile at her sadly upon her return and pat her on the shoulder.

Joining him at the door he was once again holding open for her, she realised how much she would miss the sight of him wandering amiably around the building, shaking hands with customers, stooping to admire babies in prams. He was about as caring and genuine as they come, and people like him were hard to come by. Before the action had been approved by her brain she reached up and kissed him on his cheek; it felt papery and smelt like old spice, the same aftershave her grandfather had worn.

"Oh!"

She had surprised him. He smiled and touched the spot on his cheek where her lips had pressed. "What was that for?"

"Thank you," she said, "for everything. Take care and enjoy retirement Sir. Don't give this place another thought."

"That's unlikely Anna," he chuckled, "you don't spend as long as I have in a place without forming an attachment, but, thank you."

She left him at the door to his office and paused at the top of the stairs to take a deep breath and compose herself, before descending to the familiar hum of business as usual below.

Chapter fifteen

The day dawned without any hint of the things that had happened during the night. The light around the curtains appeared perhaps a little later than it had the day before but it was mere seconds, not enough to be worried about colder and darker days just yet. Anna's back made its usual protests as she left the nursery. Her uniform, as she shrugged it on, served its usual purpose of muffling any spirit she may have felt towards the day ahead.

The day felt exactly the same as the day before, and the day before that, and the days before that.

How many days ahead would be the same? Once, after the best part of a bottle of wine, she'd tried to work out a number on the fancy scientific grey calculator of Tim's that was kept in the third drawer down in the kitchen, along with other assorted random useful things. But she didn't understand what half the buttons were for and she kept pushing the wrong things, coming up with nine digits numbers with lots of eights and sixes, so she gave up.

Anyway, it was useless trying to predict how many days a person had left, she remembered that in the cold sober light of the next day. It could just as easily be one as one thousand.

She'd thrown the calculator in the rubbish.

At the back door the ducks were perhaps a little more subdued than normal, but in her preoccupied state about the meeting to come – the one where she would have to observe Judy's smug face after the announcement was made – she failed to notice. It was only as she went to relieve Mrs Dudley for breakfast that she realised something had happened.

Mrs Dudley was not there.

Anna knelt and lifted the flax fronds completely off the ground, feeling with her hand all the way underneath just to be sure. Definitely no Mrs Dudley, and no sign of the eggs either.

She got back to her feet, dusting dirt off her stockings, and set about searching the garden, a horrible feeling of doom heavy in her heart. Upon seeing the empty nest Anna had immediately assumed the worst, a night marauder in the garden, and it wasn't long before her suspicions were confirmed. Over by the corner of the garden shed she spied a smattering of feathers, and closer inspection revealed some of the white downy ends were spotted with blood. Anna's hand flew to her mouth and she gasped. Nearby lay fragments of shell, broken and jagged like some macabre fine china jigsaw puzzle.

"Oh no!" she choked out a sob, "Oh Mrs Dudley." She covered her face with her hands and let the tears flow. The other ducks, sensing her sadness, watched solemnly from over beside the back door. When she had cried for a few minutes

Anna remembered them and wiping the tears away with her fingers she did a quick head count, feeling a small, fleeting relief when she found the rest were accounted for. She shook her head at them sadly.

"What happened last night?" she asked, desperate for answers. The ducks stayed uncharacteristically silent, heads to the side, eyes fixed on her face.

"Was it a dog? Ferret? A cat?"

Still the ducks remained silent. Anna found it eerie, compared to their normal rambunctious noise. She sagged.

"You're right, what does it matter. The end result is still the same." She turned back to the scene of carnage. "I hope it was quick," she said sadly, unable to bear the thought of Mrs Dudley suffering. She set about picking up the feathers, tears falling again, not bothering to wipe them away just letting them fall to the ground as she worked.

In the garden shed Anna found a small plastic container, green with coloured swirls like a paua shell. For a minute she couldn't remember where it had come from but then a vague recollection of a pink cyclamen plant, gifted at the time of the funerals, rose to the front. She couldn't recall who had given it to her; nor what had become of the plant.

Memories from those days were as scattered as pollen on the breeze. Days splintered into fragments; marked only by various senses. Sounds as people bustled quietly around her, swishing skirts, gentle footfalls, doors closed softly. Voices, muffled in her ears as if she were deep underwater. Various scents in her nostrils from food delivered to her door by well meaning friends and acquaintances, accepted by someone other than her and either placed in the fridge for later that day or into the chest freezer for the future. She resented those smells deeply at the time; they invaded her space and threatened to replace the normal smell of her household, the ones she was clinging to for comfort. Some of those containers were still in her freezer, white with accumulated ice, their mystery contents frozen for eternity. Anna had no interest in eating any of them, but nor could she bring herself to throw them away. People meant well. It seemed a waste to dispose of their good intentions.

Placing the feathers in the container she went back out to pick up the shell fragments, and it was then that a spot of stark white against green caught her eye. Carrying the container she walked over to the gate to investigate. The gate, she was upset to discover, was slightly ajar, and she pushed it firmly shut and nudged the latch down with an elbow, thinking sadly that it was too little too late.

Dropping her gaze to the ground she saw again the object that had attracted her attention in the first place. Nestled in the long grass was an egg. She gasped and placed the container down quickly, gently picking it up and nestling it in against her cheek. It was still warm.

Fuelled by a determination she'd not felt in a long time, Anna carried it carefully back to the house, taking care not to trip on any loose bricks in the path or over the other ducks who were still gathered near the back door. Cupping it carefully in her hands she dodged around them and made her way inside.

She had no clear plan in mind, she just knew that she had to save the egg. It was a survivor; it had shown that by surviving whatever attack had taken place the night before. Its mother and siblings had been slaughtered but by some miracle it had survived, and Anna was not about to let it die now. Not without a fight.

Right, she thought, I have to keep it warm somehow. Looking around the first thing her eyes fell on was the microwave. No, she shook her head. She didn't want to cook the poor little thing. A bowl of hot water? No, same result probably. Oven, the fire; all the normal heating options were considered then dismissed quickly as monstrously unsuitable for her needs. In desperation Anna opened the third drawer – home of all things randomly handy – and with relief spied the hot water bottle a doting Tim had bought her years previously when she'd suffered from a sore back lugging her pregnant belly around.

Placing the egg gently in the middle of the carpet where it couldn't roll or fall off anything, Anna pulled the bottle out and filled the jug with water, flicking the switch down to boil. As it bubbled away she bit her lower lip while the rest of a plan formulated.

Warmth. As far as she could tell that was all the egg required from the mother duck during the nesting period. With the sudden and tragic departure of Mrs Dudley's fluffy bottom Anna knew she would have to step in and take her place. Jug boiled, she poured the water into the hot water bottle, with a smidgeon of cold to cool it down a fraction. Then she carefully wrapped it in a clean tea towel and holding the egg carefully in place on top of the bottle she wrapped a scarf around the whole lot, holding the egg snugly in place. There, she thought. That should do for now at least, and then she placed the odd bundle into the hot water cupboard for extra good measure.

It was only then reality crept back in and she realised she was not only late for work, she was *extremely* late for work. Bordering on absent. No point in going in now, Anna thought, kicking her shoes off and peeling down her muddied stockings. She made a phone call to the branch informing them she wouldn't be in for a few days due to illness.

"What sort of illness?" Judy asked suspiciously, her tone implying she didn't believe Anna for a second.

"The kind that causes violent bouts of diarrhoea," Anna told her.

"I expect you to bring a medical certificate in when you return."

"Of course." Anna had no such intention.

Judy hung up without another word. Anna poked her tongue out at the receiver before replacing it back on its stand. "Honestly," she sighed, "why would someone choose to live their life being so miserable and mean?"

Then it occurred to her that she herself was choosing to live her life in a fashion that some might find depressing. She shook her head; it was different.

Changed into something more casual, Anna fired up the computer, making herself a coffee while she waited. She was itching to check on the egg but knew it was best to leave it alone. So while she drank she googled orphaned duck eggs and how to look after them. It was surprising how many stories came up in her search results. Some were inspiring tales where the eggs went on to hatch. Others were not as successful, the eggs rotting and having to be disposed of.

Well not her egg. She would not let it down. The egg was vulnerable, so many dangers in the world to face, but she would be its protector. She would not fail this time.

Chapter sixteen

Over the next few days, apart from when it was having a spell in the hot water cupboard, the egg barely left Anna's sight. During the day she kept it close to her person, nestled in the safety of her bra where it could absorb the heat from her body and be comforted by the sound of her heart beating. If she did an activity that required exertion and therefore posed breakage risks to the egg, she did her hot water bottle trick. Sometimes she just sat in her armchair, the egg cupped in her hands and her hands held directly in the beam of a heat lamp she'd purchased from the local hardware store.

Apart from the third day when the shrill sound of the phone shattered the silence, she remained undisturbed. She knew without answering that it would be Judy calling to find out when she'd be back so she let it ring out.

No one knocked on the door.

No one text her cell phone, although they'd have been out of luck if they had as the majority of the time she forgot to charge the thing and it faded gently, beeping softly, into darkness.

It was just her and the egg.

Curiously, she couldn't have felt less alone. There'd been times in the past when the sense of being all alone in the world had been so strong she'd even got so desperate as to go and knock on a neighbours door on the pretence of borrowing something, a hammer perhaps, even though she had two of her own, just to make sure she wasn't the last person left alive.

Most of the time it didn't bother her. She shrugged off the normal human need for companionship and wore a mantle of contended solitude instead, the ducks all the friends and replacement family she needed.

Now there was that feeling, like that feeling in the air when winter gasps out his last breaths and spring takes her first joyful steps across the grass leaving budding daffodils and ridiculously cute bouncing lambs in her wake.

When she placed the egg against her chest and felt the shell soaking up her warmth, she could have sworn she could see a light deep within. Muted and soft, but an unmistakable life force.

Anna researched everything she would need to know about caring for a newborn duckling. She ordered a bag of special food online, enough to last for a few weeks according to the website, by which stage the duckling would begin to eat vegetables and fruit and other foods. She found a website that sold pet accessories, for every pet under the sun it seemed, and even though she could easily have splurged and bought special drinking bowls and a fancy container to use as the ducklings bed, in the end she decided a bowl from the cupboard and an old litter tray she found in the garden shed would do the job just fine. She lined the litter tray with warm blankets she ripped up.

On the fourth day of Anna's absence from work the world changed again.

In the morning, far earlier than Anna would have thought was socially acceptable, the phone rang. Busy preparing her breakfast by the sink she jumped, then froze and watched the light blink with each ring. She had the silly idea that if she moved whoever it was would be able to see her, so she stayed put until the lights and noise ceased. Thank god she hadn't been holding the egg she thought, shaking her head in amusement. The poor thing would have been bounced off the ceiling when she got a fright. Breakfast over and dishes done, she was heading to the hot water cupboard to check on her small, fragile charge when there was a knock on the door. Again she froze. Her first thought was that it was Judy come to check up on her, but since when did she make house calls to check on errant staff members?

Another knock, more insistent.

Anna decided to ignore it.

But with one foot on the bottom stair she remembered the duck food she had purchased online and realised it must be the courier at the door. Just in case by some hideous chance it was Judy, she paused before opening the door to affect an injured look, all droopy and miserable as she imagined one would look when 'sick' with a tummy bug. She opened the door.

"Hello," she croaked, then "Oh, it's you."

"Good morning," Matt said cheerfully. He took in her demeanour. "You look dreadful."

"Thanks. What are you doing here?"

"Can I come in?"

Grudgingly, Anna stepped to the side and allowed him to cross the threshold. She shut the door after him and discarded her 'sick' look.

He looked startled. "That's odd. You look miles better now. Must be bad the lighting by the door? Either that or the sight of me cheered you up."

"Something like that." Anna waited to see if Matt would explain the purpose of his uninvited visit but he just carried on smiling at her like he hadn't seen her for a year.

"Is there something I can help you with? I was kind of in the middle of something - ," she let the words trail off.

"Don't let me stop you," he shrugged, "I'll just put the jug on and make us a cuppa." And without waiting for an answer he headed into the kitchen. Anna's mouth dropped open. He knew nothing about boundaries, she thought. Or was she so out of touch that this kind of behaviour was now considered acceptable? If it was she wanted no bar of it. She had never turned up unannounced at someone's house and she never would.

"I was just passing and thought I'd pop in and make sure you're ok," Matt continued, as he held the jug under the tap and turned the water on to fill it.

Anna gave up. She hadn't known this man for long but already she knew that he wouldn't leave until he was good and ready. She followed him to the kitchen island and perched on one of the stools, watching as he made cups of coffee, finding everything as easily as if it were his own kitchen and not hers.

"Why wouldn't I be ok?" she finally answered him, watching as he rummaged in the pantry for biscuits and offered her one. "No thanks," she said, "I've only just finished breakfast."

"Fair enough," he helped himself to two and dragged one of the stools around the island, climbing up himself. "I'm so used to starting work at the crack of dawn I forget other people start the day much later. This is practically lunchtime for me." He dunked the biscuit and shoved the whole thing in his mouth, only remembering to shut it when he saw her watching, fascinated.

"What?" he mumbled, a crumb dropping to the bench. He swept it onto the floor and hoped she hadn't noticed.

She had, but she'd deal with it later. "Why are you here again?".

"Just checking in on my favourite new friend." He finished the second biscuit and got off the stool to fetch more from the pantry.

"What makes you think I need checking up on?"

"A lady at your work said you were off sick," he shrugged, "and you didn't answer the phone so I thought a visit was in order. I come bearing get well gifts."

Anna looked around pointedly. "Gifts?"

"Left them in the car. Wasn't sure you were home. Wait here," he crammed a fifth biscuit into his mouth and went out the front door, leaving it ajar. Anna felt an early breeze make its way inside and curl itself around her legs like a cat's tail.

"I'll be out soon," she promised it.

"Sorry?"

She hadn't heard Matt come back inside until he was standing right behind her.

"Nothing," she spun on the stool, "look –" the words dried up in her mouth when she saw what he was carrying. Her eyes followed the string in his hand up to where a giant round balloon bobbed near the ceiling; shiny silver with bright yellow letters spelling out 'Get Well Soon!" plastered across the face.

"You like it?" he beamed proudly.

"Well," she searched for the right words, giving up when none came to mind. "*Like* doesn't even come close," she settled for.

His smile got even wider. "I knew it would cheer you up. Here," he held out the string and she reached out and took it, surprised by how weightless the balloon was.

"It's filled with helium," he said, reading her look correctly. "It'll last for weeks."

"I can't believe you bought me a balloon."

"Biggest one in the shop."

"You shouldn't have." She meant it.

"Ahh, it was nothing," he was chuffed with himself and brushed off the thanks she hadn't given. "So what gives?"

"Pardon?" Anna's attention was still fixated on the bobbing balloon above her head. She'd take it outside once he was gone, she decided. Set it free. She imagined it soaring off up to the clouds.

"What's wrong? A cold? Tummy bug?"

"Oh yes, something like that." Then a thought occurred to her. "What were you doing at my work?" she frowned.

He flushed, embarrassed. "I thought I'd check out your interest rates and stuff. I'm in the market for a mortgage."

"Really?"

"Yes, really. Don't flatter yourself thinking it's anything else."

For the second time that day a knock sounded at the door.

"Are you expecting someone?" she frowned.

"Me? It's your house."

"But I'm not expecting anyone."

"Neither am I.

"Maybe someone followed you."

"Maybe, after all I forgot your location is supposed to be secret. Damn it, I forgot to turn left and double back a few times to shake anyone on my tail."

Anna let go of the balloon and walked to the door. Opening it, she saw the last people she had expected to see, and the sight of one in particular caused her to crumple against the door frame and sink heavily to the floor.

Chapter seventeen

"Anna! Anna can you hear me?"

"Of course she can hear you. Christ, the neighbours can probably hear you."

"Don't be rude."

"Well don't be so loud."

"It's what you do when someone faints, you have to try and get their attention."

"Learnt that during your medical training did you?"

"I saw it on Dr Oz, actually."

"Oh, well if it was on TV it must be true. Nothing's *ever* made up on TV, am I right?"

Anna heard Matt give a nervous chuckle and knew, even with her eyes squeezed tightly shut, that her father-in-law had just winked conspiratorially at him. Tempted as she was to keep her eyes closed and hope they would all go away, she felt the need to explain Matt's presence in her house. In Tim's, their son's house.

"Quick, her eyes are opening, she must be coming round. Anna can you tell me how many fingers I'm holding up?"

Anna squinted at the pale hand of Barbara, her mother in law. "Three."

Barbara sat back and nodded. "She's ok."

"Of course she's ok," her husband Frank said, "she's made of sturdy stuff, our Anna."

It was not the first time he'd applied that word to Anna, and it always left her with the impression he'd just called her fat, although she knew that wasn't the case.

"Frank, Barbara," she sat up on the couch – had someone carried her there? – and smiled at them with a welcome that didn't quite reach the corners of her lips, "how wonderful to see you both. To what do I owe the pleasure?" She directed this question, as she did all her questions, directly to Barbara. She found it difficult to meet Frank's eye; had done since the funeral. He looked so much like his son it hurt.

"We thought that as you've been unable to visit us, we'd come to you," Barbara's eyes roamed over Anna as she spoke, taking in her daughter-in-law's gaunt appearance. "Don't worry," she added, placing a hand soothingly on Anna's arm when she saw a fleeting ghost of panic flit across her eyes, "we've booked a hotel. We didn't want to intrude ourselves upon you without warning."

Anna studied Barbara's hand while she composed herself, the fingers long and only slightly betraying the passage of time, thanks largely to the lotion Barbara slathered on them religiously each night before bed. Despite the lack of lines and age spots, Anna noticed for the first time how papery thin the skin was. She could see veins pulsating just beneath the surface, green and bumpy in places. She'd never noticed them before, and seeing them now she was reminded of the woman's humanity. She so seldom betrayed her emotions, it was one of the reasons Anna couldn't bear to be around her after the funeral. But blood pulsed through her as it did through us all, and the knowledge gave Anna empathy towards the older woman. She placed her own hand on top of Barbara's.

"Of course you can stay here. You will always be welcome," but was nevertheless relieved when they declined.

"We've already unpacked our bags back at the room," Barbara waved a hand dismissively, her attention already on something else. Not something, Anna realised, following the direction of her gaze, but *someone.* Matt was standing at the end of the couch, looking far too comfortable in her house for Anna's liking.

"I told you we should have called ahead Frank," Barbara said, "Anna has company. We've interrupted."

"Nothing to interrupt," Anna countered briskly, getting to her feet. "Cup of tea? Coffee?"

"Sounds great, I'm gagging for a coffee," Frank sank into her vacated spot. "That packet stuff they have at the hotel is rubbish."

Barbara held out a hand to Matt. "I'm sorry," she said, "my husband has no manners. Fancy not introducing yourself to the man who saved our daughter in law. I am Barbara, and this is Frank." She waited expectantly.

Anna stopped and turned with a frown, interrupting the introductions. "I'm sorry, did you just say saved?" she asked. Too late she recalled her mother-in-laws fondness for the dramatic.

"Yes, saved. When you fell in a dead faint this kind man carried you to the couch. If he hadn't been here you'd have been left sprawled inelegantly for all and sundry to see. I certainly couldn't have moved you."

"What am I? Chopped liver?"

"No Frank, but you know what the chiropractor said about your back. You're not allowed to strain it."

"I'd hardly call Anna a strain, the girl weighs next to nothing, look at her."

All three of them turned to look at Anna. "I think using the word saved is being a tad over the top," she said. "And I didn't faint, I just lost my balance for a moment."

In the kitchen she refilled the jug, taking the opportunity while her back was to them to grit her teeth and scream silently. She could hear Matt introducing himself. This was the last thing she felt like dealing with. Not only a surprise visit from the very people who reminded her the most of everything that she had lost, but also having to explain to them Matt's presence.

"How do you know Anna?" Barbara asked as she settled herself on the couch beside her husband.

"We met at a playground," he told her. "My son took an interest in Anna's health and, after we made sure she got home ok, her ducks. Now I can't keep him away. He keeps dragging us back here, I'm sure it won't be long before she has us trespassed."

Anna groaned inwardly. Why did he have to mention the playground? She could feel Barbara's frown from across the room. No doubt she would have something to say on the subject later. Nothing that hadn't been said before though, and nothing that Anna wanted to hear.

"Is he outside with the ducks?"

"No he's at school."

"Are you here to visit the ducks then, or Anna?" Barbara threw a pointed look at Frank, who let it bounce off. It hit the far wall and scuttled off under the sideboard.

Matt raised his eyebrows at the brazenness of the woman. "I heard she was ill so I was thought I'd check up on her and see if there was anything she needed." He turned to Anna. "Is there anything you need?"

"No thank you, I'm fine."

"Right," he glanced at his watch. "In that case I'd better get going." He smiled at Barbara and Frank, "It was lovely to meet you both."

"I hope you're not leaving because of us," said Barbara.

"Of course not. I'd better get to work before they send out a search party." He took his keys out of his pocket and jangled them as he walked to the front door. Anna followed him, conscious of Barbara's eyes on her back. At the door there was an awkward moment where neither was sure what to say.

Matt pretended to search his bunch of keys for the right one while he tried to think of something to say. It had been a whim, to come here. He really didn't know a lot about Anna, and now he'd probably just freaked the hell out of her by turning up unannounced the way he had.

"Thanks for stopping by." Anna said.

"No problem, glad you're ok."

There was another awkward silence.

"I'd better get back to my guests," Anna broke it, thumbing over her shoulder to where Barbara was not even trying to pretend that she wasn't listening.

"Of course. Go. I'd better get to work. They might not send out a search party but the firing squad could be an option."

"Oh no," Anna was horrified.

"I'm joking."

"Oh. Of course."

"Let me know if you need anything. You know, a prescription filled. A bowl of homemade chicken soup. Although

I'll be honest and confess that it would come from a packet. I will heat it for you though. I can manage that."

"Thank you, it's a kind offer. But I'll be fine."

Now the fun begins, Anna thought after he'd left. She headed back to the kitchen to finish preparing the hot drinks and started an internal countdown. Three, two….

"So," Barbara said, in a false casual tone, "did I hear Matt say you met in a playground?"

"Yes."

"Oh Anna," she said softly, "what are you doing? Why torture yourself so, it's not healthy. Hasn't that doctor you see told you that?"

"Leave it Barbara," Anna warned gently. "I know you mean well but please, leave it. We all grieve in our own ways."

Barbara refused to back down. "Grieve yes, of course, but to purposely torture yourself? It's not right. You should have moved on by now."

Anna had just put the milk back in the fridge and she slammed the door hard. "*Moved on*?" The anger in her voice made the air shimmer.

"I'm sorry," Barbara backpedalled swiftly. "That was the wrong choice of words."

"It sure was." Anna took ten deep breaths. "Because get this straight, I will *never* move on. And if you ever say that to me again you'll no longer be welcome here."

The two women held each other's gaze steadily, neither willing to back down. In the end Frank broke the tension.

"Shall we take our coffees outside and admire Anna's handiwork?" he said.

"Great idea," Barbara agreed.

Anna knew it was far from over.

They took their drinks into the garden and admired her handiwork, tension simmering gently although they all played nice. She knew they had the best intentions, but still Anna couldn't wait for them to leave. No one else dared talk to her the way Barbara did. In Anna's experience people hoped what happened wouldn't come up when they engaged in general conversation with her. She could see it in their eyes, a mild look of panic as they wondered; what the hell will I say if she mentions it? They needn't have worried, she never mentioned it.

But Barbara, well she was a whole other kettle of fish. What happened to Anna had happened to her too, and she took the opposite approach to grieving from Anna in that she was *desperate* to talk about it, to anyone who'd listen, including the boy who pumped gas into her car and the woman who worked behind the meat counter in her local supermarket. If their names weren't mentioned people might forget they had lived, and there was no way she would allow that. Not while she still had air in her lungs.

The rest of the visit passed uneventfully, apart from when Barbara excused herself to use the bathroom and was upstairs for so long that Frank got nervous and Anna realised with mild annoyance that she was probably snooping. No doubt she would have something to say about the shrine that was the nursery, and the fact that Tim's shoes still peeped out from under the bed, but if she did she kept it to herself when she eventually returned back downstairs.

The really awkward moment came when she was walking them out and Anna spotted the shirt over the back of a chair about two seconds before Barbara did. Unfortunately this wasn't enough time to do anything except hope the older woman wouldn't see it. She put a hand against the small of the older woman's back and tried to steer her gently past it, but Barbara dug her feet in and resisted.

"Isn't that- ?" she reached out a hand and fingered the fabric questioningly, letting out a gentle sigh when the feel of it invoked a memory in her fingertips. "I thought so," she said quietly. "I gave it to him the Christmas before they died. The colour looked so good on him, really brought out the blue in his eyes." She stroked it as if it were a cat, lost in the past. "What's it doing here?"

And in the ten seconds it took Anna's brain to scramble up an answer she knew that Barbara saw right through it before it was even spoken. She said it anyway.

"I wear it sometimes to garden in. Better than wrecking my own clothes."

But even saying the lie hurt. She could never destroy anything that had belonged to either of them. It would be a dishonour to their memory.

"How long are you in town for?" Anna asked when they were at their car. She tried to make it sound conversational rather than desperate like she felt. How much longer would she need to pretend their presence didn't hurt her with all the memories it provoked? Surely the fact she never visited them, never picked up the phone to call and barely even answered their emails told them all they needed to know? Yes, it was selfish, but she could live with that. Seeing Frank, who had the same sky blue eyes and forceful nose as his son, was too hard. There was a reason they were in her life now that the reason was now gone they seemed determined not to let her slip away too. This was exactly what Anna would have preferred to do.

"Only another couple of days. We need to get back by Saturday to babysit Helen's kids while she goes to an overnight wedding."

Helen, Anna's sister-in law. If the tenuous connection that made you related to someone by 'law' became severed cut, were you still related? It wasn't the first time Anna had wondered.

"How is she?" she asked, only slightly interested in the answer. Helen, formerly a syndicated journalist, was a high flying, opinionated know it all, who thought Anna was 'without ambition'. She had spent multiple Christmases pestering Anna and trying to draw out 'just what it is you want to do with your life? *Surely* you can't be happy working in a bank and being a homemaker?' the last word dripping with her obvious distaste.

"Oh she's fine. The baby's been giving her a bit of grief with teething – damn things keep poking through then popping back down again – and her eldest might be dyslexic the teachers think, but other than that she's fine. Got voted in head of the PTA last month," Barbara said proudly. "She has some fantastic fundraising ideas for the school. Just needs to light a firecracker under some of the other parents; honestly, some people are just lazy and lacking when it comes to their own children's education."

Anna was amused that Helen seemed to have become the very thing she'd once despised, "If anyone can do it, Helen can." The woman had once bought a ministerial MP to tears on TV with a vicious line of questioning; what hope did a bunch of parents have?

Frank pushed the button to unlock the car and then Anna saw him and Barbara exchange a look. She steeled herself.

"This afternoon we're going to visit the cemetery. Will you come with us?"

Anna hated that word in this situation; visit. It implied pleasantness to the occasion that didn't fit.

"No," she shook her head emphatically. "Thank you, but I prefer to go on my own."

"Are you sure?" Frank made a rare plea.

"Yes."

He sighed and shrugged his shoulders at Barbara as if to say, 'I tried.'

"What are you doing for dinner tomorrow night then?"

"Tomorrow?" Anna pretended to ponder the question, as if there were a possibility she had plans to consider. But no, her diary was free, the pages blankly stretched before her. She failed to think of a lie in time.

"Great," Frank nodded, "that's settled then. You're dining with us. We'll pick you up around seven."

"Fine." Anna accepted her fate. One evening and then it would all be over. She could handle one evening. Of course she would have to rustle up something decent to wear, she realised, as waved them out of sight. Tights were not likely to cut it at a restaurant.

Her mood darkened by the morning's encounter, she grabbed a fistful of creamy yellow freesia's that had sprung up wild beside the fence and inhaled their sharp, fresh smell. The essence of summer was contained within the smooth petals; a tangy beautiful scent that spoke of long hot days and the beach.

Instantly she felt her mood lift and her step lightened as she went back into the house. Pouring water into a vase and straightening out the stalks with a pair of scissors, Anna reflected on the effect a scent can have upon a person. The smell of the freesias had perfumed the air in the house and even the walls seemed to have brightened. Daphne; that was the other flower whose strong and sharp scent could instantly cheer her up and transport her to another place. Her grandmother had grown white and pink Daphne bushes abundantly in her garden. She adored the smell and the sight of them, and would have vases of the bloom on every windowsill in the summer. Her grandfather would complain that he felt like he was living in a 'goddamn greenhouse', but it didn't really bother him. In fact, he would joke that it saved him money buying deodorant and aftershave for the months the Daphne invaded his house he smelt like one of the bushes himself.

Thinking about her grandparents bought up happy memories for Anna, and a contented feeling nestled smugly in her chest. But it wasn't long before a dark finger flicked at it annoyingly. She really ought to make the effort to go and visit them one of these days. She'd avoided it in recent times because of the pain they couldn't hide when they saw her, but she knew they could be gone at any time. Her mother had died when she was two from breast cancer, and her father followed twelve years later, only his was in the bowel. In hindsight her dad might have been saved, but he was old school; unaccustomed to talking about things like blood in his poo. So he kept quiet until the weight loss was obvious even to the postman, and by then it was too late. Anna, an only child, had lived with her grandparents until she went away to university. They were firm and loving, but forty years out of touch with raising a teenager, so it hadn't been a particularly close relationship.

It was only when the flowers were displayed jauntily above the kitchen sink that she remembered the egg. Matt's unannounced visit had completely thrown her morning out. She hurried to the cupboard and dug the egg out from its snug little man made nest. Phew. It still felt warm. Her shoulders relaxed. Then they tightened again. Something felt different. She took the egg out to the bright light of the kitchen and peered at it.

A crack had appeared. Tiny and jagged like a lightning bolt, it marred the smooth pristine surface of the shell. Anna's first thought was that she had somehow broken it, and she guiltily searched her memory for an inadvertent knock against a wall or door frame or something else that might explain it.

Then she remembered that it was, in fact, an egg, and she smacked her forehead and said "idiot."

The egg had started to hatch. Anna popped it in her bra against the heat of her skin and bit her lower lip excitedly like a small child lying awake on Christmas Eve listening for sounds from the rooftop.

Chapter eighteen

"Anna?"

"Mm?"

"The waiter asked if you were ready to order. You've been staring at the menu for ages."

"Of course, sorry. Um, let me see," she scanned the words in front of her and settled for the first one to grab her eye. "I'll have the scallops please."

"Very good, an excellent choice." The waiter scribbled something on his notepad. "And for your main course?"

She hadn't got that far yet. She took a stab in the dark. "For main I will have the chicken, thank you."

He sighed impatiently, but being a professional he did it under his breath. "Wonderful. And which chicken would that be?"

"You have more than one chicken?"

Another sigh, deeper. "Yes, madam. We have, in fact, four." His tone implied that she would know this if she had taken the time to actually read the menu.

Anna couldn't stand pretentious wait staff, and this guy was about as bad as they got. She decided to have some fun with him. Closing the sleeves of the menu she passed it back and treated him to her most winning smile. "Tell you what, I'll have whichever one is the most popular."

"That would be the roast chicken with smashed new potatoes and a garlicky jus."

"Sounds delicious. Yes, I'll have that."

The waiter nodded, made a note, and turned to go. But before he could leave she spoke again. "Actually you know what? It's a big decision. I'd better hear about the other chicken options."

The waiter narrowed his eyes. He held a menu out towards her again. "I'll leave this with madam for another five minutes, shall I?"

Anna ignored it. "No that's alright," she said, "you can just tell madam what they are."

He knew she was playing with him then, but ever the professional he nodded. "Very well. He sniffed and took some glasses from his top pocket, then peered at the menu. "Option one is, as previously mentioned, roast chicken with smashed new potatoes and a garlicky jus."

Anna's stomach growled.

"Option two, chicken, mushroom and bacon penne pasta, sprinkled with parmesan."

Anna disliked parmesan. The smell reminded of her sick. She screwed up her nose. "Next."

"Option three, *madam,* is roasted chicken with asiago polenta and truffled mushrooms."

Asiago polenta? Anna wasn't going to order something she'd never heard of.

"And finally, option four is chicken scaloppini with sugar snap peas, asparagus and a lemon salad."

The last one sounded summery and delicious and Anna was sorely tempted to switch her order, but the mention of smashed new potatoes had won her heart.

"Hmm," she pretended to consider her options. "You know what; I think I'll take the first option."

"The roast chicken with smashed new potatoes and a garlicky jus."

"Yes, that one."

The waiter consulted his pad. "The same dish you ordered initially then."

"Is it?"

He scribbled something on his pad.

"You just wrote, "spit on this ladies food', didn't you," Anna asked. She heard Matt snort down a laugh.

The waiter's top lip curled up in distaste. "Madam, I can assure you we are not that kind of establishment."

"Good to know."

The waiter got four steps from the table when a voice piped up. "Actually you know what, that chicken dish with the spuds sounds much nicer than what I ordered. Can you change my order to that too please?" The waiter nodded to Matt, his eyes the only outward sign of his internal feelings. He drew a heavy line on his pad. "Done," he said, then swivelled on his heel and departed swiftly, before anyone else could change their mind and drag the process out any longer.

Barbara excused herself to go to the bathroom and Frank asked Matt a question about his work, kick-starting a conversation about the merits of an indoor versus outdoor career. Frank and Barbara had owned a dairy farm right up until a few years previously when they'd retired and sold it for a fortune. Anna watched them talk and wondered again what had possessed Matt to accept Barbara's invitation.

When Frank and Barbara had picked her up they'd made no mention of inviting an extra guest, and even when they'd been seated at a table for four she'd just assumed it was an oversight on behalf of the restaurant. Right up until a voice behind her shoulder had cheerfully said "Sorry I'm late, I couldn't find a clean shirt. Had to wait for this one to air out in the dryer."

Anna had watched, confused, as Matt pulled out the fourth chair and sat down, smiling broadly around the table. His hair was freshly washed and still damp and he smelt like the inside of a pharmacy; a pleasant mix of shampoo and deodorant and aftershave.

"Evening Anna," he'd dipped his head toward her. "Long time no see."

When she didn't answer he frowned. "Are you ok?"

Her confused expression gave him his answer.

"You didn't know I was coming, did you," he said. "Well this is awkward."

"Don't be silly," Barbara had said. "There's nothing awkward about it. Anna dear, we ran into Matt and thought, wouldn't it be lovely if he joined us. You don't mind do you?"

"No," Anna finally spoke. "Not really I suppose."

It was hardly the encouraging answer Matt had hoped for. He still didn't know the full story behind Anna, although when he ran into her in-laws in town and they mentioned they were off to the cemetery he figured he had been in right in thinking Anna was widowed. He thought it a little odd they were so keen for him to join them for dinner, but hey, if they were paying and Anna was going to be there, he was in.

"Where's Oscar?" Anna asked.

"Oh crap," Matt pushed out his chair and started to stand up, "I knew I forgot something."

"You *forgot* him?"

"Relax, he's in the car."

"You left him in the car?" Anna was shocked, her voice rising and the people seated at a table nearby turned to see what the commotion was about.

Matt laughed and sat back down. 'I'm joking Anna. Christ you should see your face. He's with his mother."

"You think that was funny? You have a very weird sense of humour," Anna shook her head.

"So you keep telling me."

Anna realised that Barbara was watching the exchange with a satisfied expression and wondered what had got the woman feeling so smug. Then she saw Barbara give Frank a little nudge. The woman was in match making mode, Anna realised with horror. And the inappropriateness of it all nearly made her stumble to her feet and flee the restaurant. These were her in-laws, for goodness sake. She was married to their son and they had sat forefront and centre in a sea of white chairs and watched while she declared her everlasting love to him.

Till death do us part, she had said. Didn't that count for anything?

Oh, Anna thought. Except he *had* gone and died, hadn't he.

That kind of made the whole thing moot.

Still, it was enough to give her a headache. She picked up her wine glass and took a large gulp, then another, which finished it off.

"Silly restaurants and their tiny serving sizes," she muttered, not waiting for Frank to refill her glass but doing the job herself.

She took another mouthful then sighed. She hadn't completely ruled out the prospect of a romance somewhere in her future. Sometimes she thought about it in the small hours of the night when sleep eluded her, it was only natural. But she figured that she'd know when the time was right, and that time hadn't come yet. The thought of being with another man filled her with guilt, as if she would be being unfaithful to Tim, even though she knew it was what he wanted.

They'd discussed it once, back when they were newly married. It had been a summer's day, hot and sticky and they'd spent the morning in the garden before the heat finally beat them and they'd called it a day, retreating to the river to spend a lazy afternoon. They swam when the mood took them in between drinking bottles of lemon flavoured beer that they placed in the river to keep cool. Laying on their backs in the long grass, her head on his stomach and their hands entwined, they'd watched as the sunset painted the sky a vivid orange and the first pinpricks of stars appeared in the sky. It was one of those moments that made you grateful to be alive.

"I love you baby," Tim had said, stroking her hair softly with his free hand.

"I love you too."

"No, I really mean it. I love you so much. I would die if anything ever happened to you."

She hated talk like that. "No you wouldn't," she said quietly. "Don't say things like that."

"Sorry, I just, I want you to know I'll always love you. Meeting you was the best thing that ever happened to me. I just want you to be happy."

"I *am* happy. Very happy."

"Good. Because you deserve it."

She had sat up and swung to study his face. His eyes glinted in the dusk light and she could see his face had a serious set to it. "What's brought all this on?"

"Nothing." He shrugged his shoulders. "I'm just so happy with our life right now. Is it wrong to want to freeze it and keep it this way forever?"

There was a tone to his voice she hadn't heard before. Melancholic, reflective, almost sad. "Of course not," she squeezed herself between his legs and snuggled back in against his chest. It was her favourite place to be in the world. "You can't though, you know that right?" she said after a few minutes.

"I know."

"It's only going to get better anyway, once we start our own family."

He pretended to choke. "Kids? You want *kids*?"

"At least six." They'd talked about it before they were married, to make sure they were on the same wavelength, and found they both agreed on the big stuff, like the number of kids they both wanted, (three, with the option of four depending on how traumatised they were by the first three,) and how they would be raised, (outdoors as much as possible and with manners and respect for people and the world around them). They'd already started trying, and even though the past two months had seen her period arrive Anna felt sure it would happen before too long.

"You'll be a wonderful father," she reassured him.

"Even though I'm scared shitless?"

"What are you scared of?"

"Everything. It's such a huge responsibility. I mean, they're totally reliant on you. Not just for the physical and financial stuff, but the emotional stuff. Look how many messed up kids there are in the world, what if we inadvertently screw ours up and they end up resenting us. They'll only come home once a year at Christmas and only then because we'll pay for it."

"I think you're getting a bit ahead of yourself."

"Am I though? Or am I doing the sensible thing and thinking through all possible scenarios now."

"A little of both perhaps."

"I've just never been responsible for another living thing before. How do you know I'm up for the challenge?"

She'd tilted her face up to him, studied his face now bathed in blue light from the moon. "I don't doubt it for a second."

"I wish I had your faith."

"You don't need it. I'll have faith for the both of us. Ok?"

He bent his head down and kissed her on the tip of her nose. "OK."

"Now promise you'll stop talking like this?"

His lips were warm and his breath a mix of citrus and yeast. "I promise. Sorry. Didn't mean to get all morbid on you."

But his mood remained sombre even when they returned to the house. Lying in bed that night, giggling as Anna tried to worm her feet in between his legs to warm them up and he tried his best to stop her, talk turned serious again.

"Goodnight," she said sleepily, her hands pulling his arms tighter around her. She liked to sleep in his embrace, ensconced in the warmth from his body. What she didn't know was that he waited until her breathing evened out and then extricated himself gently. He needed space and coolness to be able to sleep, and she was like a hot water bottle.

"Night baby," he murmured into her hair, inhaling the fresh scent of vanilla from the shampoo she used.

She was almost asleep when he spoke softly into her ear. "Anna?"

"Mm?"

"Promise me that if anything ever happened you wouldn't let it suck the joy from you. That'd you'd find love again, and happiness."

"Shut up Tim."

"I'm serious."

"So am I."

"I'm just saying that I wouldn't mind, you know, if you found love again. I'd rather that then you stay lonely for the rest of your life."

Anna didn't know why he was in the mood he was but whatever reason, it needed lightening. "Sorry, but if you're waiting for me to say the same you're out of luck. If anything happens to me I expect you remain single and in mourning for the rest of your days, capeesh?"

It worked and he laughed and tickled her ribs. "Capeesh. I'll wear only black too shall I?"

"I would expect nothing less."

"It doesn't matter anyway, because nothing's going to happen." And then he nibbled her ear in a way that he knew turned her on and they made love with a passion that only talking about death can provoke.

But he was wrong and something did happen. Only it was her that was left behind, not him. And she understood then what he had meant at the river because when she looked upon their peaceful faces she wanted to die too. If it wasn't for the fact her heart kept inconveniently beating she would have joined them.

"Anna?"

She blinked. Three concerned faces were looking at her from around the table. "What?"

"We were just talking about your gardens. Matt was saying they're the nicest in town." Barbara preened, taking the compliment personally.

"You've seen them all have you?" Anna asked.

"What?"

"The gardens around town. Seen them all have you?"

Matt looked taken aback. "Well no, not all."

"Then you shouldn't go around making broad statements like that."

"I'm sorry, are you angry because I said you had amazing gardens?" Matt looked to Barbara for support.

"Of course she's not angry," Barbara soothed. "Anna doesn't really do anger, she's much too sweet for that, isn't she Frank?"

"Eh? Oh yes, a real gem, our Anna."

Anna clenched her mouth shut. She wanted to tell them she wasn't 'their' Anna anymore; that they didn't need to keep making an effort with her. She didn't care if they let her fade from their lives. No more emails, she wanted to say. No more visits.

But they were right about one thing; she *was* sweet, so she didn't say any of those things.

"Thank you Frank," she murmured instead, eyes on the napkin in front of her.

"Anna is a talented crafter as well as gardener, aren't you Anna," Barbara said.

Anna frowned. Crafter? What on earth was she on about? Did she mean the driftwood wind chimes Anna had made once? The ones that fell apart in the first strong breeze?

"And she's a dab hand at a Sunday roast too, gets the potatoes perfect every time," Frank added.

"Oh yes, the potatoes. And what about her lemon meringue pie Frank, you're always nagging at me to make one as nice as Anna's."

"Unfortunately something you haven't managed yet though, haha," Frank guffawed. Barbara laughed shrilly.

Anna stared at them. She had never seen them act like this before.

"And swimming, Anna's a wonderful swimmer."

"Yes I've seen Anna swim," Matt said.

"Oh," Barbara smiled suggestively, "you have? Where?"

"In the river."

"How nice."

"Stop it," said Anna.

"Between you and me," Barbara carried on in a loud whisper. "Don't you think she has a lovely figure? I wish I had one half as nice."

Anna's mouth dropped open.

Matt was also lost for words."Um."

"Stop," Anna shouted, banging both hands on the table. The cutlery jumped and so did Frank.

"Stop what?"

What the hell do you think?"

Barbara frowned. "Don't be crude."

"*Me* crude? You're the one talking about my figure with a man we hardly know."

"But that's the point of this dinner, isn't it. To get to know each other better."

Anna took a deep breath and counted to ten before she said something she might regret. Then she took her napkin off her lap and put it back on the table, rising to her feet.

"Matt," she said, "I apologise for the less than subtle attempts to set us up."

"I'm not bothered," he shrugged. "Not often I get out for a nice meal."

"Well I *am* bothered. It's both patronising and unwanted."

"Sit down Anna, you're making a fuss."

"No. Enjoy your meal, but this is where I say goodnight." Anna pushed out her chair and picked up her purse.

"Don't be silly, how will you get home?"

"A taxi will do the job."

"Frank, do something."

"Stay," Frank implored, "eat with us and then I'll take you home."

"No thank you, I have no appetite." Anna looked directly at Barbara. "Listen carefully because this is the last time I will tell you this; stay out of my personal life. You may have accepted what happened but I haven't. Accept that I need to deal with things in my own way or *leave me alone*."

Then she swivelled on her heel and left, blinking back tears before she even got to the door.

Chapter nineteen

The next morning very little progress had been made by the egg and, fearing the poor duckling inside was weakening, Anna decided to throw Dr Google's advice to the wind – after all, man interfered in the birth of babies all the time, – and offer her assistance as a midwife. Gently, very, *very* gently, Anna peeled off the part of the shell that was attached by only a thin layer of membrane. It revealed a mass of tiny matted yellow feathers, which was a surprise to Anna as her ducks were white, and she'd assumed the duckling would be the same.

The small part of the duckling she had revealed was unrecognisable and even tilting her head both ways she couldn't figure out if what she was looking at was head or tail. Seeing the tiny feathers and glimpses of pale beige skin beneath made the whole thing become very real though, and the reality that this little things life was now in her hands, literally, nearly gave Anna cold feet and for a moment she considered calling the local animal shelter and asking them to take over parenting duties. Then she saw the duckling move slightly, and her mothering instincts kicked in.

"Hang in there little buddy," she said. "Help is on hand."

She gently peeled off another small piece of shell and revealed what was unmistakably a very small beak.

"How gorgeous," she said. The tiny glimpse of light she had unleashed into the shell, this tantalising glimpse into the outside world, gave the duckling a fresh burst of energy and as she watched the egg cracked some more, and then with a particularly large shove from within out popped a wing. Wriggle, squirm, wriggle, kick and plop, out fell the rest of the duckling. Exhausted it rested where it fell, feet curled up against its chest, a small dark eye solemnly taking in its new surroundings.

Anna felt a surge of protectiveness towards the vulnerable little duck. She pulled the adjustable lamp down lower so the duck would feel the full warmth from its bulb and she adjusted the sides of the box so that no draft could get in. Then she watched. After a few minutes she could see that the feathers were drying out, and a few minutes more the duckling transformed into a fluffy yellow ball of cuteness, and Anna was in love.

She spent the rest of the day watching him find his feet – awkwardly and with more than a few trips over his own large webbed feet – and helping it find the water bowl and the food she had placed out for it. She stroked its downy feathers and it observed her with a slight questioning look, as if it were trying to figure out how this giant, odd looking creature fitted into the picture.

The next day, which happened to be Friday, Anna called in sick again. Although she tried to motivate herself to do some gardening and housework, she found herself instead hurrying back to the box under the heat lamp every five minutes to make sure the duckling was doing ok.

It reminded her of when her son was born. He had been a good sleeper, right from the start. Other mothers from her parents class would rock up to their coffee mornings looking exhausted, smelling of sour milk and wearing odd socks, and they would mainline the coffee as they regaled tales of sleepless nights pacing hallways with wailing babies flung over shoulders, matchsticks propping up eyelids and husbands snoring peacefully though it all. Anna always felt left out, and if they asked her how she was going she would roll her eyes and pretend she was in the same boat as the rest of them. But she wasn't. Her son slept so beautifully that in the beginning she had to wake *him* in order to make sure he was getting enough milk. He grew like a text book baby, following the little dotted growth line on the plunket charts perfectly, and Anna stopped going to the coffee mornings because she felt guilty that all the other mums appeared to be struggling while she seemed to have everything so easy. But even though her journey into motherhood came naturally and she was blessed with such a good natured child, she couldn't shake the uneasy feeling that everything was just a little *too* easy. It wasn't supposed to be so effortless. The uneasiness would wake her from deep sleep, and she would lay there, heart racing, trying to convince herself that everything was ok before the anxiety got the better of her and she would rush soundlessly to the nursery to check on her baby. He was always fine; sleeping peacefully with a smile curling his lips and the soft sound of his breath the only disturbance in the night. Anna would hover above his cot and watch him while her heart returned to its normal beat and the unease would recede, but it never went away completely.

After they died, she felt it was punishment of some sort. For having had it so easy. Those coffee group mothers came along to the funeral and as they clutched her cold hand and expressed their sympathy she could read the relief in their eyes that this had happened to her and not them. Then they squeezed their babies a little tighter and went home to the noise and the chaos and for a time they were grateful for those night wakings, until the memory wore off and the sleep deprivation hit again and they forgot the life lesson they had just been shown.

The duckling brought all those early feelings flooding back to Anna, and the pressure of being responsible for his wellbeing kept her up the first two nights, dozing fretfully in the armchair beside his box, waking frequently to check he was still breathing. The worst moment was right in between waking and checking; for those seconds she could barely breathe as she panicked that the worst might have happened, and she would have to summon up the courage to make herself look. And every time she did and she could see the little chest rising and falling as the duckling slept peacefully, she would sigh with relief and subside back into the chair and think, 'I can't do this,' and she would vow to take him to the animal shelter the very next morning so that someone else could bear the burden of responsibility for keeping him alive.

But she never did.

In the afternoon she was upstairs changing the sheets on her bed when she heard a car door slam in the street outside. Hugging the curtains to remain unseen she had a look and swore under her breath when she saw the familiar silver Toyota parked outside. Frank and Barbara. Only Frank was making his way up the garden path though. She thought about ignoring the doorbell, staying in her hiding place until he gave up and left again, but curiosity got the better of her.

"Anna," he said sorrowfully when she opened the door, sweeping her up into a rib crushing bear hug. "Will you forgive an old man and his wife for their silly but well meaning behaviour?"

Anna sighed. She couldn't stay angry with them. But nor was she going to let them think she condoned their behaviour either. She frowned at him sternly. "Well meaning it may have been Frank, but it was embarrassing."

He hung his head. "I know. I really am very sorry. So is Barbara."

"Where is she?"

He stepped to one side and gestured towards the car. Barbara was sitting in the front passenger seat, her face mournful. She gave Anna a small wave when she saw them look her way.

"Why isn't she getting out of the car?"

"She wasn't sure you'd be happy to see her."

Anna suppressed an eye roll. Looked like she'd have to be the bigger person. She marched up the path and tapped on the car window. Barbara pushed the button to make it go down.

"Hello Anna," she said in a small voice.

"Are you going to come in for a coffee? Because if you're expecting me to bring it out here I'm afraid you'll be in for quite a wait."

Barbara smiled at Anna, grateful for the olive branch extension. "Coffee sounds great." She got out of the car and pulled Anna into a hug. "I'm sorry," she said, a little tearfully. "I only meant well."

"I know that. But I hope it's the last time you try anything like that, because next time I might not be so forgiving."

"Cross my heart," Barbara made the gesture.

"Good. Now it's forgotten."

They sat and drank coffee and talked about a raft of things that had nothing to do with Matt or the night before, and then she waved them off, grateful to have seen them but pleased they were gone and things could once again return to her own version of normalcy.

      By mid morning Sunday an unfeasible heat for this point in the summer kicked in and Anna and the duckling, who she was convinced was a male because of the fact that every time he took a dump he completely missed the newspaper that was his target, were too overcome by the heat to do anything but collapse in the lounge, grateful for the cool relief it offered them. She had that uncomfortable 'last day off before work' feeling, a black cloud of dread that curled around her intestines and pinched her kidneys. She stewed on how much she'd enjoyed the last few days, the peace and quiet and lack of intolerable people to screw up her day. And then she thought, 'what's to stop me taking more time?' In fact, after rummaging in the drawer and opening her payslip she discovered she had thirty two point six days of annual leave up her sleeve. How they arrived at the point six she wasn't sure. She called Mr Hedley at home and apologised for the short notice but told him that something had 'come up' and she needed to take some time off; ten point six days to be exact. Anna figured this gave her another fortnight to enjoy and then when she did have to go back she'd start at morning tea time, which ought to take care of the point six.

"Of course Anna," he said, "no problem at all. Anything I can do to help?"

She felt slightly guilty about letting him think something was wrong, but then she looked at the duckling she had nicknamed Buddy and the blue sky outside and her conscience shrugged the guilt off. "No Sir, but thank you."

After the phone call the black cloud dissipated quickly and was replaced by boundless joy. She felt ten years old, on the cusp of summer school holidays. This was the first proper holiday Anna had taken in years. Not proper as in 'going somewhere exotic where drinks come with tiny colourful umbrellas that poke your eye when you try and take a sip', but proper as in time off work that wasn't down to illness or bereavement. She felt giddy with the possibilities open to her, even though she knew she was unlikely to do any of them. It was enough to know that she *could* do them if she felt like it.

"Phew," Anna said to Buddy, who had decided her stomach was the perfect place to curl up in a little ball and rest, "I don't know about you but I certainly don't remember a hotter summer than this."

CHEEP CHEEP. Buddy couldn't either.

She watched as his little head, weighed down by the incongruously large beak, drooped against his chest while he slept. It was crazy how quickly he was growing. In a matter of days he'd almost doubled in size, and if the quantity of food he demanded was any indication, it wouldn't be long before he'd be as big as the ducks outside. This made her sad. She was enjoying having company in the house again, despite the little droppings he left everywhere *but* on the newspaper she'd laid out specifically for the purpose. His little face was impossible to scold though, yellow and fluffy and adorable as it was.

Her own chin had just headed south towards her own chest when the doorbell gave a shrill rang and jolted her awake. Buddy popped his head up and eyed her crossly.

"Don't look at me like that, I haven't invited anyone."

'CHEEP'

"I'll get it shall I?"

'CHEEP'

She scooped him up and placed him on an armchair where he shook his feathers a few times and settled down again.

Anna knew her own expression was slightly cross when she opened the door, and she didn't care. The door had seen more bloody visitors in the last week than it had seen in the whole year previously, and she wasn't exactly thrilled about it.

"Oh," she said. "I'd forgotten about you."

"The words every man wants to hear," Matt said, "Good morning to you too."

Why was he always so cheerful? Was he on something? It had to be against some natural law to always be happy. Anna was about to point this out when she noticed the small figure at his side.

"Hey Oscar," she said.

'Hi Anna, can I go see the ducks?"

"Straight to the point of our visit sorry," Matt laughed. "Not big on small talk, old Oscar here."

"Ah yes, about the ducks. I'm afraid I have some good news, and some terribly bad news."

Anna ushered them inside and waited till Oscar was seated on the couch to tell him about what happened to Mrs Dudley. As she told him she watched his face sadden, and his eyes glistened with tears he was determined not to cry.

"Stupid dog," he said angrily, wiping the tears away with the back of his hand.

"I'm only guessing it was a dog. Actually it could have been any number of predators."

"Well whatever it was it sucks."

"No arguments there."

Matt sighed heavily. It was never nice seeing your child upset, but he was a big believer that you couldn't hide them from the realities of life, both good and bad. It seemed Anna had the same idea. He remembered what she'd said at the door.

"What's the good news?"

"The good? Oh yes, I'd like you to meet someone." Anna turned to the chair where she'd left Buddy. He wasn't there.

"Now where did he go?" she muttered. "Ok, everybody freeze. Don't make any sudden movements." She got down on her hands and knees and checked under the couch.

Matt watched her, amused. "Some kind of new party game?" he asked.

"He's can't have gone far," Anna said, "I was only gone a minute." She started picking up cushions and peering underneath them.

"Dad?"

"It's alright. Who are you looking for?"

"He must be here somewhere," Anna moved a pot plant to one side to look behind it.

"*Who* must be here somewhere."

"Buddy." She lifted up the bottoms of the curtains.

"Buddy?"

She stopped to put her hands on her hips and throw him a look of exasperation. "Yes, Buddy."

"And buddy is…?"

"Let me find him and you'll find out."

"We could help if you'd just tell us what you're looking for."

"Not what, who."

"Here we go."

"Or is it whom?" she paused from moving the TV.

Matt rolled his eyes. "Don't start this again."

"I'm not starting anything. But if I tell you who I'm looking for it will ruin the surprise."

They watched Anna scan the room, which as far as he could see, was empty apart from them. "Ann, is it a good surprise? Or one of those, 'hey, meet my new friend Buddy who is a decapitated head,' kind of surprise."

"Decapitated head? What rubbish are you on about now?"

"You gotta admit you're acting a little odd. It's either that or your friend is playing the best game of hide and seek I've ever seen." He cupped his hands around his mouth and said in a singsong voice. "Come out, come out, wherever you are."

"Don't be patronizing."

"I'm not."

"You are."

"Fine, I am. But come on, it's pretty obvious there's no one here but us."

Anna was about to reply when she heard a faint, CHEEP. Given that she was listening for it, she was the only one who heard it.

"Aha!" Anna stabbed a finger victoriously towards Matt. "There he is."

"Who? Where?"

"I'm not sure. Be quiet while I listen."

Matt sighed and made a zipping motion across his lips and threw away a pretend key.

"Shush," Anna hissed. She had heard another faint CHEEP.

In the silence they all heard it.

'CHEEP CHEEP'

It came from the kitchen and as she rounded the corner of the bench Anna realised she had left a cupboard door open, the one where the bowls were kept. Nestled snugly inside her breakfast bowl and looking proud of himself, was Buddy.

"There you are," Anna cooed. "Don't you dare do that again, you hear me? You gave me such a fright."

'CHEEP'

Anna scooped him out of the bowl gently. He had left her a murky souvenir. "Thanks," she told him. "Guys, meet Buddy." She thrust out her hands to reveal the little yellow duck.

Oscar squealed with delight.

"You bought a new duck?" Matt asked.

"No I hatched it."

"Maybe you should back up a couple of steps and start at the beginning. Did you just say you hatched a duck?"

"Yes."

"From an egg?"

"That's usually where ducks hatch from, yes."

He gave her a weird look. "You didn't lay it, did you?"

"Don't be absurd."

"I hate to point out the obvious but this conversation got a little absurd a few minutes ago, and it was nothing to do with me."

"Shut up dad," Oscar said, startling them both. He stroked Buddy's back, who preened under his touch. "You ask Anna questions but you never let her answer."

Matt's mouth gaped open. His son had never spoken to him like that before. "That's not true."

"Yes it is."

"It's not. Is it?"

"Yes dad, it is. Now let her tell us how she hatched Buddy."

Anna enjoyed the gobsmacked expression on Matt's face. "There's really not that much to tell. I found an egg by the back gate and it was still warm, so I figured I'd give the poor thing a fighting chance, so I kept it as warm as I possibly could and a few days ago, out came Buddy."

"You kept it warm?" Oscar asked.

She nodded.

"How? Did you sit on it like a mother duck does?"

Matt snorted. Anna ignored him.

"No I'm a little heavier than a mother duck. I might have squashed it if I did that."

"Just a little," Matt said.

"Ok," said Oscar. "So how did you keep it warm then?"

"Sometimes I wrapped it up all warm and snug around a hot water bottle, and sometimes I put it under this special heat lamp I bought," she pointed, "that is hot like the sun."

"Wouldn't that have cooked it?"

"Ok maybe not as hot as the sun, but pretty hot. And other times I tucked it under my shirt and let my body keep it warm."

"Wow."

"Yes indeed. Wow. And it worked."

"Can I hold him?"

"Of course. Sit down on the couch so he doesn't fall."

"Can he fly?" Oscar asked as Anna placed Buddy on his lap.

"No. Besides the fact he's still a baby and his wings are just tiny tips still, see, he's a breed of duck that doesn't fly. Like Mrs Dudley and the others."

At the mention of Mrs Dudley Oscar looked sad. "Buddy doesn't have a mother anymore."

"No," she agreed. "He doesn't. Not his real mother anyway. But he has me to look after him, and if you like, you can help look after him too."

"I can?"

"Sure. I bet he'd love it if you came round every now and then and played with him."

Oscar looked hopefully at his father. "Can I dad?"

"It's ok with me if it's ok with Anna."

"I wouldn't have suggested if it wasn't," Anna said. Hadn't he realised by now that she didn't say anything she didn't mean? Of course, it would mean that she'd have to accept them in her life for at least a short while longer which wasn't ideal, but she figured she could live with that.

Chapter twenty

Somehow, when Anna had said 'every now and then,' Oscar took that as in invitation to visit every day on the days he stayed with his father. Taking full and shameless advantage of the fact that Anna was home on holiday, Oscar would put pedal to the metal and arrive promptly at Anna's house at twenty past three. Given that school was across town and the bell rang at three, this either meant he rode like a demon or hitched a tail wind on a passing car. He would arrive breathless but excited, and before the helmet was even off his head he would have mumbled "Hi Anna" and have pushed past her into the house on his way to find Buddy.

"Nice to see you too," Anna would say to the air in his wake.

After a few days of this, Buddy's internal clock kicked in and at twenty past three he would be waiting at the front door, chirping eagerly in anticipation.

"I could take it personally you know," Anna told him, "that you're not as excited to see me in the mornings."

'CHEEP'

"Yes I know I'm not an eight year old boy. Don't hold it against me."

'CHEEP CHEEP'

"That's not fair. We have our fun too, don't we? Didn't you enjoy the bath last night?"

Anna had. She'd forgone the daily showers, fitted in around work constraints, in favour of a long and leisurely evening bath. With a glass of red wine in one corner and a scented candle (frangipani) in the other, she would roll up a hand towel for neck support and run the water as close to the top as she dared without it spilling over. Then she would sink in and let her body soak until her fingers were wrinkled like prunes and the wine was all gone. Each time the water got cold she would prise up one end of the plug enough to let an inch or two of water out and run the hot tap until the water reached the desired temperature once more. She had a small footstool beside the bath to place her magazines or books on when she wasn't reading them. Two nights previously, lulled into a semi slumber by the warm water, the book had fallen to the floor and she was laying there with her eyes shut when she heard a scramble beside the tub and then there was a plop! Water splashed onto her face.

"What the - ?" she'd sat up, feeling for the rolled up hand towel – which had fallen into the water – and failing to find that using what she thought was the sleeve of her top off the floor but which turned out to be her knickers, to dry her eyes, but not before she burnt her toe on the candle and knocked the, now thankfully empty, wine glass into the water.

The culprit was now paddling happily up and down the bathtub admiring his reflection in the polished porcelain.

"Buddy," she said, "how lovely of you to join me."

'CHEEP'

"Yes I know I left you all alone. I was enjoying a bath as you can see."

'CHEEP CHEEP'

"No I don't think it's selfish at all. You can't begrudge me a little pampering."

'CHEEP'

Buddy felt deserving of a little pampering too. Anna enjoyed sharing her bath tub with him, right up until he used it as a toilet that is, the little white splodge emerging from under his jaunty little tail, and mingling in with the bath water. Anna briefly wondered if it would sink or float but she didn't hang around long enough to find out.

Thinking about the bath with a smile on her face, Anna jumped when there was a knock at the door. She checked the clock on the oven as she dried her hands on a tea towel.

"Three twenty," she noted, "right on time."

"Hi Anna," Oscar said craned his neck impatiently to see past her to where Buddy was turning in excited circles.

'CHEEP CHEEP CHEEP CHEEP'

"I could be wrong, but I think someone's happy to see you," Anna said, watching the duckling trip and somersault over his feet. Oscar dropped his school bag and jersey on the floor under the coat rack and for a split second Anna caught a glimpse of the future that should have been. She took a sharp breath.

Don't scare the boy.

"How was school?" she asked, her tone even.

Oscar shrugged as he picked Buddy up. "Ok."

"Learn anything earth shatteringly exciting?"

It was a question her father used to ask her. Anna didn't even know she remembered that until the words came out of her mouth.

"Nope." Buddy nibbled lightly at Oscar's cheek with his beak, as if searching for bugs in the grass. Oscar giggled.

"Really? How disappointing. What's the point of going to school then?"

"To eat your lunch."

It was a joke Oscar had heard his father say many times.

Anna laughed then stopped when she heard a strange beep. Unaccustomed to the sound, it took Anna a minute to work out what it was as she'd forgotten she'd set the timer on the oven, a complicated business she wasn't even sure had worked until that moment.

"It's ready," she declared, sliding her hands into a pair of blue oven gloves. They had a picture of a red rooster on one side. It had the expression of a rooster heading for the chopping block. She didn't even know she owned oven gloves. She'd half-heartedly on a whim decided to clean out the fourth drawer that morning, - mainly because of a mountain of plastic supermarket bags that were threatening to overflow and take control of the kitchen – and underneath them all the oven gloves sat serenely, apparently unused apart from one small, unidentifiable stain. The sight of them had given her an idea.

"What's ready?" Oscar, buddy safely ensconced in hand, climbed up onto one of the stools at the breakfast bar. Anna had stopped worrying about him carting Buddy around; he was more careful than she was. Also with each passing day Buddy increased in both size and robustness. She was genuinely surprised each morning when she looked into his box at how much bigger he seemed than when she'd put him in there the night before.

"You, my friend, should count yourself lucky. I've only baked one other cake in my life before today, and it was a terrible flop." She paused with her oven-glove-clad hands on the oven door handle to give him a hopeful look. "Let's hope this one is more successful."

The door fell open with a flourish and out wafted a small cloud of smoke. "Oh darn," she said, waving it away. "I knew there was a reason I didn't do this."

But when she pulled out the cake itself she was pleased to see it was unscathed, the smoke traced to an old oven fry that lay forlornly burnt to a crisp on the bottom element. Anna used a pair of tongs to pick it up and throw it out the kitchen window.

"Well will you look at that," she said, pleased.

Oscar looked.

"What is it?"

"What do you mean, what is it? What does it look like? It's a cake of course."

"I meant what flavour is it. Like chocolate, vanilla, or something else?" Oscar couldn't off the top of his head think of any other flavours of cake. The only 'cake' he ever ate was on his birthday, and it came from the supermarket. A slice that came in a box with fluorescent frosting and a candle that his father would replace with one of those comical ones that would magically relight itself every time you blew it out. His father thought they were hilarious. Every single time. Oscar had discovered through trial and error that the only way they could be extinguished once and for all was by flushing them down the toilet. His teacher had once said that in the event of a nuclear explosion only cockroaches would survive. Oscar was pretty sure that when the cockroaches crawled out from beneath the burning rubble those candles would light the way.

"It's banana."

"Well it looks nice."

"Nice? Oscar, this cake looks better than just *nice*. It looks exactly like the cake in the picture." She thrust the open page of the recipe book in front of his nose as proof.

He studied it. "Almost but not quite," was his verdict.

Anna turned the book around and studied the picture, comparing the two. As far as she could see the cakes looked identical; golden and plump and dewy and flawless.

"What's different?" she asked, baffled.

"It's just, no. Nothing."

"Spit it out Oscar."

"Well in the picture, see," he leant over the top of the book and pointed, "there's a big bowl of chocolate icing ready to be put on the cake. And, see here, a cup of hot chocolate to the side. With tiny marshmallows."

Anna hid a smile. He was right. It was the first time she had really seen a glimpse of his humour, and she liked it. He looked up at her like a Labrador puppy.

"I can do the icing and the hot chocolate," she said. "But the marshmallows are pushing it."

"Deal."

For the second time that day Anna morphed into a domestic goddess and, following a recipe at the back of the cake section, she made a big batch of butter chocolate icing – most of which they ate off spoons and very little of which made it onto the actual cake – and, because of the heat from the day outside, two cups of cold milk with spoons of milo.

"You do the honours," Anna said, passing Oscar a knife.

"No way, you baked it, you should be the one to cut it." He tried to pass the knife back.

"I can't. It looks so good. You'll have to do it."

So, tongue between teeth and forehead furrowed in concentration, Oscar carefully measured out two slices – 'how big?' he asked Anna. 'Not too much for me. Bit more than that, bit more, bit more, yep that ought to do it,' she answered when the piece was as wide as a jumbo slice of pizza - and they ate in silence, enjoying every moist delicious crumb and licking every trace of icing off their fingers.

"Another slice?" Anna asked.

"I'd like to, really I would, but I'm stuffed."

"Are you sure? There's heaps here and it'll get wasted with only me to eat it."

"I can't fit any more in".

Anna shrugged. "Ok but if you change your mind let me know. I can always wrap a slice for you to take home."

She picked up the two empty glasses and started rinsing them under the taps, using a brush to scrub the stubborn bits of milo that had stuck to the bottom. She was feeling a sensation she could only describe as cheerful, and was therefore completely unprepared for the question when it came.

"Why don't we ever see them?"

Anna didn't hear him clearly at first, he said it so quietly. She picked up a tea towel and started to dry a glass. "Pardon?"

He spoke louder, but not more confidently. "How come we never see them?"

"Who?"

"Your husband and baby."

Anna winced.

Husband. Baby.

Two innocent words that stabbed at her flesh like shrapnel from the grenade he had just unknowingly lobbed into the room. She turned and looked at him.

"How do you –?" she couldn't finish the sentence, but he understood anyway.

"The clothes –" he pointed towards where one of her husband's shirts was draped casually over the back of the couch – "and the toys." Her eyes followed his to the toybox in the corner. There was a colourful ball and a tin drum set sitting on the floor in front of it, but only one drumstick; she'd been unable to find the other one.

How could she even begin to explain? She couldn't. She doubted she could explain it rationally to the highest trained therapist in the world, let alone an eight year old boy.

"It's complicated," she said.

"You mean I wouldn't understand because I'm just a kid." There was no disappointment or resentment in his voice when he said it. It was said as a matter of fact.

"Well, yes. I guess so. Although to be honest, I'm sure many adults would struggle to understand it too."

"It's ok, you don't have to tell me." He looked back towards the toys. "They're messy though, aren't they. Every day they leave things lying around. Do you always tidy up for them? My nana used to nag me to pick up my things when I was smaller. I'm much better at it now."

"Does your nana live with you?" She wondered if he meant Matt's mother.

"She used to. But then she got sick," he continued.

Once upon a time she might have asked questions, these days she had a policy of 'don't ask, don't tell.' If someone wanted you to know something they would tell you. But he had opened up to her and she didn't like to leave it hanging, as if she didn't care about what he'd said.

"I'm sorry to hear she's ill," she said.

"She's not anymore."

"Well that's good to hear."

"She died."

"She— *what*?"

"She died."

"Yes that's what I thought you said. I'm sorry to hear that."

Oscar studied the counter top where Buddy was preening himself, trying – and failing – to balance on one foot and falling comically. "Thanks." He'd heard it before.

There was an awkward silence. Being the only adult present in the conversation, Anna again abandoned her policy, just this once. "When did she –?"

"Two years ago."

"Was it –?"

"Cancer."

"Oh."

She looked at his little face, eyes still downcast. Her heart, relatively unscathed for the majority of her life, had taken a hammering over recent years. Until now, she'd even doubted there was much left of it that wasn't blackened by grief and pockmarked by pain or stained with sadness. But hearing Oscar tell her that his grandmother had died, she felt a familiar jolt inside as something withered and died with a familiar dying wail of "life isn't faaaaaaair!" trailing off into silence. Well, she thought, that ought to have taken care of the rest of it.

She spent some time drying the glasses while she considered what her next words should be, which was ridiculous because she of all people knew what it was like to hear meaningless platitudes or, even worse, nothing at all. It was odd how people she had previously considered to be excellent conversationalists were suddenly lost for words when she ran into them in the street or the supermarket. Sometimes she'd see someone she knew at the other end of the aisle and she'd brace herself for the inevitable head tilted to the shoulder, the suck in of air between the teeth sadly and the sympathetic, "So, how *are* you?"

It got to the point where she could tell they were hoping she wouldn't do as she'd done the last time they'd run into her, which was answer the question honestly. It was just plain awkward when she did. She came to realise that they didn't actually want to hear how she couldn't sleep, or eat, or even shower some days. That she cried more than she'd even known was possible, at the drop of a hat – oh look, see, here I go again – and that her body was so tight and wound up in knots that it had started to emit strange noises, from places she didn't consider polite nor pleasant. She realised they absolutely did not want to hear this and so she took pity on them and would turn and go back down another aisle to spare them her ugly grief.

Now here she was, afraid to ask an eight year old boy about his feelings on death. She was treating him the way people had treated her. Steeling herself, she opened her mouth to ask him a question when –

KNOCK KNOCK

"Dad's here."

She expelled the question unspoken into the air gratefully.

"Yes, I think you're right. At least I hope it's him," she babbled as she moved to open the door, "and not some salesman or Jehovah's Witness because I have no money and as far as I'm concerned God can shove his brochures about the afterlife up his…" she remembered who she was speaking to, "well, where the sun doesn't shine."

Oscar picked Buddy up and carried him over to the large rug in the centre of the lounge, placing him down gently. As he did every day he got on the floor beside him to whisper his private goodbyes. Anna opened the door.

"Hi," she said.

"Hey," Matt smiled. "Boy been any trouble?" He asked the same thing every night when he came to pick Oscar up.

"Of course not, he's very well behaved," she said, as she did every night.

"Good, good." He stepped past her. "All comes down to excellent parenting." He crossed the room to where his son knelt. "Hey you, had a good day?"

"It was alright."

"School any good?"

"School is school dad. It's never good."

"Ah I remember those days well. How's Buddy?"

Only then did Oscars face become more animated. "He's great, look at him. He's growing so big. Soon we'll be able to take him outside to play with the other ducks."

Anna watched as Matt knelt down beside his son and the two of them discussed their day and Buddy. They had the same blond hair, a mix of honey and straw and sand. She was becoming fond of them, well, the boy in particular. She wasn't sure if she liked that though. It was a complication and she didn't need any of those.

They were out the door before she remembered something and called them back. "Wait, she called, disappearing back into the shadows of the house. She remerged minutes later, a wrapped bundle in each hand.

"Here," she said, holding them out. "You forgot your cake."

They took them. Matt peered at his. "You baked us a cake?"

She didn't like the warm way in which he said it. "No," she set the record straight, "I didn't bake you a cake. I baked *a* cake. If you don't want it pass it back."

"I didn't say I didn't want it," he tucked it behind his back protectively; in case she should snatch it from him.

She gave him a look. Why did he have to read things into situations that just weren't there? Why couldn't he just accept a slice of cake without assigning meaning to it?

"It's really yummy dad."

"You already had some?"

"We had a piece for afternoon tea."

"Perfect. You won't be needing any dinner then."

"You can't be serious. A piece of cake is not enough for a growing child's evening meal, besides it was an hour or so ago." Anna frowned at him.

"I was joking. Don't worry, I have dinner under control."

"What are we having?" Oscar asked.

"Fish and vegetables."

Oscar sighed. "You mean a McDonalds fillet of fish burger and fries, don't you."

"You're too clever for your own good."

"So you keep telling me."

"There's nothing wrong with a bit of McDonalds every now and then," his father said defensively. "Hasn't done all those American kids any harm has it."

"Every now and then? More like once or twice a week."

"Do you know how many kids in Ethiopia would be grateful for a McDonalds happy meal?"

Oscar had heard this before. "Millions, apparently."

"That's right. And don't forget it."

Anna knew that she could do two things. One, she could take pity on the poor boy and invite him and his father in for dinner, again. Or two, she could stay completely out of it and let them sort themselves out.

"Goodnight," she said.

Chapter twenty one

"Suspended?"

"Yes." Judy's voice was smug, her excitement ill-concealed. She'd been waiting for this moment a long, long time. "You might have been able to get away with crap under Mr Hedley, Anna. But I'm in charge now, and I'm not putting up with it."

"Suspended on what basis?"

"I asked you to supply a medical certificate. You failed to provide one."

"Oh for god's sakes Judy, no one's bothered with those before."

"Exactly my point. Things have been too lax around here. You lot treat this place as a joke. I mean come on, you decide you need a holiday and just don't bother showing up?" Judy scoffed. "This is the real world Anna. It's hardly professional behaviour and it's against the terms of your contract."

"I called Mr Hedley and he approved it. Go and sort this out with him."

"You haven't heard?"

"Heard what?"

"Perhaps if you'd bothered coming to work you'd know."

"Know what?" Anna had a bad feeling.

"The old guy had a heart attack." Judy didn't sound at all sorry to say the words.

Anna gasped and a hand flew over her mouth. "Is he – ?"

"Dead? No. Lucky bastard. Collapsed in a restaurant and a doctor happened to be dining nearby. Gave him CPR till the ambo's got there and jump started his heart with a defibrillator."

"Oh thank god," Anna relaxed against the counter top. "Is he in the hospital?"

"Not any more. He's at home under strict orders to take it easy. I'm in charge," Judy brought the conversation back round to the topic of business, "and that's why you, Anna, are suspended pending an investigation." It was her way of saying that she was fully intent on firing her but only after she dragged it out for a period first.

If she was hoping to crush Anna with the news, or invoke a flood of tears or pleas for forgiveness, she was disappointed.

"Oh well," Anna said, "You do what you have to do."

"I don't think you understand what I'm saying. This is a very serious matter. Once I tell the board about your behaviour it's more than likely you'll face dismissal."

"If they feel it's justified there's not much I can do about it is there." Anna, although a little perturbed at the path events had taken, was too concerned about Mr Hedley to care much about the threatened unemployment right then.

"Don't pretend you don't care."

"Judy, as my grandfather used to say, shit happens." Anna didn't swear often but had no problems doing so when it was called for.

"You're just pissed off because I win."

"You win? It's not a game to play with people's lives, Judy. One day you'll figure that out but I have a feeling it'll be too late. Don't you wonder why you have no one in your life? It's because no one wants to be around someone who is so miserable and mean and vicious." Anna figured she had nothing to lose by letting Judy in on a few home truths. Sometimes, she knew, it was kinder to be cruel.

"Um, hello? *You* don't have anyone either."

"But I did. There's a difference."

"Whatever. Good luck finding another job without references."

Anna hung up. There was nothing more to be said.

So that was that then. She was now permanently on holiday. She figured she should probably feel a little sad, after all she'd been at the bank for a long time. But she really couldn't bring herself to care. It was a toxic environment. She should have moved on long ago. In fact, she thought, maybe this was the rocket up the ass she'd been waiting for.

In the back corner of her garden, half grown into the hedge, Anna found the big metal half drum that her husband used to light fires in when they had company for dinner outside on balmy summer evenings. As the sun dropped and the temperature sank with it he would chuck a few pieces of kindling and a few fire starters in there and rub his hands with pyromaniac glee as the flames licked the night sky. It was rusted from exposure and still bore the ashes from the last of those dinner parties – Anna couldn't recall the names or even faces of their guests – so she tipped it on its side and used a spade to scrape the majority of the ashes out.

When it was empty she righted it and filled it with torn up newspaper and scrapings of wood from the bottom of the woodshed. Her husband would turn in his grave if he saw the state of the shed now. He'd kept it pristine, which was kind of ridiculous when you considered its purpose, and the wood was always neatly stacked according to the level of dryness. Now, Anna called a man once a year who backed his truck up beside the house with a chorus of BEEPS. He'd push a button and the back of his truck lift would crank up to dump a load of wood in her driveway. She paid him a small amount extra to wheelbarrow the wood around to the shed. She didn't go so far as to ask him to stack it though; thought that was asking too much. The state of the shed would have offended her husband's obsessive compulsive tendencies.

She lit a match and threw it into the drum and when the fire was well established and a nice bed of embers glowed she went upstairs to her wardrobe and pulled the grey and green shirts and skirts from their hangers. Then she opened the drawers and pulled out all the pairs of stockings that she owned. She found her name badge on her bedside drawer and added it to the pile. After one last, lingering look to make sure she had everything, she went back outside and threw it all into the fire.

The ducks fled to the safety of the hedge and she called an apology after them. Then Anna poured herself a wine - tucking the remainder of the bottle under her arm - fetched a warm blanket from the linen cupboard, and curled up in one of her white cane chairs on the back lawn to watch as it all burned down to ashes.

Chapter twenty two

Her husband had wanted to be cremated. It was the only thing she ever denied him, but seeing as he was dead there wasn't an awful lot he could do about it. It had come up one morning in one of those conversations that appear random and unlikely at the time, but weigh heavily when it actually comes into question.

Flicking open the newspaper at breakfast, he'd read out loud a story about a woman who had been battling her husband's family for ten years for the right to bury his body in the town they'd called home, rather than the town he'd grown up in and where his family felt he belonged.

"Meanwhile the poor bugger is stuck in limbo, unable to rest while they bicker over him like dogs over a bone," her husband had said.

She'd been tired. Her son had been given his three month immunisations the day before and he hadn't slept well. She was so unaccustomed to restless nights that when they occurred they left her barely able to function.

"Mm," she'd said.

"I mean, can't they allow the poor guy some dignity? Fancy spending ten years in limbo because your family can't sort their shit out and come to an amicable agreement."

"Fancy. Coffee?"

"Please. They should cremate the guy. Split the ashes, half each. Everyone's happy then."

"Were you cold last night? My feet are like ice blocks from pacing the floor. Have you seen my slippers?"

"No. Maybe. I think I might have used one to hold the door open in the garage."

"You owe me a new pair."

"Fine." He was still stewing over the newspaper article. "I guess *he* wouldn't be happy though."

"Who? God?"

"No not him, the guy whose coffin has been stuck in a chiller for a decade."

"Chiller?"

"Freezer at the funeral home."

"Oh. Right. God how long does it take a piece of toast to cook?" She yawned.

"Probably just as bad to be split over two parts of the countryside," he mused. "I know. They should cremate him and spread his ashes somewhere he loved."

"Can you pick up some more bread on your way home from work?"

"Sure. Like his favourite hunting or fishing spot. Somewhere that meant something to him."

"And milk. And tomatoes."

"Ok. That's what I want, ok?"

"Tomatoes?"

"No, to be cremated. Don't bury me in a box for the worms to eat," he shuddered. "I can't think of anything worse."

"What makes you think you'll go first?"

"Men always die before the wife. I read it somewhere."

"Really?"

'Yeah. It's to escape all the nagging," he laughed.

She threw a tea towel at him.

And that had been the extent of the conversation. Just one of the many that made up their daily life, falling somewhere in between "did you pay the power bill on time?" and "your son started to cut his first tooth today." It barely registered and was not at all important, until it was. Until he died and the funeral director had sat her down to ask her all the important questions.

"Cremation or burial?" he'd asked gently.

"Burial." Then the conversation from that morning had come back to her and she'd paused, "no, wait," while she tried to recall his exact words.

But even once she did she couldn't do it. She couldn't have them gone entirely from this world. She needed them near in some small capacity, so she'd had the two of them interred together; her son wrapped in his father's eternal embrace. She could picture them like that. It was after all her final glimpse of the two people she loved most in the world, before the lid was placed on the coffin and the screws were turned into place.

Chapter twenty three

Buddy was restless. Now the size of a large kitten he'd grown bored with the limits of his domain and had started hiding behind furniture so that when Anna opened the door he could make a mad dash for freedom. This usually resulted in him either tripping over his own feet in excitement or splattering beak first against the door as Anna shut it swiftly in his face.

'QUACK'

Even his voice had deepened, and Anna guessed from his mood swings that he was going through the human equivalent of puberty. He would stagger back on his feet like a drunk at pub closing and cast her wounded looks through the glass.

"I'm sorry," Anna would mouth back at him. "But you're just not big enough yet."

The truth was she had no idea how to go about introducing him to the outside world, and even if she did she wasn't ready. In her eyes he was still the vulnerable little duckling she'd help break out of the shell, despite the fact that now when he joined her in the bath she had to squash up with her knees under her chin so he had enough room to swim his laps. As far as she was concerned the outside world loomed large with potential predators. At some point she'd have to face it, and probably sooner rather than later, but she would put it off for as long as she could.

She went to visit Mr Hedley. He looked bored and uncomfortable on his couch, unaccustomed to sitting still in one place for long periods of time.

"Doctors orders," he told Anna sadly. "But I'm hoping to get out for a game of golf before too long."

"You'll do no such thing," his wife's head popped around the door. She entered the room and fussed over him, placing a blanket over his knees despite the temperature in the room being in the twenties. He tolerated it for a minute before swatting her away like an annoying fly.

Some wives, upon their husbands' retirement, found themselves resenting the constant and intrusive presence in their lives. For some, when retirement struck it was as if they'd gained themselves a rather large toddler. One who whined that they were bored or sulked around the house when told to find something entertaining to do. Some wives found the sudden flood of half finished DIY projects annoying, or the repurposing of their herb garden for their husbands' plant grafting experiments mildly frustrating.

But not Shirley Hedley. She'd been waiting for this moment for some time now, and she finally had her husband right where she wanted him. Born to be a nurturer, she'd been so bereft when their only son left home she'd almost had a clinical breakdown. To fill the hole, she'd started sponsoring one of those African orphans, sending gifts and paying the dollar a day. But it just wasn't the same. She had considered getting a dog but she'd finally got the cream carpets she'd been coveting for years and wasn't about to ruin them. When her husband keeled over, taking his entree with him, she'd naturally been terrified. But the moment the doc declared him well enough to come home she'd rolled up her sleeves and sighed happily. He was hers now. She was *needed*.

Mr Hedley, on the other hand, was finding the constant fussing irritating, to put it mildly. He'd had enough sponge baths to last him a lifetime, and this was despite the fact he was quite capable of bathing himself. There wasn't a room in the house, he'd discovered, where he could hide from his wife's watchful eye, and she hovered around ready to plump his cushions or lift his feet onto a foot stool. If he sneezed a tissue would be pressed into his hand before he'd even opened his eyes. If he coughed a thermometer would be shoved between his lips while she felt his forehead and fretted he was coming down with something.

It was driving him crazy.

So when Anna arrived to visit he was as grateful as a puppy when its master arrives home from work.

"OK," he rubbed his hands together gleefully. "Tell me everything and don't leave a single detail out."

"About?" Anna was confused.

"The bank of course," his face assumed a sad, wistful, expression. "I think I spent more time there in the last forty years than I ever did here." He looked around the room with its floral wallpaper and collection of photos of relatives, both alive and deceased. He had no idea who some of them were, let alone whether they were from his side of the family or his wife's.

Anna realised he hadn't heard about her suspension so she filled him in. When she finished he was outraged, his lip quivering and a spittle hovering in one corner.

"She can't do that," he said. "She can't. I've a good mind to go down there and sort this matter out."

Shirley reappeared at the sound of his raised voice. At the sight of him, animated and angry, she frowned.

"Now what's got you so riled up," she tutted, pushing him back into the couch and straightening the blanket over his knees. "You know you're not allowed to get stressed, it's bad for your heart."

"But Shirley, you have no idea what's happened —"

"No I don't and I don't care either," Shirley cast a dark look Anna's way.

"I'm sorry," Anna said, getting to her feet. "I'd better go."

"That's probably for the best," agreed Shirley.

"You'll do no such thing," growled Mr Hedley. "Sit back down. Make us a cup of tea please Shirley, we have business to discuss."

"I'm sorry," Anna repeated, when Shirley had reluctantly left the room. "I didn't come here to upset you. I just wanted to make sure you were ok."

"You've always been such a sweet, caring person Anna," he smiled at her fondly. "You didn't deserve what happened to you. And you don't deserve to be treated this way. I don't know what the devil Judy is playing at."

"I probably shouldn't have called you at home like I did," Anna admitted.

"It was unorthodox, certainly. But I didn't mind so why should she? Leave it with me," he told her. "I'll sort it out."

"No please don't worry about it," Anna regretted telling him now. He was still recovering and was supposed to be enjoying retirement, not fighting her battles for her. "Honestly, I'm not worried. After all, what will be, will be."

"Que Sera Sera," he smiled. "I love that song. My mother used to sing it to me when I was a wee lad."

Anna's breath choked in her throat as a memory flitted across her mind. She was in the nursery, rocking her son in her arms, his little eyes growing heavier as he was lulled to sleep by the gentle sound of her voice.

'Que Sera Sera, whatever will be, will be, the future's not ours to see, que sera sera'

When does it stop? She wondered. Would she ever be able to see something, hear something, or smell something that reminded her of them, without feeling the heartache all over again, as fresh as if it had just happened?

Chapter twenty four

The twenty first of the month.

This one was slightly harder than the others, as it marked the anniversary of another year gone by. Another year they had been in the ground. Another year they hadn't celebrated a birthday. She wasn't able to bake them a cake or throw them a surprise party or wrap and hide a present somewhere they'd no doubt find before the big day because, as her husband used to joke, she was rubbish at hiding presents.

Another year where they were frozen in time and in her memory, yet diminished in the memory of others. It bothered her, this thought. How many people still remembered them? Did her husband's old work colleagues' ever stop to think about the man who once sat in the corner office and who was the first to volunteer to dress as Father Christmas for the Christmas party? Not because he bore any physical resemblance, but because it was his favourite time of year. Family aside of course, who else out there stopped from time to time to remember Tim, husband of Anna, father to Ben and a generally nice bloke?

She doubted the people whose lives he touched on a daily basis in little ways did. Like his dentist, or the guy who pumped petrol into his car. Or the nice Japanese woman behind the counter of the sushi shop who always nodded enthusiastically and greeted him with a loud, "Hey! You come again!"

Did she ever stop and wonder what had become of him?

Or the people he'd gone to school with. When they held their reunions and he failed to show did they wonder where he was and why he wasn't there.

The thought that she might be the only person left in the world, apart from his family, who ever thought of them or missed them, made her terribly sad.

Life goes on. Anna stopped listening after the fifth person said it to her in the wake of their deaths. They were right though. Life does indeed go on. When all was said and done and the funeral was over, Anna curled up in a corner while the grief ate her from the inside, while everyone else returned to their normal lives as if it had been nothing but a blip on the radar. Eventually the frozen meals stopped being delivered and the phone stopped ringing. The sympathy cards in her letterbox dribbled to a stop and the flowers, the elaborate bouquets that made her lounge look like the lobby of a florist shop, withered and died.

With these thoughts heavy in her mind, Anna was more depressed than usual for the twenty first. She paid for the flowers without exchanging her usual pleasantries. She quite frankly didn't have the energy to pretend to be happy when she was not.

At the cemetery she went straight to their graves and did her usual tidy up. She could barely see the headstone through her tears, the names and dates a wavering blur. Days like this there was no hiding her grief. No pretending that she was coping ok, or moving on with her life as everyone expected her to. On days like this the pain was as raw as if it had happened yesterday.

Memories flew at her. Standing over the cot, watching her baby sleep. Listening to him breathe and feeling an indescribable love, one so strong that at times it felt like a physical grip in her chest. She would be unable to resist touching his soft blond hair, stroking it, and then freezing as he murmured and moved in his sleep. Other times she'd creep in and he'd be laying so still she'd feel real fear, and she'd quickly lick a finger and hold it under his nose to feel the cool air of his expelled breath, rather than scoop him up and call his name which is what her motherly instincts wanted to do.

Memories of his birth; her first sight of him as he was lifted up from between her legs and her husband spied the unmistakably swollen genitalia and whooped and said, "it's a boy!" although she knew he would have been just as pleased if it had been a girl. She had held him against her naked skin, marvelling at his tiny little arms and legs, wrinkled from his time floating in amniotic fluid, and his indignant angry red face. The following weeks and months; nuzzling his sweet skin, smelling his delicious baby smell, smiling at every coo and gurgle he made, convinced he was trying to communicate with her, quite certain he was cleverer than any other baby in the world. Closing her eyes now she could still feel the weight of his small head on her shoulder as she rocked him slowly to sleep, his fine downy hair tickling her chin. She remembered the sensation of his lips on her breast as she fed him, watching as his tiny jaw milked her, in awe of this perfect person she had created.

Memories of the first time she saw her husband, like some cheesy cliché. A party, the crowds parted and there he was, standing on the opposite side of a darkened room. Drinking a beer and laughing at something someone else was saying. She'd been unable to look away and he must have felt the weight of her stare because he stopped laughing and looked straight at her.

Three dates and that was it. She'd moved in with him and they hadn't spent a night apart until he died. When she gave birth to their son he'd camped out in a grotty old armchair in the corner of her hospital room, determined not to miss a second of his son's early days in the world. When her son had a mild reaction to his six week immunisations and had to spend a night in hospital under observation, her husband refused to go home without them, even though she knew he really could have done with a night of uninterrupted sleep. The nurses tried to tell him there was only enough space in the room for their son and Anna, but he'd just shrugged and said 'whether I sleep in the hallway or your office, I'm not leaving,' so they relented and let him squish up on the extra bed with Anna, even though it was against hospital regulations.

All these memories and more assailed her. It was like a mental slideshow of their too brief time together, the slides in no discernible order. She flicked through them at random, pulling forth the memory of her baby's first smile here, then with a swipe of a mental finger she was looking at her husband's beaming face when he turned at the top of the aisle and saw her making her way towards him. The triumphant smile when the first tree they planted together bore fruit, his tears when her first pregnancy ended in miscarriage.

Of course it wasn't all perfect. She remembered the bad times too. They fought. Both stubborn, both determined, both certain they were right about most things. There had been arguments that festered until one or the other turned to trusty Google for the answer, or called a friend for an impartial point of view, then informed the other with ill concealed glee that they were, in fact, wrong, and here was the proof.

He'd been incapable of closing a drawer or a cupboard after himself, and it drove her nuts. He talked with his mouth full and scratched himself without being aware he was doing it, and over time the rasp of his nails against his skin made her want to batter him.

But of course the good moments outweighed the bad, and they'd been happy. Certainly happier than some other couples they knew. Every few months they'd be climbing into bed and one of them would say, "You know Bill? Works at the council, drives a red Audi? Does that weird shaved thing with his beard so it looks like his mouth is in the shape of an arrow?" and the other would fluff up the duvet and murmur that yes, they did indeed know Bill.

"His wife just kicked him out."

"Nooo. Really?" (the voice would be suitably scandalised.)

"Yes. In such a clichéd manner too. Changed the locks while he was at work. Came home and all his stuff was on the front lawn, well, what was left of it. Some of the neighbours' kids had already rifled through and helped themselves to a fair bit."

"That's terrible! That poor man." (Sympathetic.)

"Don't feel too sorry for him. Turns out he's fond of clichés too. Been having it off with one of the fluffy blond typists at work."

"That bastard." (Shocked outrage.)

"I know, right?"

"Can you reach the light switch? Thanks."

They would snuggle down together in the darkness, each lost in their own thoughts. Eventually, just when one thought the other was asleep a voice would break the silence.

"I'd never cheat on you," it would say.

"I know." (Contentment.) "I'd never cheat on you either."

"I know."

Then they'd drift off to sleep in each other's arms, an island of security in an insecure world.

These memories played in a loop through Anna's head, as she lay on the ground with her eyes squeezed shut and her tears pooling at the corners of her eyes before they overflowed down her cheeks, past her ears, and into the earth beneath her.

"Anna?"

The voice seemed to come from faraway, like another room or across the street. She barely registered it.

"Anna?"

Closer this time, more insistent. Anna refused to open her eyes. This was her time to mourn, her sanctuary from the outside world, a place to remember her loved ones and everything she had lost. Any moron who couldn't see that was not deserving of her attention.

"I knew it was you." The voice was above her now, triumphant until the last second when its owner saw the state she was in. "Shit," it said, "you're busy. I'm sorry –"

But it was too late. Anna emerged from inside her cocoon of memories, bereft at having her journey cut short, annoyed with the voice for doing so. She opened her eyes and looked up. Matt was already starting to back away.

"What do you want," she said.

"I'm really sorry, I didn't stop to think you might be busy."

"Busy?"

"Yeah, you know,-" he gestured at the headstone above where she lay. His words deserted him.

Anna sat up. Her back protested. "What are you doing here?"

"Working."

"Working?"

"Yes."

"You work in the graveyard?"

He pointed towards the church. "I mow the lawns and trim the hedges, that sort of stuff. This might seem like a stupid question, but what are you doing here?"

"You're right. That is a stupid question."

"Sorry, I'll rephrase. Who are you here to visit?" and he tilted his head to try and see around her to the headstone.

"If you don't mind," Anna said in a voice positively dripping with capital letters, "I WOULD LIKE TO BE LEFT ALONE NOW."

"Say no more." Matt held up his hands and backed away.

She didn't watch him leave but she sensed after a time that she was alone again. She also knew without a smidgeon of doubt that he would be back. Not while she was here maybe, but once she had gone.

And she was right. When she departed the cemetery by the side gate an hour later, her tears spent, the slideshow completed, there was no sign of him. The buzz of his lawnmower had come to her on the breeze occasionally, and the 'snip snip' of a pair of long handled hedge trimmers as he worked his magic on the Ivy, but she hadn't looked. She was annoyed that he had disturbed her. The cemetery was not a place for social niceties.

From around the other side of the church Matt watched as Anna slowly got to her feet and picked up her bag. She stood for a long minute, her eyes drinking in the headstone in front of her, before raising her fingers to her lips and kissing them. Then she pressed her fingers against the head stone and left without a backward glance. He ducked back out of sight as she left but he needn't have bothered as she kept her eyes firmly on the ground in front of her. When enough time had safely passed that he knew she would already be down the road, he moved out of the shadows of the building and straightened, feeling like a spy in a James Bond novel. The night was approaching and with it the light was fading, so he moved quickly to where Anna had spent the last few hours.

The grave was clearly well visited and maintained. Two bouquets sat each side of the headstone, one colourful and extravagant, the other pale and sedate. The names and dates meant nothing to him, but when he did the maths in his head and realised that one of those names belonged to a child less than one year of age, he felt all the air leave his lungs in one long, sad breath.

"Oh," he said. "Oh hell."

He thought about what his life would have been like if he'd lost Oscar in his infancy, and the tremendous fear and grief at just the thought made him groan out loud.

How could a parent survive such a thing?

"Matt, I'm glad I caught you," Reverend John had approached, his footfalls silent on the fresh cut grass. He came up alongside him. "I've been meaning to thank you," he said, "for the advice. My lawn is the best it's looked in, well, in as long as I've lived there anyway."

"Your lawn -?" It took Matt a moment to collect his thoughts and catch up to what the reverend was saying. "Oh yes, your lawn. No problem Rev -,"

"John."

"- John."

"You should branch out you know, start your own business. I know a few gentlemen who'd be grateful to have their garden and lawn maintenance taken out of their hands. We're not all blessed with your green thumb unfortunately." He realised his audience was not paying attention. "Matt?"

"Hmm? Sorry." Matt shook himself. "Reverend did you know, -" he didn't want to say 'the deceased' so he simply gestured to the grave.

Reverend John followed the direction of his finger.

"Ah," he said. "Yes. A real tragedy, that was." He closed his eyes tight for a minute and Matt realised that he was praying. It felt wrong to ask for the story when it was so clearly still a sensitive subject.

He checked his watch. "I'd better get going, still have one more lawn to do before nightfall."

The two men walked side by side along the grass aisle towards the church. The Reverend waited until they were at the door to speak again.

"Sometimes things happen that defy understanding. Even for a man in my line of work." He shook his head sorrowfully. "I know I'm supposed to toe the party line and say that everything HE does, HE does for a reason. But occasionally even I struggle to understand." He stared off into the middle distance, remembering something.

They heard a phone ring inside the church.

"I'd better get that. See you next time, oh and Matt, think about what I said will you. Could be a lucrative business venture." Then he disappeared through the side door and was gone, leaving Matt staring after him and mulling over his words.

Chapter twenty five

"I'm sorry Anna," Mr Hedley said ruefully on the phone the next morning, "but Vanessa in human resources says that once the disciplinary process has been started, it must go through the official channels to its natural conclusion. Load of codswallop if you ask me."

Anna tucked the phone receiver under her chin so her hands were free to shoo Buddy off the couch. He glared at her reproachfully. "It's alright sir," she said. "I do appreciate you trying to fix things."

"Between you and me, she mentioned that a lot of the staff are unhappy with Judy's management. I wish I had seen this side to her before she was promoted," his voice was frustrated. "She always seemed so dedicated."

"Oh she's dedicated, dedicated to making sure I'm unemployed."

"I'm so sorry Anna."

"It's fine sir, really. Please don't let it upset you. Honestly, whatever the outcome is I'll be fine. Perhaps this is the wakeup call I needed. Let's face it, I haven't exactly been the banks best employee."

Mr Hedley nobly sprang to her defence. "Nonsense Anna, you are a very diligent worker."

If he knew how much time she spent on google researching pointless information he might think differently, Anna thought. "Thank you Sir, I appreciate you saying so."

Anna heard Mrs Hedley mutter something in the background.

"I'd better let you go," she said.

"Yes, ok. Seems it's time for my medication again, horrible stuff. I will be following what happens, Anna and for what it's worth I've made the board aware of my feelings. It may hold some sway."

"Thank you."

"Goodbye Anna. Take care won't you."

"I will, and you too."

Anna hung up the phone and pulled the cord out of the wall. She'd had more than enough communication with the outside world for the day. As well as Mr Hedley and his heroic efforts to defend her character, she'd received a letter in the mail that morning. It came in an official looking envelope, with the words Private and Confidential stamped across the top left hand corner in blue ink. Inside was a summons to the bank, a week from tomorrow. She was to meet with the board and HR.

She would simply tell them the truth, that she'd felt like some time off and yes, she was well aware that she hadn't followed the correct channels and yes, she knew it was hardly responsible behaviour and went against the rules of her contract. But was she sorry? She couldn't honestly say that she was and frankly hoped the question wouldn't arise. But she would apologise for any inconvenience and leave it to them to decide her fate. There was no point in worrying about it she'd decided. Worrying was not going to change the outcome. In the meantime she would continue to enjoy her extended holiday. She'd already replanted the vegetable garden, uprooting the lettuces that had gone to seed and sowing agria potatoes for winter. The fence and gate had looked so good with a fresh lick of paint that she'd decided to do the front porch as well; a decision she almost regretted once she started. It took her two full days and the heat nearly saw her give up several times, but she was proud once she'd finished.

    She sprayed all the weeds along the garden paths and cleaned out the gutters, a job she'd been meaning to do for the last five years but always forgot about until it rained and they flooded and it sounded as if she lived under a waterfall.

    Inside the house, spurred on by the satisfaction she had got from burning her uniform, she'd had a spring clean of her closet, throwing anything she hadn't worn during the last year into a plastic rubbish bag, ready to be donated to the local charity shop. She couldn't bring herself to touch Tim's side.

    Then, with time on her hands that she felt obligated to fill, she'd set about spring cleaning the house too. She scrubbed off the cooking oil that had accumulated on the splashback, gave the walls a good wipe down with some soapy water – wondering the whole time where all the fly poo had come from and how it was she hadn't noticed it before when it was suddenly *everywhere?*- and gave the skirting boards a quick wipe for good measure. Instead of dusting around objects, as she usually preferred to do because she figured how dusty could they get underneath, really? She lifted everything off and gave the wooden shelves a thorough polish. Any ornaments - horrible things that she couldn't see the point of but which were usually gifted therefore unable to be thrown away in case the gifter should visit- she took to the kitchen and gave a good clean with soapy water, removing years of sticky grime. Books got a quick wipe down and anything else -random detritus she had collected over the years; pretty feathers, unusually coloured stones, ticket stubs, - she threw away.

When she was finished, a job that took her three days, she stood in the middle of the room and congratulated herself. She hadn't realised how much she'd let the place go, although the fact that she hadn't got around to replacing her vacuum cleaner after it blew up a few months prior was a good indication.

'QUACK'

She snapped out of her reverie. Buddy was weaving his way round her ankles like a puppy. A piece of paper rustled under his feet and she bent to pick it up. Scanning it, she realised it was the letter from the bank about her meeting. She had stuck it on the fridge door with a magnet that read 'life's short, drink more wine' to keep it in place but it must have come loose. Reaching for the magnet to reattach it her finger landed in something wet and sticky.

"Oh yuck," she said, seeing the now familiar splodge and realising that Buddy had used the letter as a toilet. Poetically, the bulk of it was on the third paragraph, right where Judy's name was mentioned. She laughed.

"Nice one buddy, nice one."

'QUACK'

Buddy thought so too, and so did Oscar when she told him about it later.

"You didn't think it was so funny when he did it to your homework," Anna pointed out.

"That's because that book didn't belong to me. It belonged to the school library and Mrs Turnip goes nuts if you damage one."

"Seriously? Your librarians name is Mrs Turnip?"

Oscar flushed. Sometimes when he was with Anna he forgot she was on the other team, i.e an adult. He found her really easy to talk to. She never talked down to him like he was just a dumb kid, the way some adults did.

"No, not exactly," he said. "That's just what we call her."

"Dare I ask why?"

"Have you ever seen a Turnip?

Anna searched her memory banks. "Yes," she said. "I have."

"Well that's pretty much exactly what she looks like."

Anna tried to reconcile the image she had in her head of a wrinkled white vegetable, with that of an aged school librarian. "Is she old, this Mrs Turnip?"

Oscar nodded. "Yeah about forty I think?"

Anna wasn't sure if he was joking or not. "Watch it," she said. "Don't you know forty is the new twenty."

"Says who?"

"Says anyone who is forty."

"Dad says forty means your life is half over, if you're lucky."

"Who in their right mind would say such a thing to a child?"

"Dad says after forty, your body starts packing in on you and it's all mid life crisis's and dying your hair and aerobics and stuff."

"Your father has a rather warped view on aging."

Anna was dumbfounded. Was the man a total idiot, or just a partial one? As far as Anna was concerned, children should be sheltered as long as possible. They should live in a happy bubble of carefree days playing outside in the fresh air without a care in the world. Where the worst they had to worry about was getting the odd prickle in a foot.

Of course she knew this was being unrealistic. She knew that kids were becoming more and more exposed to things she considered, 'adult matters', at a very young age. One of the ladies at work had a daughter who had recently started her period. She was nine. Anna was horrified when she heard the girl's mother casually mention it in the lunch room.

"That's nothing," the mother, Louise, said when she saw the look on Anna's face. "These days, they even give them the sex talk at primary school."

"They don't."

"They do. Year six, or standard four as we used to call it. Of course, you can opt for your child to sit out but their friends are just going to tell them about it anyway so what's the point. They may as well hear the proper version from the teacher instead of some botched version in the playground."

Anna put her sandwich down on her plate. She had lost her appetite. "I don't believe it," she said.

"It's true," Louise insisted. "She's also put herself on a diet would you believe? At nine years old. Breaks my heart because she's beautiful, and I'm not just saying that because I'm her mother. But you know what kids can be like. Cruel, some of them. Someone called her chubby and now she won't let anything sugary past her lips. Spends half her time on her phone googling calorie counting apps. It's terrible. I'm so scared she'll end up anorexic or that other one, you know, when they chuck up their food, what's it called?"

"Bulimia."

"That's the one. I watch her like a hawk when she goes to the bathroom. I shouldn't have to do that, not at her age."

"No," Anna agreed, "you most definitely should not."

"You know kids lose their virginities younger these days too, right? My son, the idiot, thought if he hid the condoms under his mattress I wouldn't find them. Who does he think makes his bed?"

Anna searched her memory of the last staff family picnic and came up with a tall, thin, pimply adolescent with a few stray stubbles of hair on his chin and a permanent sulky expression. "Michael?" she ventured, and was rewarded with a nod. "But he can't be more than sixteen, surely?"

"Fifteen and a half."

"No."

"I know, believe me, I know. After that I just couldn't look at him as my baby anymore, not once I knew what he was up to." She shuddered. "Of course, his father was bloody useless. Just said boys will be boys. You know, I think he was actually proud of him in a way?"

Anna murmured her disapproval.

"I had to sit Michael down and tell him that if gets someone pregnant I won't be saving him when her father comes beating the door down, or getting up in the night to feed it. What else can I do?"

Anna shrugged sympathetically. She had nothing she could offer on the subject.

"I tell you it's not easy," Louise concluded, "this parenting lark. You're lucky you don't have –" She stopped, horrified, as her mouth caught up to her ears. "Oh Anna," she said, ""I didn't mean – I'm really sorry, - I can't believe I said that." Tears pooled in the inner corners of her right eye.

Anna watched, fascinated, wondering why the left one remained dry. Was it some kind of condition? "That's ok," she said. "I know what you meant."

Conversation was stilted after that and Louise made a quick getaway back to her desk not long after, ten minutes before she was required to. Anna spent those ten minutes inside her head, thinking about how her son had never had the chance to disappoint her in such a way and how she would happily have gotten up in the night to any children he may have sired, given half the chance.

She studied Oscars bent head as he played with Buddy, laughing delightedly when the duck nibbled his fingers. His hair curled into delicate wisps at the bottom; fine tendrils that made his neck look so thin and vulnerable and she felt a strong compulsion to lean over and kiss it. She actually leant forward before Oscar, sensing something was amiss, looked up.

"Are you ok?" he asked.

Anna pretended to pick up a piece of fluff off the carpet by Oscars knee as if that had been her intention all along. "Yes."

"Are you sure? Your face has gone a bit white."

"I'm just a little tired," Anna got up from the floor and made her way to the kitchen to start preparing her dinner. She checked the time. "Your father is late," she said, changing the subject.

"Yes, he said he might be. He had something to do in town I think. At the library."

"Oh. Did he say how long he would be? I mean, should I feed you?"

"No it's ok," Oscar was wary of overstaying his welcome. "I'm sure dad has something planned."

"Takeaways, you mean."

"Probably," Oscar admitted.

Anna made a decision. "I'll make us a stir fry, you need some healthy vegetables. In fact, you're probably lacking in every vitamin under the sun. I'm surprised you manage to stand upright, with the rubbish he feeds you."

"He's not that bad," Oscar defended him. "I know we joke around but he's a great dad."

The fierce loyalty in his voice stopped Anna from her rant. "I'm sure he is," she said. "SorryI didn't mean to imply otherwise."

Oscar shrugged, she was forgiven. "It's not his fault he's not the world's best cook. But he makes sure I have fruit for lunch every day. He does the best job he can."

"I'm sure he does. And obviously he's doing a great job, because you are one of the politest young men I've ever met. Manners are a rarity these days. Please and thank you will be on the list of endangered words if we're not careful."

"There's a list of endangered words?"

"There should be. As well as please and thank you, common courteous phrases such as 'how are you' have gone out of fashion."

"You sound like my granddad."

"I do?"

"Yeah, he's always going on about the good old days as well."

"He sounds like a wise man."

"Yeah, he likes to think so. But he's also like, eighty."

"What's that supposed to mean?"

"Well, aren't you like, a bit young to be so cynical?"

"You know what cynical means?"

Oscar gave her a wounded look. "Please. I'm eight, not four."

Anna hid a smirk. "Sorry. Do you have any homework?"

"Some maths, unfortunately."

"Why don't you pop up at the table and get started on it while I cook. That way you don't have to worry about it when you get home."

Oscar pulled a face. "I guess so." Reluctantly he left Buddy on the floor and fetched his school bag from where he had dropped it on his way in. He chewed the end of his pencil studiously for five minutes, occasionally stopping to look at the roof in concentration, or use his fingers as a calculator.

"I hate maths," he finally admitted, stalling. "Are you any good at it Anna?"

"Not really."

"Don't you work in a bank?"

She nodded. "Yes but I have a flash calculator, and a computer. It does everything for me."

"You're lucky."

He bent his head to his book again. "Do you have a favourite number?" he asked a minute later.

"No."

Oblivious to the upset he had caused with one simple question, Oscar blithely carried on talking.

Anna didn't hear him. She had stopped stirring and stood with her eyes squeezed shut.

She didn't have a favourite number. But she had one she hated.

Eighteen.

Eighteen hours. The memory of each of them etched into her memory. Eighteen hours that had altered the course of her life.

No, she shook herself. Come back, don't go down that path. She finished whipping up a quick chicken stir fry, with fried egg and noodles.

"Dinner's up," she placed the bowls on the table. "Eat it while it's hot."

With obvious relief Oscar shoved his books back into his bag and they were just about to tuck in when there was a knock on the door.

"Dad's here," said Oscar. He looked at her, fork half way to his mouth, unsure whether he should still eat or not.

"Eat." Anna got up to answer the door. "You're late," she told Matt.

"Am I?" Matt made a show of checking his watch. "Sorry. Time got away on me."

Anna checked over her shoulder to make sure Oscars attention was on his dinner before lowering her voice. "You know I don't mind Oscar coming over to see Buddy," she said. "But I think you're starting to take advantage."

Matt's froze, one foot through the door.

"You don't even check to see whether I'm home before you let him come over, what if I had plans and he arrived to find an empty house?"

"Did you?"

"Did I what?"

"Have plans?"

"When?"

"I don't know, you're the one who mentioned them."

Anna shook her head, frustrated. "My point is that I seem to have become an unpaid babysitter for your son."

Matt pulled out his wallet and opened it. "What's the going rate these days?"

"The going rate for what?"

"Babysitters, isn't that the point you're making? Aren't we having the same conversation here?"

"No," she said frustrated. "You're missing the point entirely."

"Do you think you could get to it a little faster?"

Anna sighed and stepped aside to let him in. "Forget it."

He could tell he'd pushed her too far. "Look, I'm sorry. I promise I'll check ahead in future, and pick him up on time. Ok?"

"Thank you, yes. That's all I'm asking."

"Hey mate," Matt crossed the room and bent to kiss his son's head in greeting. Anna was reminded of her earlier compulsion to do the same thing. "Holy mother of Mary, what is that divine smell?" Matt sniffed the air and peered into his son's dinner bowel.

Anna took the hint.

"Oh go on then," she sighed, "pull up a chair."

Chapter twenty six

"Anna, come in," Barry Ferguson extended his hand. Anna shook it – she never knew whether to go firm or limp in these situations so settled for somewhere in the middle – then surreptitiously wiped her hand down her jeans leg. His hand was damp and clammy and she knew she would spend the entire meeting now wanting to wash her own.

She followed him into the boardroom and took a seat on the left side of the table. She would have preferred the right which was closer to the door therefore a quicker escape route, but that side was already taken by the imposing bulk of Harold, the regional HR manager, and another man who Anna had never seen before.

"Anna, thank you for coming in today. You know Harold of course –"

Anna nodded and smiled at Harold, who nodded and smiled back.

"- and this is Peter Bentley from head office."

Anna nodded and smiled. Peter nodded and smiled back.

"I'll get straight to the point Anna," said Barry.

Anna held her breath. This was it. The guillotine blade was about to fall on her banking career, such as it was. She had never been fired; had no idea how to respond. Should she cry? Beg for forgiveness? Or shake her fist and storm out creating a scene, vowing revenge. She quite liked the sound of that last one. It was a long time since anything vaguely exciting had happened in the branch. She imagined the looks on the other ladies faces as she strode from the building, knocking over pot plants and ripping posters out of the window. She smiled.

"Anna?"

"Yes?"

"Do you understand?"

She realised she had missed whatever had been said. Her first dismissal and she had completely missed it.

"Oh, um , not exactly," she said. "Could you please go over the main points again?"

Barry sat back in his chair, loosened his tie. "Obviously we're not thrilled with the way you went about taking annual leave, Anna. It was against company procedure and did rather leave the other staff to pick up your slack, cancel and move appointments and what not."

Anna felt suitably ashamed. She hadn't stopped to consider the extra work she was dumping on the others.

"However, while in breach of your contract, we've taken onboard a glowing recommendation from Mr Hedley and all things considered, we feel that a suspension was unjustified."

Anna blinked. "You mean I'm not fired?"

"Fired? Of course not." Barry looked at Harold, perplexed. Harold shrugged his shoulders to signal that he was just as confused as Barry was. Peter looked at a spot somewhere over Anna's left shoulder, his thoughts elsewhere and his purpose at the meeting unclear.

"Oh. I must have misunderstood her."

"Her?"

"Judy."

"Ah." Barry and Harold exchanged another look as comprehension dawned. "Yes, Judy has been, how shall I put this," he squinted at the far wall while he searched his vocabulary for the right words, and settled for, "a bit fast and loose with her newfound power." Harold nodded in agreement. Peter shook his head, which Anna took to mean he was also in agreement but expressing his displeasure.

"Has she?" she said. "There's a surprise."

The men stared at her. Finally one ventured, "Sorry, was that, *sarcasm*?"

"Yes."

"Ah."

"Sorry, it's just that you only had to consult any of us worker bees on the shop floor before you went and promoted her. We could have told you what she's like."

"Oh." Heavy sighs. More looks exchanged.

Anna took pity on them.

"Of course, she's very good at her job," she proffered up and they clutched at it gratefully, nodding like nodding dogs lined up on a dashboard.

"Yes," they said, "she is. The figures for this branch are looking good. We've recently been announced as the best performing branch in the region."

"Well there you go, it's not all bad then. If you can iron out the other issues, like the fact that she despises us all and we're not overly fond of her either, you might be able to salvage something."

"Yes," they nodded. "Maybe."

Formalities over, the meeting wrapped up. Anna was free to return to work immediately. The suspension would be erased off her work record, although a verbal warning would remain in place.

"After all," Harold said, "where would we be if everyone decided to take a holiday on a whim and no one showed up for work one morning?"

Anna accepted the warning gracefully and apologised. Then, emboldened by the new sense of freedom her time off had given her, she asked if she could pretty please, if it wasn't too much trouble, have the remainder of the week off? Just to tidy up a few loose ends? She would of course complete the correct request form and leave it in Harold's tray, she promised.

She had learnt her lesson. Everything would be by the book and above board from now on. T's crossed and I's dotted.

"Well," Barry said, looking to the others for any objections, of which there were none. "I guess that will be ok. I'll let the tellers know they can start booking you in for appointments as of next Monday." He stood up. The others followed suit. "Anything else or are we done?" he looked enquiringly around the table. Harold and Barry shook their heads.

"Thank you Sir." Anna said, resisting the urge to curtsey.

"No thank *you*, Anna, for being so understanding. You have a long history with this company, and whether you know it or not you are highly thought of. When the others caught wind of what Judy had done we almost had a mutiny on our hands."

"Oh?"

"Yes. They held a meeting of which the end result was, and I quote, 'sack Anna and you'll have to sack us all.'"

This gave Anna a lovely warm feeling. She got on well with the other ladies and there had even been a time when she had socialised with them out of work hours. Baby showers, happy hour drinks, the occasional naughty boozy lunch. When the collection tin was passed around for someone leaving, or someone's birthday, she dug deep in her pocket, happy to contribute.

As she walked down the stairs she saw upturned face after upturned face, all smiling at her expectantly.

"Well?" Nadia called as she reached the bottom and her foot stepped onto the carpeted surface. "Don't keep us in suspense, are you staying?"

Anna nodded. "I am."

There was a chorus of happy sighs and congratulatory smiles.

"Welcome back Anna," said Rochelle. "We've missed you."

"I've missed you too," Anna said, realising it was true as she spoke the words. She hadn't missed the place, but her co-workers? Yes.

"I'm so glad you're coming back," said Yvette. "We've missed your sense of humour in the staff room. It's been a bit on the boring side without you to be honest. No offense," she aimed this last bit at the others.

"See," said Lorraine, "that's what happens when enough people take a stand against bureaucracy. The little people win."

"Woo hoo! Down with the establishment!" called out Holly, who had always been the most rebellious of them all. She pumped a fist in the air triumphantly. "We did it!"

"Thanks guys," said Anna gratefully. "You really shouldn't have put your own jobs on the line though."

"Bullshit," said Holly, caught up in the moment and forgetting where they were and that a line of impatient customers could hear every word. "You'd have done the same for any of us."

Yes, Anna thought, she was right. She would have.

And *that* made her realise that the ladies now looking at her with warm affection were, in some kind of way, a family.

On the walk back home she mulled over this revelation and the knowledge that it was possible to be part of a family that weren't, in the true sense of the word, your family.

This thought made her feel slightly less alone in the world.

Chapter twenty seven

The thing that Anna had spent quite some time dreading happened, in the end, with barely a fizzle to speak of, like a disappointing wet firecracker.

Buddy, increasingly frustrated with the terms of his confinement, had taken to following her everywhere and quacking at the top of his voice indignantly. It was doing her head in. The solution involved, as so many things often do, a door left ajar. She had gone outside to take scraps to the compost heap early one morning and before opening the door she checked to make sure the coast was clear, which it seemed to be, so she went ahead and opened it, juggling the ducks bread and the scrap bowl as she did.

She greeted the ducks and threw out the bread before continuing on to the compost. She took her time, enjoying the crisp, unsullied air of the new morning, stopping to pluck a few weeds from amongst the lettuces, and was just weaving a loose tendril of her pea plant around the trellis when an almighty racket kicked up at the back door.

'QUACK QUACK QUACK QUACK QUACK'

'QUACK!'

'QUACK QUACK!'

Anna picked up the nearest weapon to hand, a little hand trowel as it turned out, and hurried back to the house expecting to have to fight a stray cat or dog that had gotten into the garden. But it wasn't a stray cat or dog that was causing the ruckus amongst the ducks, it was Buddy.

A quick glance confirmed that Anna had left the door ajar and Buddy had somehow managed to prise it open. She stood there, fretting, unsure whether to swoop in and grab him or let nature take its course. As there was thus far no bloodshed she decided to wait and see what would happen, but she was remained poised to wade in and grab him if the need arose.

"Guys," she said cautiously, "meet Buddy."

'QUACK'

"Buddy, meet the rest of the gang; Rodney, Sophie, Daffy, Princess and Marty. In my defence they were already named when I got them."

One of her two large male ducks, the one named Rodney and the one she'd long suspected to be the alpha of the pack, circled an excited Buddy warily. They did the dog equivalent of sniffing one another.

'QUACK'

'QUACK'

'QUACK?'

'QUACK'

And that was it. No drama. No, 'this is our territory back off if you know what's good for you' like she'd been worried about.

Just a few quacks, a few inquisitive pecks, one kick that may or may not have been accidental, and just like that Buddy was accepted as part of the family. The ducks waddled off together in the direction of the water bowl.

"Oh," Anna watched them go. "Ok. Well, right. I guess that's fine. Only he's still quite small," she called after them, despite the fact he was now the size of a rugby ball. "And he likes his food in his special bowl and his blanket puffed up before bed and -" she choked up. It was how she imagined some mothers' might feel sending their children off on a sleepover for the first time.

For the rest of the day she stalked the ducks around the garden. When they started to get annoyed with her she retreated to the inside of the house and stalked them from behind the curtains. The house felt emptier and full of strange echoes again. Even her sighs seemed embarrassed to break the silence, dropping to the floor and scuttling off under the sideboard with barely a murmur.

"I guess it just us again," Anna said to the walls. They acted like they hadn't heard her.

But then as the sun fell and Anna nursed a large glass of red wine while half-heartedly watching a cooking show on TV there was a tap tap tap on the back door. She hurried to it and there was Buddy, hopping from foot to foot impatiently. He barrelled past her, full of news from his day.

'QUACK QUACK QUACK QUACK'

"You're back," she smiled, happier to see his feathery little face than she'd ever thought she'd be. She fed him, although he only managed a small amount as his eyes were heavy with fatigue. Then she fluffed up his blanket and watched as he nestled down, tucked his beak under his armpit, and went happily to sleep, snoring gently. That night, Anna did the same. And when she heard the dawn chorus and realised that for the first time in eleven hundred and seventy eight nights she hadn't woken in the early hours with terror in her heart she wasn't sure what to think.

Chapter twenty eight

Eighteen hours.

Not a particularly lengthy amount of time in the grand scheme of things. Not when you compared it to say, a week, a year, or a lifetime.

But Anna knew different. Anna knew that eighteen hours could seem longer than a lifetime. Longer even than an eternity.

They'd been on the way to his parents for Long weekend. The car was packed to the gills with all the paraphernalia that goes along with having a baby; high chair, portacot, baby bath. The thing – she'd forgotten now what it was called – that she placed him in the middle of and it supported him because he was too young to stand, and it had toys hanging off it all around him in a circle. He'd sit in there happily and babble away while she did dishes or folded washing, and he'd bash away at the toys and gurgle in delight when they made noises. She couldn't remember why they'd thought it so necessary to drag that along with them, but they had.

Now, looking back, she wished she could add up all the time he spent sitting in that odd contraption and have him in her arms for that time instead.

They'd decided to go up on the Thursday night after work so as not to lose half of Friday travelling. Anna had her usual quiet misgivings, she hated travelling in the dark and by the time they got there it would be bordering on twilight, but she trusted her husband to get them there safely. He was a very conscientious driver. He abided by all the road rules, travelling the appropriate car length behind the car in front - extended further if the weather was wet - and only overtaking if the road was clear for a very long distance ahead. He always pulled over to the left to let faster traffic pass and he dipped his lights so he didn't blind oncoming traffic. He was not a man to take unnecessary risks.

The headlights came out of nowhere.

They were only twenty minutes from their final destination. Twenty minutes from where a set of eager grandparents were waiting, with the table laid and roast chicken and vegetables keeping warm in the oven.

When the oncoming campervan crossed the centreline taking the corner, Tim took the only evasive action open to him, jerking the steering wheel to the left as hard as he could. In those seconds, when Anna realised what was happening and looked to her husband for reassurance, she saw real terror on his face and she knew then that they were in trouble. She turned in her seat to see her son's curved cheeks, his eyes closed in sleep, and she had only time to try and reach to protect him before she heard the car hit gravel and become airborne as it sailed out over the bank and into the gaping void below. It felt like it hovered there forever before it finally fell, into the trees below, heavy and with enough momentum behind it to drive it still forward, crashing through undergrowth before it hit the thick trunk of a Wattle. The bonnet folded in on itself like a concertina. A branch pierced the windscreen and the glass shattered inwards.

Anna heard her own voice scream before it was cut off abruptly by the impact. Her head snapped forward and then back against the headrest violently .

And that was it for awhile.

She would never know how long she was unconscious for. It could have been an hour; it could have been a minute.

It was the silence that woke her, a deathly silence apart from a gentle hiss as steam escaped from the mangled bonnet. The headlights were somehow still going, and they lit up the macabre sight of their car wrapped around the tree. She noticed the tree seemed to have survived relatively unscathed.

Anna's body was in an awkward sideways position in her seat, and as she became more aware of her surroundings her neck let her know it was in a bad way with an agonising sharp pain. She figured that must be a good sign though, it meant she was alive, and it probably meant she wasn't paralysed. The front of the car had compacted so much that the dash which was normally a comfortable knees distance in front was now in her lap, and she couldn't move her left leg although she realised she could, with relief, wiggle her foot. A moan sounded beside her and she wriggled and twisted some more until she could see her husband. She gasped.

"Tim," she croaked, her voice hoarse from the screaming. "Tim!"

He looked in a bad way. There was blood everywhere from where his head had impacted with the side window. It was all through his hair and staining his face a crimson red. There was so much of it she couldn't make out any of his features. He looked like a character in a horror movie, with no face just a bloody, gory mess. He was making a horrible rasping sound, and she could hear blood gurgling in his throat as he tried to breathe.

"Tim!" she attempted to undo her seatbelt but her fingers couldn't make it happen. She looked over the back and felt relief, her son was ok, his peacefully sleeping face exactly as it had looked when she'd last checked on him. His expensively cushioned car seat that looked like a miniature lazy boy and which had cost almost as much as one had done its job, and she thanked her lucky stars that they had not scrimped when it came to his safety.

"It's ok baby," she soothed, "mummy's here. Daddy's here, everything is going to be ok." She felt certain that the driver of the campervan who had caused them to go off the road was at that very moment peering down at them from the top of the bank, calling for help on his cellphone. If not him then someone else, someone would have seen what happened or the tyre marks leading off the road.

"Hang in there Tim," she said, "help is coming. Any moment now, it won't be long. Can you hear me?"

But Tim didn't answer, and she realised with horror that his breathing had quietened and was now shallow; small gasps rather than breaths.

"No." She made a renewed effort to free the seat belt clasp so that she could reach as far as her trapped leg would allow her. "No Tim, don't you dare leave us, don't you dare. You hang in there, you hear me? Someone is coming, they'll be here any minute. You just need to be strong a little bit longer, ok? Just a little bit longer baby, stay with us."

She shook his shoulder. His head was lolled forward, his chin on his chest at an unnatural angle.

She tried cajoling. "Tim? Baby? Answer me. Please? I need you. *We* need you. I can't do this on my own."

Reassurance. "I know you're hurt baby but help is almost here, I can hear them. They're just trying to figure out a way down the bank then they'll be here. Any minute ok, just stay with me."

Anger. "Tim! Answer me! Don't you dare die on me, you hear? Don't be so selfish! Ben and I need you, we need you!"

But nothing provoked a response. In front of her eyes his body relaxed, and she realised he was only taking every other breath. With horror, she realised she was literally listening to the life ebb from his body, and there was nothing she could do to stop it.

"I love you," she told him. "I love you so much."

And then he went completely limp and she never heard another breath from him again.

It was hard to take it in. She wanted to fall to pieces but she knew she couldn't; she had to stay strong for the sake of their son. She turned her attention back to him, moaning as her leg sent pain coursing through her body in waves as she reached out for her baby. Her fingertips grazed the buckle on his seatbelt. She strained some more, fresh pain blossomed, and managed to free her leg enough that she could push the red button to release the straps holding him in his seat. They sprang open and she sobbed with relief.

"Come here baby," she cooed, "come to mummy."

For the first time, it struck Anna as odd that her son hadn't been woken by the impact. "Oh no," she moaned, "no no no no no." Forgoing all attempts at gentleness, she tugged at one of his chubby legs, each tug more insistent and rougher than the last.

"Ben," she said, "Ben baby, wake up sweetie. Mummy needs you to wake up now."

She grabbed his leg tighter and pulled him towards her, and his little body slid down the seat without any resistance, until he was near enough for her to take hold of him with both hands and with some effort lift and drag his small body through the gap in the seats to her lap.

All pain was forgotten.

She forgot that she had just watched her husband die.

Everything in her life, in the world, came down to that moment; the moment she lifted her son up to her face and held her breath as she listened for any sound of breathing. There were none. She wrapped her fingers around his chubby little wrist and swore at herself when she failed to find a pulse; certain it was because she was doing it wrong. How could she be so useless at a time like this? She was angry, so angry at herself. This was her baby, he needed her. She had to pull herself together. Holding his head up awkwardly in the crook of one elbow, she placed her mouth over his and she breathed the air from her lungs into his, over and over and over again. She infused each breath with her deep and endless love for him, and as she passed it from her body to his she begged him with every single fibre of her being to accept it. To take it into his lungs and let it absorb into his body and for it to bring him back to her.

She would never know how long she tried. At some point she couldn't breathe anymore, her sobs ripping the air from her lungs and then she just held him to her, as tight as she could, not caring whether she hurt him or not, because maybe pain would invoke a response where her breaths had failed. She wept. She wept more than she had ever wept in her life, her tears soaking his hair and skin, the way they had when he was born and she'd wept tears then too, only then they had been tears of happiness.

She held him to her tightly and smothered him in kisses; the tiny curves of his ears, his soft, sweet little lips, forehead, cheeks, and the tip of his nose. His long dark lashes rested against his chubby cheeks like they always did when he slept, and she tried to convince herself that he was just resting. He cooled beneath her touch and she cried and kissed him some more. His little head lolled loosely, and she realised his delicate neck must have snapped and she prayed that it had been swift and he had felt no pain. This precious little boy who she had carried in her womb for so long, nurturing him, and who she had suffered through the worse pain of her life in order to bring him into the world, but pain that had of course all been worth it in the end. She would go through ten times that pain again now for just one more glimpse of his gummy smile.

At some point the headlights dimmed and disappeared all together, and she was left in the darkness with the bodies of her husband and her baby and she wished with all her might that her own injuries were bad enough that she would soon die with them, because she couldn't see how she could ever live on. Not without her precious baby, her perfect, sweet and innocent boy who had never harmed anyone. What had he done to deserve this?

Only hours before she had been part of a happy family, a little unit of people who she loved and who loved her unconditionally and unreservedly. She had a husband who, despite their differences, adored her. And she had the baby she'd dreamt of for years; a tiny piece of her that she had felt such a fierce love for she would have happily laid down her own life to have saved his.

And now they were both gone. Just like that. Here one second, gone the next. It was the kind of thing you heard about happening, but to other people. How could someone be gone just like that?

Eighteen hours she spent trapped in the car. She dozed fitfully in and out of conscious but she never once let go of her baby. Even when his little body became cold and stiff and started to smell unrecognisable, she never let him go. She kissed him. She told him how much she loved him, how thankful she was to have had him, and she told him how sorry she was that she hadn't been able to stop this horrible thing from happening to him. One minute she was calm, then next she screamed so loudly she scared the owls from the trees nearby, their frantic wings in the air the only other sound in the night. Any road noise was muffled by the thick vegetation and she wondered whether anyone would ever know what had become of them. Would she die of exposure or blood loss or thirst or shock? She wanted to. She wanted to stay here with her family. In this car. Their own family coffin. She wanted to die. She wasn't a religious person but right then she clung to the hope that when she died, hopefully in this car and soon, she would be reunited with them again.

But some time the next day she heard voices. And not long after that she saw faces at her window.

Her memories of what happened after that are hazy and fragmented. She remembers the sound of the machine they used to prise open her car like a tin can, freeing her leg. She remembers a voice, male, saying sadly, "this one's gone, poor guy," and she knew he was talking about Tim.

She refused to let go of Ben, so they belted her on to the stretcher with him in her arms and carried the two of them up the steep bank to the waiting ambulance, where she refused to let go of him again.

A bumpy drive, then a long corridor, fluorescent lights above her, a doctor talking to her as if she were a child while he examined her leg – "This might hurt a little bit, Anna, but I'll try to do it as quickly as I can, ok? You just let me know if you need me to stop" – murmurs around her as people tried to figure out the best way to get her to release her son's body, because she threatened to hurt anyone who tried.

In the end they sedated her, the bastards. There was a prick as the needle penetrated her vein and then she felt herself drifting away and she was powerless to resist. She tried to scream because she knew what they were doing but she was asleep before her mouth could even form the shape.

When she woke, after a lengthy surgery where they put a pin in her ankle and stitched up her leg from ankle to knee, her son was gone. And she told the nurse in the recovery room that they should have cut out her heart, because she wouldn't need it anymore.

Chapter twenty nine

The feeling of contentment that she had felt that day at the bank was hit and miss, and she still woke more nights than not, but she was ok with that. In fact, she preferred it, it was familiar.

Buddy would be waiting at the door when she came downstairs in the morning to be let out, jumping from foot to foot and quacking furiously. The others would be waiting as usual on the other side of the door but after a few days they learnt to stand to one side unless they wanted to be bowled over by a large uncoordinated duckling going twenty miles an hour.

She started back at work with very little fanfare, although the girls had bought her a cupcake and a card with a cross looking cat on the front and the slogan, 'Don't let the bastards get you down!' Everything was the same, but different. HR supplied her with a new set of uniforms, accepting her story that she'd mailed the old one back and it must have been misplaced by the notorious postal system. The lunchroom still smelt the same, a combination of microwaved curries and old, unidentified food lurking in the depths of the fridge that no one laid claim too and everyone else was too lazy to throw out.

The first week back, Anna surprised herself by managing to be on time every morning. It wasn't too great a struggle, merely requiring a greater level of organisation and time keeping and less dilly dallying and pausing to smell the flowers. But where was the fun in that? She resented it with a passion. Arriving at work she would pause to suck in a lungful of the beautiful warm fresh air, before heading glumly through the doors into the recycled air conditioning.

At night, she went home to her quiet house and stood for far too long perusing the contents of her fridge in the carnivorous silence of her house. She messed the house, tidied the house, fed the ducks, showered and slept -or not slept - just the same as she had been doing for the past few years. She felt as if she were merely watching seconds pass on the clock of her life.

Everything was exactly as it should be, how it had been for some time and how she wanted it to be, yet the thought of going home now to an empty house and another endless night of meals for one, some bad TV and sleeplessness left her feeling cold.

The one bright point was Oscar's visits. Matt and the boy's mother had a fairly flexible custody arrangement, but the bones of it were that he spent week on week off with each parent. The first week Anna was back at the coalface, he was with his mother, and Anna rattled around the house talking to herself and taking her loneliness out on Buddy until even he was sick of the sound of her.

"Did I tell you about my day?" she would ask him.

'QUACK'

And then he'd waddle off in pursuit of his reflection in the shiny surfaces of the house, as was his latest obsession. Anna took this to mean 'No, and don't feel you need to either,' which she thought was pretty rude when she considered all that she did for him. She could even hear the hum of the TV when it was on standby, such was the lack of other noise.

Five o'clock Friday, exhausted from pretending she cared which superannuation scheme someone picked or helping sort out budgets for people who were, frankly, either too stupid or too reckless to sort it out for themselves. In the past she'd been capable of mustering up the correct amount of concern, empathy and professionalism. But now all she could think was; is this it? Just as she was contemplating shoving a pencil in her ear, anything to escape the monotony of the humdrum around her, Matt came into the bank and asked her if she'd mind if Oscar hung out with her for a few hours the next day, as the warm weather meant he was behind on his work and would have to work Saturday. Although they'd seen each other twice since the cemetery, Matt hadn't mentioned it and therefore neither had she. She assumed he wasn't interested and this came as a relief. It was refreshing to be able to talk to someone who knew nothing about her past.

"Of course," she said, pleased he'd thought of her.

"Are you sure? You don't have anything else on?"

Anna pretended to consult her online diary, although she knew without a doubt she had nothing more exciting planned than cleaning the bathroom and shovelling over the compost pile. "Nothing that can't be rescheduled," she said.

Saturday morning she was up with the dawn as usual, and she got on with cleaning out the bathroom and turning over the compost so it was out of the way. When she finished she could feel a line of sweat trickle down between her shoulder blades and thought of the cool temptress that was the river. This gave her an idea.

She biked to the supermarket and bought a slapstick picnic dinner; French bread sticks, cheeses, cold deli meats and a couple of containers of salads (coleslaw and an Italian pasta, she kept a wary eye on the stickers to make sure they stayed attached until she was through the checkouts). Back at home she found her old picnic basket in the bottom of the linen cupboard and added some paper napkins. While getting the basket from the cupboard she noticed a box of solar powered fairy lights. It made her melancholy for a moment, as she recalled buying them with Tim one day with the intention of using them for a BBQ at Ben's first Christmas, the one he didn't live long enough to see. She paused, fingers lightly tracing the letters on the box. The thought of all the missed Christmases and birthdays was devastating. She would never see his excited face when he saw the presents under the tree for the first time. So many things he never got to experience. It broke her heart.

Just after lunch there was a knock on the door and she opened it to see Matt and Oscar.

"How's Buddy?" were the first words out of Oscars mouth.

"And hello to you too," she said, "come in and see for yourself."

He didn't need the incitation though and was already half way into the lounge.

"Sorry about that, he gets his manners from his mother. Are you sure this is ok? Matt asked.

"Yes of course."

"Great. Thank you, I really appreciate it. Normally I'd farm him out to my brother but between you and me —" he leant forward to peer into the house to make sure Oscar wasn't listening, " — he's not a fan. My brothers four boys are rough little buggers and all they want to do is wrestle all day. I don't know if you've noticed but Oscar is more of a thinker. Poor boy ends up somewhere on the bottom of the pile every time."

"That's horrible."

"Oh they're just boys being boys, but I have to trick Oscar into going there. He's not very happy when I do that though."

"I don't blame him."

"No I guess I can't either. Anyway, thanks again, you know for looking after him. He's really missed Buddy; nagged me solid on the phone each night to bring him here this weekend."

"Buddy has missed him too."

Matt checked his watch. "I better get to it, I'll be back around four, five at the latest. That ok?"

"Yes it's fine. Would the two of you would like to stay for dinner."

"Let me just check my calendar," Matt frowned as he pretended to think about it just as she had the day before. "Nope, calendar's clear," he grinned. "Dinner sounds good. Need me to pick anything up?"

"No it's all sorted."

"Great. See you in a few hours." He leant around Anna again. "See you soon," he called to Oscar. "You be good or else."

"Yes dad," Oscar rolled his eyes.

"Or else what?" Anna asked.

"Dunno. He's never pushed me enough to find out."

Buddy and Oscar played happily on the lounge floor while Anna floated around, dusting and tidying. At one point they went out into the garden with the other ducks and Anna felt a tiny pang of jealousy at the connection he had with them, but it was only tiny. Around three she remembered the solar lights and fetched them from the cupboard.

"I just need to go and do something," she called to Oscar, "will you two be ok on your own for a few minutes?"

"I'm eight, not five," said Oscar. "We'll be fine."

Anna stopped by the garden shed to collect a couple of old wooden crates and some empty jars she knew were lingering in the back under a heavy layer of cobwebs, and then made her way – closing the gate firmly behind her which was no easy task considering the load she was carrying – to the river. Near the bank grew a pink Manuka tree, its small blossoms littering the air like confetti.

Standing on one of the crates Anna wove the fairy lights around the lowest branches. It was a box of 500, so this took some time. Then she shook out the blanket and placed it on the flattest piece of ground underneath the tree and put the crates on opposite corners to stop it from blowing away in the wind. Lastly, she placed the jars around the base of the tree. Satisfied, she went back to the house where she found Oscar and Buddy in exactly the same place she had left them.

"See?" Oscar said. "We're still alive. The house hasn't caught fire. I didn't open the door to any strangers."

"Well that's good. I appreciate that."

When Matt turned up at just after five Anna was all prepared and ready to go.

"Phew that's some heat out there," he exhaled as he came in. "Do you mind if I have a quick splash before dinner?"

"Splash?"

"You know, a shower. The grass sticks everywhere, I don't want to dirty your sofa or chairs."

"I have a better idea." She threw Tim's shorts and two towels at him. It was the same pair he'd borrowed the last time they'd been swimming. He caught them and gave her a quizzical glance.

"We're going swimming? Now?"

"Yes, unless you don't want to -?"

"No, a swim sounds good. But what about dinner? I know I'm fairly lax but I should probably feed the boy something."

He sniffed the air. There was a distinct lack of cooking smells.

"I have something special planned," she said.

"Something special, really." He winked at her.

Anna realised he had the wrong idea. "Not that kind of special. Just something a little different that I thought Oscar might enjoy."

"So, *not* a date then."

"A date? Of course not."

He sighed. "Can't blame a guy for trying."

Anna fetched the cold foods from the fridge and added them to the basket. "Let's go."

"Can Buddy come?" Oscar asked.

"No not tonight, he's still a little young to be venturing far from home."

As she led the way through the gate and the paddocks to the river, the three of them were caressed by the gentlest breeze. For Anna, it invoked a deep feeling of satisfaction, a sense of earthiness and grounding in the here and now, and she soaked up the pleasure that was the present moment. She turned her face skywards and the breeze traced its fingers across her cheek and her lips parted with the pleasure. It was the one thing she missed the most from her former life.

Touch.

Until it was gone she took it for granted. Cuddles from her husband, his lips on her cheek on his way out the door. His hand placed gently in the curve of her back as they walked somewhere, their fingers laced together as they stood and watched their baby sleep. The feel of his chest against her as they made love, his lips on her neck, murmuring in her ear, nibbling at her bottom lip.

She missed the touch of her son. His head against her chin as she rocked him. The way he used to hold one of her fingers firmly in his hot little grasp while she fed him, his lips on her breast. She missed the reassuring weight of him in the crook of her arm. He was a hefty little sod, all rolls and chubby deliciousness.

She couldn't remember the last time she had touched someone. Apart from shaking hands of course, but that hardly counted.

"Here we are," she said, placing the basket on the ground and waiting expectantly for them admire her handiwork.

"Is this where you disappeared to before?" Oscar asked, taking in the little picnic area Anna had set up.

"Yes."

"Cool."

It would do. "Do you want a swim before or after you eat?"

Oscar looked at his dad, who shrugged, "Before, I guess. Isn't there some rule against swimming within an hour of eating?"

"Hm yes that does ring a bell. Well you two jump in. I'll join you in a second."

Matt, grinning, moved behind the tree to change into the swimming shorts. He remerged a minute later and called to his son, "Last one in does the dishes!" before performing a perfectly good bomb off the bank into the waters below.

"Hey that's not fair you had a head start!" Oscar complained before joining him at a more sedate pace.

Anna unpacked the food and eating paraphernalia from the basket and set it up in the middle of the blanket from where they could all help themselves. Then she joined them in the water. She floated on her back and admired the twilight sky, wishing on the first star that twinkled into existence just like her mother always had. Even with her ears under the water's surface she could hear the muffled laughs from the other two as they set about building, then knocking down, another stone dam.

"Time to get out," she called when the water started to cool down.

"Do we have too?" Matt moaned. "The water feels so good."

"No you don't have to. You can stay in if you like. Of course the eels will be out cruising for their dinner soon," she added casually as she towelled herself off.

Matt shot up the bank so fast she barely saw him move.

"What?" he protested defensively when he saw her smirk, "I've seen documentaries, they grow to insane sizes!"

"It's because of all the children they eat," she laughed when Oscar hightailed it out of the water so fast he almost knocked his father to one side. It was a deep bellied laugh, one that left her cheeks aching when she finally caught her breath and wiped an escaped tear away. She clutched at her stomach, "Oh I haven't laughed like that in a long time."

Oscar was surveying the water, his face white. "Do they really eat children?" he gulped.

"Have you ever seen a stray sandal just lying around on the beach?"

"Yes."

"Well there you go. Washed down rivers and out to sea, their hapless owners never to be seen again."

Oscar gulped harder. "*Seriously* dad?"

Matt laughed. "Sorry to bust up the party Anna, but if I ever want him to dip his toe in the water again I'd better come clean. No," he shook his head to reassure his son, "it's not true. Besides, I think they're vegetarians."

Anna couldn't help but smile sadly as she unpacked the food onto the blanket. This was how she imagined her future would be. Excursions like this with her boys and any other kids they'd been blessed enough to have. She wondered if she would ever do anything ever again that wasn't a painful reminder.

"Tuck in," she said when she unpacked everything.

Matt whistled loudly threw his teeth. "You've gone to quite the effort. What have we done to deserve this?"

"Done? You haven't done anything. I just thought it would be nice to have a picnic dinner. It's something I used to do a lot in summer." If Matt sensed the sadness behind the voice he didn't say anything. "I almost forgot," she added, getting to her feet –kneeling in the spilt coleslaw in the process, "Oh yuck," she said, and wiped it off with a napkin, - "stop eating for a second and look at this. Ta da," she flicked the switch on the solar powered fairy lights and with a flourish they sprang to life, illuminating the tree and the air around them like hundreds of luminous fire flies.

Oscar swallowed his sandwich. "Wow," he said, eyes wide, "that's pretty cool."

Matt nodded in agreement. "Very nice. Did you put them up there yourself?"

"No," she said. "Fairies did."

"Fai -? Oh, I see. You're being sarcastic."

"Are they electric?" Oscar asked.

Anna sighed. The magic was being stifled by stupid questions. "Yes," she said. "There's a six hundred metre extension cord running back to the house."

"Where?" Oscar looked around them.

"I think she's being sarcastic again," Matt laughed.

"Pass the matches out of the basket," Anna told him. She lit tea light candles from a packet and placed them in jars dotted around the tree. "There."

The lights looked lovely but their full effect wasn't apparent until the sun dropped behind the trees and stars started to sparkle in the immense sky above and the light deepened into a vintage denim colour. It was then that Anna's handiwork became alive. The lights shone like little stars themselves, and combined with the flickering candles the picnic area looked magical and like something out of a story book. Anna's earlier comment about fairies suddenly seemed entirely possible.

They ate in peace, the gentle babble of the water as it travelled steadfastly on its journey to the river mouth and beyond that, the sea was the only sound to disturb the silence. When she finished eating, Anna lay down on the blanket and closed her eyes and imagined she was a leaf taking that journey.

She loved the sea and tried to remember the last time she'd been. Ah yes, it was when Ben was only a few weeks old. She'd been wildly optimistic. A day at the beach would be good for them all, she declared. Some salt air and a vigorous walk would clear the cobwebs, with Ben in the mountain buggy pram that had cost them the earth but which had thus far done nothing apart from clutter up the hallway and stub her toe on two occasions.

They'd packed up the car with all the essentials, plus a few hundred things they didn't need but wanted to have on hand just in case, because as they were fast learning, with babies you always needed the one thing it turned out you'd forgotten. Then they'd set off, spirits high, anticipation making them giddy. They sang 'The wheels on the Bus' for the time the journey took, making up new things on the bus as they went along. But when they got there, a southerly wind was blowing in off the ocean, and despite having three sorts of mosquito repellent Anna realised she'd forgotten to pack the sunscreen, so spent the entire time fretting about wind burn and sun burn and covered poor Ben in so many thick layers of muslin that the poor boy never even saw the beach, let alone got a dose of healthy sea air. The buggy, while impressive in appearance, proved utterly useless and Tim cursed more that day than she'd ever heard him curse before as he had to dig the tyres out of the sand one too many times, and strain to overcompensate for the buggy's tendency to steer right – towards the water – when he wanted it to go left. By the time they arrived home a few short hours later, nursing aching forearms and feeling more exhausted then when they'd set out, they decided not to repeat the experience until Ben was at least old enough to appreciate the experience his parents were trying to give him.

She wished she had thrown caution to the wind and dangled her baby's toes in the water, and let him feel sand on his bottom.

Before summer was over she would go, she decided. Catch a bus or maybe even call up one of the ladies from work, or a friend she hadn't talked to in years and see if they wanted to make a day of it.

"Anna?"

"Hmm?"

"Thank you."

"You're welcome."

"I mean it. This was just what I needed." Matt leant back against one of the crates, watching as his son used one of the jars to try and catch a large moth that was circling the light.

Anna opened her eyes and pushed up onto her elbows, arching her back and yawning. The physical exertion from the swim, coupled with the good food and fresh air had made her sleepy right through to her bones. She contemplated the walk home and wished she'd brought a sleeping bag with her. Before Ben came along, she and Tim had done that a few times, slept by the river under the stars. She had always found it an incredibly grounding experience. Nothing like the great expanse of the universe turning above to remind her just how small her little pocket of the earth was.

"Sometimes I forget to just stop, you know." Matt continued. "Work, paying bills, all that grown up stuff; I needed this little reminder to stop and enjoy life. Hell, I can't remember the last time I took the boy camping. We used to love doing that, when he was little. Me and him, we'd take off for the night, sometimes into the forest, sometimes the beach. Pitch a tent and cook on a small camp stove." He shook his head. "Why did we stop doing that?"

"Because mum didn't like it, remember?" Oscar said quietly. Matt hadn't realised he was listening. "She thought it was dangerous."

"Oh," Matt remembered the arguments then. "Yes." His face clouded over in the flickering light from the candles. Then he brightened. "Still, she can't stop us now eh? We should do it again, soon. Would you like that?"

"Yeah, that would be cool," Oscar grinned and paused from waving a stick at the moth. "Can we go next weekend?"

"I don't see why not."

"Cool," Oscar repeated, his face shining with excitement.

"Well guys," Anna reluctantly started to pick up the picnic things, "I guess we should be heading back. It'll be dark soon and my bed is calling." She yawned as she packed up the basket, although packed was a loose term as she merely threw everything in and resolved to sort it out the next day.

"Yeah I guess we should," Matt agreed, getting to his feet and picking up the blanket, folding it in one swift move and tucking it under an arm. "Are we going to try and take those down now?" he asked, eyeing the lights in the tree above.

"No," Anna shook her head. "I think I'll leave them there. They look pretty. Who knows, it might entice me to dine out here more often."

"Can we come again too dad?"

'If Anna will have us, sure."

"Of course I will. Why wouldn't I?"

"It's a saying Anna, like a rhetorical question."

"Oh. I knew that."

They blew out the candles in the jars, leaving one each to carry to light the path home, although the moon was so bright they almost didn't need them. The air was soft and warm and the scent of night blooming jasmine came to them on the breeze. It was heady and sweet and made their heads woozy with a natural intoxication. At least, that's the excuse Anna came up with the next day when she thought about what had happened next.

Seeing them off at the front door, Oscar walked ahead up the garden path and she was just about to close the door when Matt turned suddenly and hurried back to her. He stopped only an inch away, surprising her with his proximity. He smelt of grass and the river and the night, and she inhaled this essence of him without thinking. She was unaware that when she did so her pupils dilated into big, black puddles and her lips parted involuntarily.

Matt noticed. Longing seized him and before he could stop to think about it he acted, leaning forward to kiss Anna.

She was so shocked and so out of practise in the ways of anything romantic that at first she just stood there, stiff like an ironing board. Matt was just beginning to think he'd made a terrible mistake when he felt her soften and lean in to him, and her lips pressed against his as gently as a whisper. She was the sweetest thing he had ever tasted; sweeter than chocolate, or champagne, or summer strawberries. A small, embarrassed cough from the end of the garden path reminded them of where they were and whose eyes were right then being exposed to this spontaneous romance. Anna jumped back, her fingertips flying to where his lips had been seconds before.

"Goodnight," she said in a high pitched voice, and closed the door.

Matt stared at it for a moment, and his hand lifted up to knock but then he heard his son's voice in the darkness.

"Yuck dad," it said.

His hand dropped. He smiled at the door then turned and walked to his son, slinging an arm around his shoulders as they walked to the car.

"What's the matter?" he said, "You think your dad is too old to kiss girls?"

Oscar shrugged his arm off. "Yes. Thank god nobody else saw you."

Matt laughed as he put the key in the lock and unlocked the car doors, "get in you," he said. "Honestly. You act like I'm bloody ancient."

Chapter thirty

Back inside the house Anna also stared at the door for a moment. Her heart was racing in her chest and her lips felt as if she'd dipped them in sherbet.

"What on earth?" she whispered.

Turning off the downstairs lights – after checking on Buddy who was nestled snugly in his box and snuffling softly – she made her way upstairs where she showered with her shower cap on, selected the blue striped pyjamas that always made her feel like a sailor, and slid into her bed, pulling the sheets up under her chin.

But sleep wouldn't come because she couldn't stop thinking about the kiss. It had all happened so quickly she wasn't even really sure it was happening until it was over. It had been so long since she'd kissed anyone she wondered if she'd done it right. Maybe things had changed in the last few years and she didn't know and right now Matt was somewhere thinking, 'well that was odd.'

It had felt right, though. Well, it had felt nice, and surely that was the same thing. The weirdest part was that she couldn't decide how she felt about it. Was she happy it happened? Did she regret that it had happened? Or was she ambivalent? "Ugh," she moaned, turning on to her side and punching up her pillow a little more aggressively than normal. Only now she remembered the angst that came along with all things romantic. Married life had been so easy in comparison. Having someone who you could just be yourself around was underrated, it really was. She had taken it for granted, as many people most likely currently were.

Her eyes focused on the pillow in front of her. A very small indent remained, though as not as pronounced as it once was. She reached out a hand and tentatively touched it. Squeezing her eyes shut she pictured his sleeping face, as she'd seen it so many times. So many times that she hadn't ever thought to stop and appreciate it. Sometimes in fact she'd grumbled at it. Sometimes, and she was ashamed to admit this, she'd resented it deeply for snoring and keeping her awake. On those occasions she even felt like stuffing a pillow over it.

A tear rolled out of one eye, across the bridge of her nose and down past the other eye to soak into the pillow below. It felt wrong, to be here, beside Tim's memory, having done what she'd just done.

"I'm sorry baby," she whispered. "It was just a kiss. It doesn't mean I love you any less."

Her guilt kept her tossing and turning and sometime around three am she gave up and got out of bed, passing the blue door – she couldn't face that accusing room either – and made her way downstairs where Buddy was still fast asleep. He quacked and gave her a reproachful look when she turned the light on.

"Sorry," she said and turned it back off. She flicked the light switch on the small rangehood over the oven instead – less intrusive - and made herself coffee before curling up on the couch and turning on the TV.

Celebrity apprentice reruns were on, and she watched with half her attention until the Don finally pointed his finger and said his immortal words and a celebrity – who'd she'd neither seen nor heard of before – flounced from the room refusing to shake the hand of her triumphant rival.

Anna sighed and hit the kill switch, the silence wasting no time in rushing back to fill the void. There was only one thing for it.

The dawn found her amongst the roses, still in her pyjamas, muddied and weary. She had pruned and weeded beneath the light of the moon, and the physical activity had kept the guilty thoughts at bay. As the town came to life around her, noises carried to her on the soft morning breeze, she stood and stretched, arching her neck so her face was upturned to the brilliant colours of yet another sunrise.

In the new light of day she made a decision.

Across town, Matt emerged from his blankets with a stretchy smile and a contented sigh. He kept his eyes firmly shut so he could bask in the memory of The Kiss. It was unlike any other kiss he'd ever experienced, but not in a way that he could put his finger on. As far as kisses go it had been fairly standard; lips here, pressure not to firm as to be aggressive, not so soft as to be construed as weak. Tongues had been gently introduced while teeth were kept at a polite distance. Yes, it had all been run of the mill as far as kisses go, and yet most magnificent at the same time.

Even his alarm failed to pop his happy little bubble. He bounded out of bed with an energy his body hadn't felt since his early twenties. When Oscar arrived at the breakfast table shortly after he had to rub his eyes to check whether it was indeed a feast in front of his eyes or some mirage brought on by pent up hunger.

"You cooked?"

"Don't sound so surprised."

"But I *am* surprised."

"Your old man's not completely useless."

"Seriously, *you* cooked all this?" Oscar took in the plates of crispy bacon, golden hash browns, sunny side up eggs and steaming hot baked beans. It wasn't a gourmet meal by any means, but it may as well have been the finest French dining as far as this table had ever seen.

"Look, keep sounding surprised like that and I can just as easily take it away."

Oscar shut up and sat down quickly lest this feast be snatched from in front of him. He devoured the whole lot in five minutes, sneaking sideways glances at the man who to all intents and purposes *looked* like his father, but who suddenly cooked and hummed while he washed dishes and even flicked Oscar playfully with a tea towel as if they were on some fancy butter commercial.

"Are you feeling ok dad?" he asked, watching his father arrange the tea towel tidily on the oven door instead of just scrunching it up and wedging it in there as he normally would.

"Hmm? Yes, never felt better," Matt beamed. And it was true, he hadn't.

Oscar couldn't ever remember seeing his father look so happy. "Is it because of Anna?" he asked, and nearly fell off his chair when his father blushed. Oscar had never seen his father blush before.

"humpftsghtydyghst," his father mumbled, which Oscar assumed meant yes.

After dropping Oscar back off at his mothers, Matt decided to tackle the supermarket for a big shop, something he hadn't done in quite some time. He did this with a bounce in his step and a whistle on his lips. He smiled at everyone he saw and if he'd been wearing a hat it was entirely probable he would have doffed it. When he thought about Anna and that kiss he couldn't stop himself from beaming like some kind of village idiot.

Under the fluorescent lights of aisle four, in front of the chocolate section, he made a decision.

Chapter thirty one

"A simple coffee, at a cafe?" His voice was desperate. Anna had already turned down, in no particular order, dinner, the movies, and a home cooked meal at his house, although he couldn't blame her for not being overly keen on that last option.

"No."

"What do you mean, no?"

"What do you mean, what do I mean? No is a fairly self explanatory word. It's as basic as they come. Any three year old could tell you the meaning of it."

"There you go again, insulting my vocabulary."

Anna sighed. "I'm not insulting anything. I'm merely confused as to why you keep questioning my decision."

"Because it's a stupid decision, that's why."

"So now you're insulting my decision making skills?"

"You better believe I am." He lowered his voice and turned his back on a young couple walking hand in hand past him up the cereal aisle. He'd called Anna from the supermarket to propose a date for that night. The last thing he'd been expecting was a response in the negative. "I don't understand. Did I do something wrong?"

"No," She took her frustration out on an ant trailing across the bench top carrying a crumb three times its own size.

Squish went her thumb. Then she immediately felt awful. After all it was hardly the ants fault. "But I don't want to discuss it anymore. Look, Matt, you're a nice guy, and your son is delightful. But there's just no room in my life for any kind of, -" she floundered, trying to think of an alternative word to the only one that came to mind. She failed. "Relationship," she finished reluctantly.

"No room?"

"No room."

"Anna, I'll admit I haven't known you all that long. But it seems to me all you do is work and garden. How can there not be room for a couple of dates in amongst there? Or am I missing something."

"What I do in my spare time is none of your business. Now if you're done, I need to go now."

"No I'm not done. You're going have to be a bit more explicit. I thought we were getting on great, I thought you enjoyed the kiss as much as I did. I assumed, wrongly it seems, that we might be at the start of something here,"

"Matt, you're making too much of a big deal of things. We barely know each other for goodness sakes. I'm just not interested in taking things any further, and I think it's best if Oscar stops coming over. Buddy is becoming too domesticated. I plan on introducing him to the wild soon."

"By the wild I take it you mean your garden?"

"Yes."

Matt sucked in a breath and let it out again in one long, confused, exhale. The young couple turned to look at him and he scowled at them. They moved quickly away.

"So, if I understand this correctly, you don't want to see either me *or* Oscar anymore?"

"Correct." Anna felt a pang when she said this, and the thought of Oscars sad little face at being cut off from Buddy nearly made her change her mind, but then she caught sight of Tim's jandals by the back door and her resolve strengthened.

"Was it something I did?"

"No."

Something *he* did?"

"Definitely not."

A thought came to Matt. "Oh."

"What?"

"Is it...because of, you know-?"

Anna was slow on the uptake. "You'll have to be more specific."

"You know, what happened, to your husband and kid."

Anna sagged against the counter top. So he *did* know. "Goodbye Matt. Feed Oscar properly and make sure you tell him how much he's loved each night. Please don't contact me again."

And she hung up.

Matt stared at the flashing screen. *Call ended,* it mocked him. He considered calling her back but her voice had become angry with the mention of her family, and he thought the best thing he could probably do right now was to give her some space. Any other woman and he would probably decide at this point that she wasn't worth the grief and cut his losses.

After a few days he sent her a text message. She didn't reply. He sent her a bunch of flowers, the nice ones from the florist, not the cheap ones from the supermarket. He attached a card that said, '*I'm sorry. Can we meet to talk things through? Venue of your selection and time of your choice.*'

He assumed she got them, he'd paid five dollars extra for them to be delivered, but still he heard nothing. He started to feel annoyed. Ok, maybe it was as simple as her deciding he just wasn't her type. Fair enough. He could live with that. But the very least she could do was tell him that and put him out of his misery. The worse part about the whole thing was Oscar. The boy couldn't understand why he suddenly was no longer welcome at Anna's, and at the breakfast table he was filled with questions that Matt had no answer for.

"Doesn't she like us anymore?"

Matt winced with his back turned to Oscar. It was heartbreaking. "Of course she does. Well, you anyway. Me, I'm not so sure."

"Did I do something to upset her dad?"

"Definitely not."

"Was it because you kissed her?"

"Maybe. "

"Did you do it wrong?"

Matt choked on his coffee. When he could speak again he smiled at his son and reached out to ruffle his hair. "I don't think so, but who knows. Maybe look it up in the library next time you're there."

Oscar didn't laugh.

Matt sat down at the table put his arm around Oscar's shoulders, pulling him in close. "Look, I don't know why Anna doesn't want to see us right now. But I *can* tell you that she's had some pretty, -" he searched for the right word and remembered something the reverend had said, "tragic things happen in her life. She may just need a bit of time."

"You mean like what happened to nana, don't you."

"How did you know that?"

Oscar shrugged. "Something Anna said."

"It's not exactly like what happened to your grandmother. We had time to say our goodbyes to her. When someone gets sick and then dies, at least you have a little bit of time to come to terms with what's happening. You can say the things you need to say. With Anna's family, she didn't get that chance."

"That's sad."

"I know," he squeezed his son tighter. "It really is."

Chapter thirty two

Work, while never satisfying, had become unbearable. Anna felt stifled at her desk, like she was shackled there. Every time the front doors opened the breeze would reach in to touch her with its soft, delicate fingers. It smelt of the big outdoors, warm currents that smelt of the muddy river and traces of salt that had come from the sea. It was delicious, and on more than one occasion she found she had risen off her seat and was half way to the door, her nose lifted to the breeze, her hands already reaching to peel the constricting polyester shirt off her back.

"Anna?" one of the other ladies would say, snapping her from her trance.

And she would return to her seat, feeling sweat glue her stockings to her legs, and dream of escaping this hellhole once and for all.

Her phone rang and she recognised the number as Matt's. She ignored it. It stopped ringing after six rings when the answering machine picked up. Ten seconds later it started ringing again, the number his again. Anna busied herself on her computer as if she couldn't hear it.

"Aren't you going to get that Anna?" Judy snapped from her desk when it rang for the third time.

"What? Oh the phone? No, I wasn't planning on it." She didn't tell Judy it was a personal call, letting her assume that Anna was ignoring a potential customer. She just couldn't be bothered anymore, not with Judy and not with this place.

"I guess you'd like a written warning to go with that verbal one then."

"What?"

"Don't think because Hedley saved you that your job is safe. It just means it'll take a little longer to get rid of you than I'd thought."

Anna swivelled in her chair to look at Judy. Her fluffy blond helmet of hair gave Anna an idea. She swivelled back to her computer and did a quick google search.

"You know Judy," she said. "I've been trying to Keep the Faith, but honestly, sometimes I just feel Shot through the Heart."

She heard Louise snort.

"What are you on about?" Judy snapped.

"I mean, I know this job can't always be a Bed of Roses, but lately I feel really Misunderstood, you know?"

"No I don't know. You're talking crap, as usual."

"It's ok Anna," Holly piped up from her desk, "I'll Be There For You,"

"So will I," said Rochelle, barely concealing her laughter, "Always."

Anna smiled gratefully at the girls. The joke was much funnier knowing they were all in on it. She looked at the Bon Jovi song titles on her screen.

"Judy," she said, "I've Been Living on A Prayer, but it's clearly too much to ask for you to Have a Little Faith In Me."

The other ladies laughed. Judy knew there was a joke going on and that it was aimed at her, but she couldn't figure it out. "Just shut up Anna," she said. "Get back to work."

"No." Anna stood up. She picked up her purse from under the desk and her pot plant, which she tucked under her armpit. "It's My Life, and I don't want to waste another minute of it in here looking at you. So if you'll excuse me," she couldn't bring herself to knock her computer to the floor nor do any real damage so she settled for knocking the magazines off the waiting table onto the floor, "I'm outta here," she announced, "In a Blaze of Glory." Then she took a bow to the applause of the others, and laughing at the bewildered expression on Judy's face she swept out.

It was the most satisfied she had felt in a very, *very* long time.

On her way home she stopped at the supermarket and bought herself a pizza in a box. She couldn't be bothered cooking. At the crossroads that led to the playground she paused and considered heading that way, but in the end she resignedly took the turn that led home. There was always the risk that Matt and Oscar might be there, and if she saw them her resolve might crumble.

The pizza had cooked and she was just settling down at the outside table, alone, with two slices and a large glass of wine when the phone rang inside the house. She frowned and checked the time, just after 6, and decided not to answer it, knowing it would either be Matt or a telemarketer or someone with an Indian accent telling her there was a major issue with her computer and unless she let them remotely log in to 'fix' it, she was screwed.

It rang for twenty rings then stopped.

It started again, this time for thirty rings, before it stopped.

Two minutes later she had just started to relax when its shrillness disturbed the silence again. When it hadn't stopped after a minute she threw her pizza down onto her plate, annoyed, and stalked inside intending to unplug the cord from the wall. It came as a surprise when she found herself picking it up and pushing the green talk button instead.

"Hello?"

"Anna?"

"Yes?"

"It's Matt."

She bit her bottom lip in frustration and mentally kicked herself.

"Matt please stop –"

"Anna, please!"

Something in his tone made her pause and listen.

She heard him take a deep breath and let it out with a shudder. Her pulse quickened. Something was wrong.

"What is it, what's wrong?" she asked.

"It's Oscar," his voice caught, "he's been in an accident."

She gasped and put a hand over her mouth. "What happened? Is he -?" she couldn't finish the question.

"Ok? I don't know. I honestly don't know."

Anna could hear the desperation and panic and uncertainty heavy in his voice.

"I don't know what to do Anna, tell me what I can do? They told me I just have to wait, let them do what they need to do. How can I just stand here and wait? How can I leave my little boy's life in the hands of others? Oh god Anna."

It was the first time she had heard him swear, but she didn't begrudge him it. She didn't have a clue what she could say that might help him. The irony wasn't lost on her. All those times she had resented people for saying the wrong thing to her, or in some cases even nothing at all, and now here she was in the same situation unable to think of a single suitable thing.

"Anna?"

"I'm here," she cleared her throat. Her heart wanted to ask questions. She wanted to know what had happened, but she really didn't know if she could handle the answers. To her shame, self preservation took over.

"I'm sorry," he continued, "I didn't know who else to call. Can you come? Please?"

She didn't answer.

"Anna? Please?" His voice was broken, needy.

She had nothing she could give him. Her reserves were all depleted. "No," she said in a small sad voice, "I'm sorry, I can't."

And she hung up the phone. Then she stared at it as if unable to believe what she had just done. "Oh my god," she whispered, her hands to her cheeks. She couldn't go through this again. It was too much to expect from one person. A person who had only just started to claw their way out of a very deep hole, with grief and depression shovelled on top of her. She had *just* started to catch glimpses of light; to think maybe she could live some semblance of a life again. Now this had happened. She wondered what she had done in order to attract such awful karma, then she felt mortified that she was thinking about herself at this time instead of the poor boy somewhere in a hospital bed and his father pacing the hall outside.

She reached for the phone to call him back but her fingers stopped just short.

No.

Yes.

No!

Yes. She would call. Then as her fingers grazed the receiver again she heard a noise outside.

'WOOF! SNARL'

She dashed to the door and in less than five seconds she clocked the situation. A dog was in the garden, and he was circling an anxious Buddy. A large black and brown dog of undetermined breed, he had his head lowered and his teeth bared. A low growl emanated from between his lips. He looked feral and vicious, and Anna froze, before searching with her eyes desperately for anything that she could use as a weapon.

"Get away with you!" she yelled, picking up a sandal and throwing it with all her might. It fell a few metres short of its target and the dog barely glanced her way, before it moved in for the kill. Before Anna could react she saw movement out of the corner of her eye. It was accompanied by a deafening chorus of quacks, angrier than she'd ever heard them before.

'QUACK QUACK QUACK QUACK QUACK QUACK QUACK QUACK!'

The other ducks rushed at the dog, a tangle of sharp beaks and angry wings, and with a yelp it turned on its heel and fled the garden, Rodney waddling furiously after it as far as the gate. The dog leapt over the gate and was gone, and Rodney said 'QUACK QUACK QUACK' which Anna translated to mean 'and don't you ever come back!'

She sank against the door frame feeling an enormous flooding of relief. Buddy was ok. The other ducks circled him protectively, soothing him with their voices and gentle touch until he was calmed. Anna watched. It was as if they were saying, "We're here for you Buddy, no matter what. We've got your back."

Something in Anna fell back into place.

Chapter thirty three

The hospital smelt the same as it had back then; a combination of boiled food, heavy duty disinfectant and sickness. Anna sucked in her breath for as long as she could but of course couldn't hold it forever, so she placed the sleeve of her jersey over her nose and mouth and breathed in the smell of her fabric softener instead.

"Can I help you?" the man on the front desk asked. He leant forward with his elbows on the desk, pretending he hadn't just been reading the magazine on the counter in front of him.

"Yes please. I'm looking for a boy who was bought in tonight."

"Name?"

"Oscar."

"You have a surname?"

Anna couldn't for the life of her remember it. "I'm sorry, I can't remember," she said lamely.

The man's eyebrows met in the middle. "Are you family?" he asked, his tone suggesting he knew the answer to this already.

"No. A friend."

"Ah." He looked at her as if he doubted this claim also.

"All I know is that he has had an accident. His father, Matt, called me and asked me to come up. There can't have been many eight year old boys named Oscar brought in tonight surely?"

"Well," The man wasn't giving anything away.

"Please," Anna decided to appeal to his human nature. "I just need to know he's ok. Can't you just click on a few buttons on your keyboard and look it up? Oscar. He's eight. His father's name is Matt."

"You must be Anna."

The voice came from behind her. It was flat and unfamiliar. Anna turned and took in the woman who had spoken. Blond and probably at any other time considered pretty, right now her eyes were red and inflamed and her face was haunted.

"Yes," Anna answered her.

"This is your fault, you know." The woman's voice turned bitter. "He was on his way to see you, even though I'd told him he wasn't allowed."

Anna realised this was Oscar's mother, Kate. "I didn't know that. I'm sorry."

The woman looked like on the brink of launching into a tirade but before Anna's eyes she subsided. She immediately looked small and frail. "It's alright," she said, barely louder than a whisper. "I don't really blame you. His father should never have let him ride his bike around town. I had no idea."

Anna stayed silent. She recognised a mother in turmoil. It was a reflection she'd seen in the mirror many times.

Kate rubbed her eyes. "Anyway. It's doesn't matter right now. Nothing matters except getting my son better."

"How is he?" Anna asked.

Oscar's mother grimaced. "He's critical, they said. He was in a serious condition but they downgraded him to critical. That's got to be a good thing right?"

Anna nodded. She would have given her life for her own son to have been critical. At least then he'd have stood a fighting chance.

"I'm going up there again now. You can come if you like but you won't be able to see him."

"Is Matt there?" It was a stupid question. She regretted it as soon as she spoke the words.

"Of course." If she was curious about the relationship between her ex husband and this woman standing before her, Kate didn't show it. But then Anna figured she had bigger fish to fry.

"I'll just say hi." It sounded feeble and inappropriate.

Kate shrugged. It was unimportant to her.

They travelled up in the lift to the ICU in silence. In the confined space Anna realised why Kate had been away from her son's bedside. She reeked of cigarette smoke. The smell was marginally better than the hospital. The doors chimed open and Kate led the way into a dimmed corridor. The waiting room outside the ward was a different story, brightly lit and sterile. A vending machine manned the wall and plastic chairs were scattered in no particular pattern. If only they could tell tales, Anna thought, they must have seen and heard all sorts of triumph and tragedy in their time.

There was a smattering of people gathered and Kate joined them, speaking in hushed tones. Anna realised she'd already been forgotten. She looked around for Matt. He was pacing back and forth near the double doors that led into the ICU unit. Seeing him, Anna wished she hadn't come. She had no place here. At a time like this families needed to be together. She quietly turned to leave.

"Anna,"

Too late, he'd seen her.

Matt was at her side in seconds. He stopped short of touching her. His face seemed gaunter than the last time she'd seen him, although she supposed that was only the result of worry and shadows.

"Matt, hi."

"You came."

"Yes."

"I didn't think you were."

"Yes, I'm sorry about that."

"It doesn't matter, you're here now."

"How is he?"

Matt ran his hands through his hair. "He's better than they first thought, thank god. The helmet protected his head from the worst of the impact."

"What happened?"

"A car hit him from behind. Police said he was thrown quite a distance, ended up in a heap in the gutter," his voice choked up and he sunk his head into his hands.

Anna reached out and embraced him. Whatever was happening or not happening between them, it seemed the right thing to do. She held him while he cried, patting him on the back and murmuring soothing tones into his ear. There was nothing she could say to make him feel any better, she realised that. It was enough that she was here.

He drew back after a while and pulled a wad of tissues from his pocket. They were soaked and ineffectual. He used his sleeve instead.

"He was on his way to your house," Matt said. "Left me a note saying he was going to fix things."

"Fix things?"

"He took it pretty hard when you didn't want to see us anymore. He missed you, but more so Buddy, he's been missing Buddy a lot."

Anna felt dreadfully selfish. Matt saw it in her face and sought to comfort her. "It's ok," he said, "I told him it was my fault, not his."

This made Anna feel worse.

"Hey it's ok," Matt picked up one of her hands and squeezed it. "I get it. I mean, I didn't at first. But I know what you've been through. I thought I had an inkling of how horrendous it must have been for you, but I didn't have a clue until tonight." He took a deep breath. "When I thought I was going to lose Oscar I nearly lost my mind. I swear to god, I don't know what I would have done if he'd died. Probably jumped in front of the first truck I saw."

Anna had thought the very same thought many times. She nodded.

The doors opened and a doctor came through. "Matt," Kate called, and he hurried over to join her. They conferred with the doctor quietly. Kate started sobbing and Matt collapsed into a chair with his head in his hands. Anna stopped breathing. No. She felt the walls closing in.

But then an older gentleman – a grandfather? – asked what had happened and Kate lifted her head. Anna saw she was smiling, and she started to breathe again.

"He's ok," Kate choked through happy tears. "He's going to be ok."

The people in the room started to hug and rejoice, and Anna took the opportunity to slip quietly away. In the elevator on the way down she let her tears fall easily, only for the first time in a long time they were tears of happiness, and tears of relief.

The air outside was sweeter than she could ever remember tasting it. The stars were the brightest they had ever been, and everything felt aligned exactly as it should be. Oscar was going to be ok, and that was all that mattered.

She had caught a taxi to the hospital and he had asked if she wanted him to wait but she'd said no, not knowing how long she'd be. She knew she could ask the man on the desk, now openly reading his magazine, to call her another taxi, but she felt like a walk. Her feet took her in the direction of the cemetery and she made her way through the gate and to the grave easily, despite the darkness. The light from the stars and the crescent of moon was enough to light her way, but even if they hadn't been there she would have found the way by the feel of the ground beneath her feet. Walk a path often enough and every step becomes familiar.

"Hey guys," she said softly. It wasn't the first time she'd visited the grave under the cover of nightfall. In the early days she'd often found herself here upon waking. Curled up on the damp dewy grass, with no memory of how she'd gotten there.

Anna let out a deep sigh. Something had shifted in the universe that night. A weight had been lifted from her.

Second chances.

Oscar had been given one. He had hovered on the knife edge between this life and the next and returned. Anna didn't know why, but when it came down to it, she actually didn't care. All she knew was that he was lucky enough to still be here.

And so was she. Until now, she'd been so consumed by the fact that Tim and Ben had been unfairly taken from her that she hadn't stopped to be grateful that she hadn't died with them. It didn't feel right to be grateful, not when she'd lost so much and wished so hard for so long that she had also died in the car that night.

She placed her hand on the cool surface of the headstone and turned her face up to the stars. She closed her eyes and took a deep breath. A second chance. She could hear Tim's voice in her ear, scolding her for squandering the life she'd been gifted.

After the funeral, someone had said something to her that, at the time, set her teeth on edge. What was it? Oh yes. They'd hugged her awkwardly then looked at her with eyes laced with sympathy and told her that God only leaves the strong ones behind, the ones that can survive a loss.

What a load of bullshit, she'd thought angrily at the time. And she'd had to bite her tongue to stop from telling them exactly what she thought of a God who took babies away from their mothers. Besides, she didn't consider herself strong at all, and when she thought back on her behaviour in the time since they died she knew she should probably feel ashamed. But she didn't. She knew that right or wrong, she had coped the best way that she knew how. She had done what needed to be done in order to get through the days and the nights, and now she had arrived here at this point. She had realised two things.

The first, that family can be family, no matter if they are related or not. The ducks had shown her that, when they adopted orphan Buddy without any drama and a minimal of fuss. It was if they had sensed how much he needed them, and they'd been happy to step up.

The second realisation was that, like Oscar, she had been gifted a second chance.

It was now up to her to make the most of it.

Six months later

The phone rang.

Anna scooped it up on the third bell.

"Buddy's nursery and garden maintenance, how can I help you? Mm mmm, aha, yep, sure no problem, let me just grab the book." She put a hand over the receiver and gestured to Matt, who was sitting in a chair with his feet on the desk, eating a sandwich.

"Pass the book, will you. And get your feet off my desk."

He grinned at her and passed the book, but kept his feet firmly where they were. She frowned and pushed them off. They landed on the floor with a thud. He dropped his sandwich.

"Hey watch it!" he said, picking up the sandwich. He inspected it, decided it passed the ten second rule and took a large bite. He laughed when Anna grimaced.

"Right sorry, where were we," Anna turned her attention back to the phone. "Yes we can fit you in this week. How does ten on Thursday suit you? Perfect? Great, just give me the details and we'll see you then." Matt watched as she scribbled the name and address into the book. Business was going great, and they'd only officially been open a month.

After Oscars accident and the realisation that she had been sleepwalking through life, which was a crime in itself and a lousy way to honour the memories of her husband and son, Anna had set about swiftly making some changes.

Firstly, she tried to figure out exactly what it was she wanted to do with her life. A psychology magazine she purchased from the bookshop had some ideas on how to go about doing this, but after she became fed up with mood boards that didn't put her in 'the mood', and career quizzes that came up with obscure results such as 'you are a creative people pleaser who will have success with an artistic pursuit', she gave up and retreated to her sanctuary. There, with the sun warm on her back and the earth under her fingernails, she had an epiphany.

Buddy's garden nursery was born. When, over dinner, she excitedly filled Matt in on her idea, it was Oscar who suggested why didn't his father go in on it and they offer a garden/lawn maintenance service as well?

She had a fair amount of money left from Tim's life insurance for start up, and the bank was happy enough to lend Matt the rest. Opening day they attracted a curious crowd, gathered to see what the widow and the lawn mower guy had come up with. Anna's green thumb ensured the plant life flourished, and Matt's services were in such demand that he got carried away and booked himself so much work that Anna had to step in and firmly stop him from booking himself seven days a week solid for the foreseeable future.

"Ok you're all booked in" Anna wrapped up the phone call. "You have a wonderful day," she smiled into the receiver before she replaced it. "Phew," she said to Matt, pushing his feet off the desk again, "for a small town there sure is a heck of a lot of business. Anyone would think the men of this town don't like mowing their own lawns, the number of repeat calls we've had." She paused from scribbling in the book and frowned thoughtfully, "funnily enough it's the wives who do most of the booking though."

"What can I say," Matt winked. "I just have a special talent for it."

Anna snorted. "More like you have a special talent for taking your shirt off."

"What on earth do you mean?" He tried his hardest to look indignant.

"Don't play Mr innocent with me. I heard from Celeste at the last school fete meeting that you've been mowing lawns half naked."

"It's hot out there," he defended himself.

Anna laughed. "Yes, well I have a suspicion that it could have something to with the increase in calls from housewives."

"Hey if it works -' Matt shrugged.

She swatted at his chest and he laughed and grabbed her hand, pulling her in close for a long kiss. When they broke apart, breathless, he kissed her eyelids softly, then the tip of her nose. "Would you like me to take my shirt off right now?" he teased in a whisper.

Anna shivered as he nuzzled her neck. "You'll distract me from my work," she protested half heartedly.

Matt checked the clock. "Near enough to knock off time," he said, "Oscar's with his mother tonight, how about we lock the door and pull down the blinds and make ourselves comfortable." He pulled her in close enough that she could feel the heat radiating off him. Holding her tight, he moved forward until she was backed against the desk, and he lifted his eyebrows at her in question.

Anna arched her back into him and smiled. It *was* nearly closing time and she doubted anyone would be shopping for plants at six o'clock on a Monday.

"Oh go on then," she smiled.

Printed in Poland
by Amazon Fulfillment
Poland Sp. z o.o., Wrocław